ONLY ROCK IS REAL

Sandra Miller

"I sometimes choose to think . . . that man is a dream, thought an illusion, and only rock is real."
Edward Abbey, *Desert Solitaire: A Season in the Wilderness*

This book is a work of fiction. Any similarity to real people or events is pure coincidence, unless referenced. While most of the geology, geography, medicine, and astronomy are correct, there may be inaccuracies, either intentional or unintentional, in order to accommodate plot.

ISBN 9781521386279

Dedication

To Ted, who puts up with a great deal, and to Katie, who puts up with very little.

CHAPTER 1

For the second time that morning, Abby resisted the urge to swerve from her jogging path and cross the road, to cut through the sun-spattered woods and follow the deep pull of gravity she felt from the canyon, to go gaze again into those burnished depths, those shattered cliffs. She reminded herself that the canyon wasn't going anywhere and there would be plenty of time once she was settled to ponder those elaborate layers, sliced open like the most astonishing confection ever fabricated. The incense of pine filled the air, and the soft slapping rhythm of her sneakers steadied her mind.

Starting over was no small thing.

Starting over after nearly losing yourself, even more.

Early light splashed her face through the trees as she reviewed her relaxation mantras. There would be no room for anxiety today. Breathe deep, and capture the day.

Abby moved past the campground as tourists began to rise, the fragrance of coffee and bacon drifting through the woods. Glancing over, she imagined who might show up in her clinic that morning. That paunchy middle-aged man, struggling to lift an overloaded ice chest into his truck, was at risk for a bad back strain. That older woman, hunched at her picnic table sucking on a cigarette, had the gray complexion of a heart patient, and this altitude could easily trigger her angina.

No distractions, she chided herself. She dropped into a walk, panting softly in the thin air at seven thousand feet — a drastic change from Phoenix. Hurrying into her house, she skimmed off her running clothes and showered quickly, pulled her chestnut hair back into a messy bun. Maybe a little severe, she thought, but very professional. As she strode out the door, she fingered the shiny new key in her pocket, the key to the back door of the Grand Canyon Clinic.

She was early, staff just arriving. First days were rarely good days for Abby, who realized she was too cautious, too self-critical. Her recent loss of confidence didn't help, but she knew the only way past it was through it. Abby swallowed hard and introduced herself to the busy nurse who was straightening supplies in the exam rooms. It felt like home, the familiar smells of antiseptic and soap, the spotless floors and counters.

"Dr. Wilmore," she said, shaking the nurse's hand. "Abigail Wilmore. But everyone calls me Abby."

"Dolores Diaz," the nurse replied, taking Abby's hand warmly in both of hers. She was fiftyish, stout, her kind face framed by short dark hair laced with silver. "Welcome to the asylum! I'm so glad to meet you. I've heard such nice things."

"Really?" Abby smiled. "Rumors, most likely."

"Come on, follow me. I know Dr. Pepper is anxious to see you."

Abby kept a straight face. In his place, she probably would have changed her name. Dr. Pepper — how could he tolerate the inevitable teasing, such a convenient source for witless puns? Dolores led her down the hall to a small office crammed with two tiny desks, the shelves stuffed and overflowing with papers and medical journals. Everything looked unbalanced and dangerously close to collapse.

John Pepper, the clinic supervisor, unfolded his lanky frame and extended his hand, his light blue eyes coolly appraising. Abby tugged her white coat straight. She didn't always wear a white coat at work, but today she needed that shield, that universal symbol.

"You're early. I like that." He smiled nicely enough, a little guarded, the cautious smile of a cynic. He couldn't be more than five or six years older than her, she thought. He was dressed casually and had thick brown hair, a bit long and unruly, and he looked too thin — his jeans clung to his hips like a bull-rider's. All he needed was a silver prize buckle, Abby thought. She gave his hand a strong squeeze.

"One of my few assets," she remarked lightly. "Being on time."

"It's a good one. I know some people think I'm too . . . demanding. For being out here on the edge of the world, as we are. But it's a slippery slope if things get too loose, so I'm a little bit all about the rules, I'm afraid."

Was he looking for a reaction, or was she was imagining it? Abby had been honest with him about her problems when she applied for the job, so she hoped he wasn't having regrets.

"I've made some room here for your books." He indicated a shelf, an open space a few feet wide. "You'll probably need more, but this is yours for starters."

Abby shook her head and pulled her computer tablet from her pocket. "I only have a few books I use, mostly for procedures. Everything else is online. You know, DynaMed, UpToDate."

"Right," he nodded. "I've got UpToDate, but I still need DynaMed."

"It's based more on scientific evidence," Abby pointed out, feeling a need to prove something.

"So I've heard. You can apparently show me a few things. That's good." He smiled again, more kindly this time. "Anyway, I'm off today for admin work, so I'll get out of here and leave the place to you. Dolores will take good care of you in the back, and the women up front will show you all about the scheduling and billing and the business end of things. You're familiar with our electronic records program, right?"

Abby nodded.

"Okay then. I know you've got my number, so let me know if you have any problems or questions. And if things get crazy—and believe me, they can get crazy really fast—just call me. I'm only a few minutes away, and I'll be sticking close by for the first couple of weeks until you get your feet under you."

He left abruptly, and just like that there she was, alone on her first day at her new job. His swift exit surprised her, left her feeling adrift. She shook it off and reminded herself that patients here were like patients everywhere, and that she knew what she was doing. Their bodies were put together in the same ways, and malfunctioned and fell apart in the same ways, no matter where.

Efficient and funny, Dolores gave Abby lots of tips. Some people didn't believe in tetanus shots, but everyone would want antibiotics for everything. Some tourists started drinking early, so those injuries would begin showing up by noon. And there was a heat wave coming, so get ready for dehydration and heatstroke. Besides the incidental illnesses and injuries of tourists, the clinic also managed the routine health care of several thousand people who lived and worked in the area.

Abby had only seen one patient, a woman with sciatica, when Debbie from the front desk leaned into the hallway and called out in a dolefully loud voice, "Trauma coming in! Three minutes! Gunshot wound."

Of all things on her first day. Incredible, Abby thought. Dolores glanced her way, threw her an encouraging smile and said, "Buckle up."

Abby's pulse had jumped up her throat. She nodded back at Dolores and stepped into the tiny office, her back to the door, and took a moment to focus. You're fine, she told herself, you can handle this. She closed her eyes and slowed herself down, inhaling long, deep breaths. She pictured the oxygen molecules as they trickled in through her nose and tumbled down inside her lungs, imagined the red blood cells snatching up the oxygen and swapping out their carbon dioxide, releasing it as she exhaled. Her pulse slowed a little.

Capture the day, gunshots and all.

The door crashed open and the hall suddenly filled with uniforms and a stretcher. A noisy crew of men surrounded her with sweat and boots, calling out vital signs and looking her way, checking her out.

"Hey, new doc!"

"Nice to meet ya!"

"Welcome to the canyon!"

They wheeled the patient to the trauma room, and Abby pushed her way to the head of the stretcher. A thin man in his forties grimaced and groaned, reaching for his leg, which was elevated and wrapped heavily in dressings. An IV was already running.

"What's the story?" she asked.

The ranger introduced himself, grinned cheerfully, and consulted his clipboard. Short and burly, with a thick neck and close-cropped dark hair, the ranger looked like a small bull but he touched the patient gently with his hand, calling him by name and restraining his arm to keep him from grabbing the bandages. Dried blood coated everything, flaking on the sheets, staining the patient's hands and sleeves, crusted on his foot, and saturating his jeans which had been cut off at the thigh on his injured leg.

"Well now," the ranger drawled happily, planting his feet and grinning at Abby. "This here fellow just drove up to the rim last night and set up his camp around midnight. Hang on, Matt, let go of that. Anyway, he was a little worried about the wildlife—you know, the vicious chipmunks and possum and such—so he decided he'd better keep his sidearm strapped to his hip this morning when he visited the john. Matt, listen to me, lie still. Only problem was that when he was pulling up his pants something got tangled with something else and boom! that big old pistol fired itself right into his calf. Looks like the bullet went clear through, but man, there's a lot of blood on that outhouse floor right now. I mean, a whole lot. I'm glad I'm not on the cleaning crew."

Abby settled in, adjusting IV fluids, ordering labs and X-rays. She gave the patient morphine and he began to relax. Fortunately the wound had nearly quit bleeding, but he was seriously anemic and would need to go to Flagstaff Medical Center for a surgical wound flush and possible blood transfusion. The patient, now dull with narcotic, sleepily protested the transfer because it had taken him a year to get that campground reservation, but he was overruled.

The rangers cleared out, and Ginger up front called for an ambulance.

"Ready to jump back on the treadmill?" Dolores asked, smiling and pointing to the next exam room.

Abby nodded. She was no stranger to a busy pace, and preventive visits were her favorite encounters. She relished the task of trying to keep her patients healthy, find the tiny abnormalities before they became bigger problems, uncover the destructive habits and search for what key might change the course for each person. Endlessly challenging and sometimes rewarding.

Her next patient had been waiting a long time because of the trauma case: Ada Cheshire, a cheery, obese fifty-five-year-old woman who drove a shuttle bus up and down the rim, carting tourists to the far western overlooks where traffic was no longer allowed because of congestion. She was new to the job, just six months.

"Here for my yearly Pap!" Mrs. Cheshire announced loudly, pulling off all her clothes before Abby could step out of the room. "Nah, don't leave. It's just us gals. My first time with a lady doctor, and I think I like it. Dr. Wilmore, was it?"

Abby quickly handed her a gown and sheet to cover her ample body. "Mrs. Cheshire, I don't know if you realize, but Paps aren't recommended every year anymore. Only every five years at your age, if your past Paps have been normal and if you don't have HPV. HPV is that virus that causes cervical cancer."

"Say what? I've got a virus in my hoohaw?" She stopped undressing and her eyebrows shot up.

Abby smiled. "No, I'm saying you probably don't, since your Paps have always been normal. We'll test for it to be sure."

"Honey, I think I'll just stick with the old schedule for now. Because I'm ready for this Pap, and I've cleaned up for you down there, so let's do it." One of her dimply breasts kept slipping out of the paper gown, which was not large enough to contain her, so Abby handed her an extra gown to cover her front.

"We'll do it today for sure." Abby knew not to push new information too quickly. "And when was your last mammogram?"

"Nope, nope, none of that for me." Her head wagged emphatically. "I've heard terrible things about those mammograms. Why, honey, they can actually cause breast cancer! Besides, I heard they hurt like the devil."

"They do hurt a little." Abby nodded. "But in reality, you're more likely to get breast cancer, family history or not, than cervical cancer. For you at your age, a mammogram is more important than a Pap. And mammograms don't cause cancer, by the way."

"Well, I'll think about it, but no promises, because I'd probably have to drive all the way to Flagstaff to get the dang thing done. And let's get on with this, 'cause my shift starts in thirty minutes." She plopped herself on the table with a loud groan and flopped her legs open wide.

Abby grabbed the sheet to cover her lower half. A few minutes later, after changing to a longer and wider speculum to accommodate the woman's large proportions, Abby finally located the smooth shiny cervix, peeking at her from the top of the vagina, and swabbed for the Pap.

"Whew. Glad to have that over." Mrs. Cheshire heaved herself upright and wiggled off the table, casting aside all the drapes and reaching for her clothes. "And you know what, Dr. Wilmore? I think I will take a year or two off, since you think it's okay."

"Excellent," said Abby, taking the specimens and sliding discreetly out the door. "I'll leave you a list of all my recommendations, like the mammogram."

The rest of the morning was similar. There were blood pressures behaving nicely and blood pressures behaving badly, and medications had to be adjusted. Some diabetics were managing well, but most had sugars off on a rampage, creating havoc. A few tourists with minor complaints, ruddy rashes and puffy knees and watery bowels. A fairly slow day, Dolores commented.

Abby took a moment to meet the two women at the front desk, bubbly red-blond Ginger, who laughed easily, and her somber counterpart Debbie, whose straight black hair fell in a curtain to her waist. Debbie never once let a smile crack her face, and her ghostly pale complexion made Abby think of vampires. They were signing out the last morning patient when Debbie leaned into the hallway for the second time, calling out mournfully, "Trauma coming—ten minutes! MVA, four patients!"

Dolores appeared, shaking her head sourly and motioning Abby over. "We've asked her before not to do that. She should come back and tell us, not bellow down the hall like a cow. Dr. Pepper would be upset—she wouldn't do that if he was here."

Really? thought Abby. That's what Dolores was worried about? MVA meant motor vehicle accident, which could be anything from a neck sprain to a fatality. It was beginning to feel like the morning might never end. And it wasn't ten minutes, the time estimate was wrong, because the doors banged open immediately and patients and rangers clattered in. So much for relaxation mantras—Abby barely had time to snatch a breath. The worst of the injured went to the trauma room, and Abby found herself there again without even feeling her feet move. People were moaning or calling out or talking on their phones while the rangers asked questions and filled out reports. Dolores was directing supplies to those who needed them while holding a crying woman's hand.

"Hey, Doc Wilmore! That's you, right?" A ranger stood at her side, adjusting the IV of the elderly man on the exam table, slipping oxygen prongs onto his face. The patient breathed shallowly, carefully, as if each inhalation hurt, his worried eyes darting back and forth.

"Might be a broken rib, or maybe a pneumothorax," the ranger was saying. "He was driving along minding his own business when the other car crossed the line and smacked him head-on. Hit his chest pretty hard against his airbag."

"Was the other driver drunk?" Abby wondered aloud. She turned to the patient and touched his hand. "Take it easy, now. I know it hurts to breathe, but your oxygen level looks fine, so that's a very good thing." The old man gave her a weak smile and closed his eyes.

"Nah. The other guy was watching a doe and her fawn grazing in the woods and he sort of forgot he was behind the wheel. He wasn't hurt at all, of course."

The ranger took her under her arm and pulled her out of the room with him during the X-ray. "Saving our gonads for the future," he quipped when they had moved out of range of the radiation. His sandy hair fell to his hazel eyes, flecks of green and brown like the forest, and his full lips curved into an appreciative smile as he looked at her, still holding her arm. His high cheekbones gave his face a Native American cast, and he smelled of pine trees and coffee, leather and earthy musk. Abby was aware of his large hand encircling her upper arm, of his fingers in her armpit brushing the side of her chest along her breast.

"Nice," he said, breathing the word out.

"Excuse me?"

"Nice to meet you, Dr. Wilmore. I'm Jake Peterson."

"Abby." She pulled out of his grip, stepped back. "Good job with this patient."

"Let's see if the X-ray shows I guessed right."

Surprised, Abby saw Dr. John Pepper poke his head out of an exam room door and ask for Dolores. Someone must have called him because of the multiple traumas. He gave Abby a quick nod.

"Nothing looks too serious, except maybe the guy you're seeing," he remarked, glancing at Peterson and back to Abby. "You need any help?"

"Thanks, just waiting for the X-ray. He's stable enough, but I'm sure he'll need to go to the hospital."

"Tell Ginger up front, she'll start the arrangements," Pepper said, disappearing back into the exam room.

"The friendly pepper-upper," Jake murmured in a singsong way that made Abby want to laugh, but she quickly stifled herself. When the X-ray was processed, she brought it up on the computer in the tiny office, Jake crowding in next to her to see. There it was, a small pneumothorax, just as he had suspected. No fractured ribs, fortunately. She studied the black space around the inner ribcage where the lung should have been, and with her fingertip she outlined the thin membrane of the partially collapsed lung, its normal cobwebby tissues condensed and opaque.

"A small pneumothorax, but it's definitely there," she said. "Nice job."

"Every now and then I guess right. They'll be wanting these X-rays in Flag for sure."

He leaned past her to hit the copy button, and she felt his chest press against her back. As he waited while the image printed to the disc, his arm still extended around her, she could have sworn that he leaned against her. The moment was prolonged and peculiarly intimate.

Dolores bustled in. "Flagstaff ER is on the phone for you, Dr. Wilmore. They're ready for your transfer report. Line two."

Abby turned and ducked around Jake, hustling to the telephone in the trauma room. She gave the report and lingered with the elderly patient, explaining the transport and reassuring him that he would likely be fine after a short observation, although there was an outside chance that he might need a chest tube. Then she explained what a chest tube was, all the while silently hoping that Ranger Peterson would leave the clinic and get back to doing whatever manly things he did. At this point the patient's daughter had joined him, and she expressed her relief and gratitude.

By the time Abby left the trauma room, the afternoon patients were waiting to be seen. So much for lunch; she would have to remember to bring a supply of snacks for days like this.

She pulled a clipboard from another door and was turning the knob when Jake Peterson appeared at the back end of the hall on his way out. His brawny frame filled the narrow corridor, and he lifted one hand in farewell. "Hope to see more of you, Dr. Wilmore," he called. He spoke carefully, polite and professional. Then his lips curled into a playful grin and he turned and was gone.

Every now and then that afternoon, his words recycled through Abby's brain between her busy tasks. Hope to see more of you. Hope to see *more* of you.

Ridiculous. He was just another macho guy like so many others, and she would probably never encounter him again. She had never been drawn to his type, the rugged six-pack outdoorsy Paul Bunyan sort of man. Let's face it, the man she almost married last year was considerably more suited to her, an indoorsy pale number-crunching accountant whose sense of humor had been filed away with his investments years ago.

Like you were so perfect, she reminded herself. Be real.

The best thing was that she had survived her first day in good order—the staff had complimented her and genuinely seemed to like working with her. She walked home through the trees, enjoying the toasty fragrance of the forest, eager to start unpacking the boxes and suitcases that had arrived that afternoon. Squirrels chittered and scolded furiously from high in the Ponderosa pines, making her smile.

Tomorrow would be even better. And the next day.

The past was past. She left it behind in the dry haze of Phoenix with its pitiless prickly vegetation and its precipitous summer storms flashing across the harsh landscape. Those violent downpours, too much water falling too fast, running over the baked ground without soaking in, leaving the world thirsty again.

This was her place now, and she was determined to make it work.

CHAPTER 2

Abby rubbed her aching temple with her fingertips. It was turning into one of those days. Things had started out well, genuine people coming in for all the right reasons: young women craving birth control and older women swamped with hot flashes, acutely twisted ankles and chronically aching knees, burning bladder infections and swollen leaky prostates. Worrisome weight loss and curious weight gain, blinding migraines and tricky thyroids. She enjoyed the variety of challenges. Then the last patient had become difficult in another way.

"I'm sorry," she repeated, "but I can't give you a prescription for Ritalin without your medical records. It's against our policy. I would at least need a call from your personal doctor to confirm that you have been diagnosed with ADHD and that you've been getting regular prescriptions. Or if they could fax a copy of your last three or four appointments, that would work too."

The man glared at her, his jaw hard. "I live in Ohio," he rasped between clenched teeth. "Those offices are closed now."

"So they could call in the morning—"

"I'll be in Colorado by morning. Are you even listening to me at all?" His voice rose. His mouth twitched and his foot jiggled up and down. Initially he'd been pleasant and polite, abashed about letting his prescription run out while traveling.

Abby heard Dolores walk down the hall and pause by the door. She knew Dolores was listening, knew she would try to help if this kept escalating.

"Here's the deal," Abby said, carefully calm. "We won't charge you for the visit because you didn't know you couldn't get the prescription. Okay?" She stepped back, moving toward the door. She should have left it cracked open, like she sometimes did if a patient seemed troublesome or chancy, but this man had fooled her. He was nicely dressed, pressed shirt and slacks, and he looked like a businessman.

"What the hell is the problem? I'm not a drug addict, for crying out loud. Just give me a few so I can concentrate on my driving."

He was gesturing now, his hands chopping up and down, and he stood and moved toward her. Abby backed out the door, her pulse quickening, and he followed, getting louder. Dolores stepped next to her, and Ginger from the front desk appeared in the hallway, grimly red-faced and carrying a large industrial stapler in her right hand. She had heard the voices getting louder.

"Just a few pills to get me through, that's all I'm asking. Are you even a real doctor?" He leaned toward her, thrusting out his jaw. "Do you want me to file a complaint with the medical board?"

The back door thumped open, and here came Ranger Jake Peterson, pushing a wheelchair containing a lobster-red, tearful young woman. Jake paused, barely a hitch, parking the wheelchair against the wall and taking in the scene at a glance. He moved steadily toward them, filling the hall with uniformed authority, badge glinting, eyes narrowing as his hand went to his hip.

"Is there a problem?" Jake asked the man in a growl.

"Uh, no. No problem at all. Never mind." The man shrank back, slid behind Ginger, then melted out the door to the waiting room. They heard the outer door slam shut. Debbie's pale face appeared in the small connecting window from the front reception desk, devoid of expression, and then she returned to her desk. Debbie rarely left her desk.

Jake cocked his head at Abby.

"Well," she said, inhaling deeply, "that was certainly good timing. Although we could have handled it ourselves, of course."

"I'm sure." Jake smiled. "Want me to go after him?"

"No. I don't think he'll be back. Besides, Ginger's got her stapler loaded and I know she won't hesitate to use it."

Everyone laughed and Ginger flushed, her freckles brightening and her sunny hair bristling around her head. She raised the heavy stapler up high and waved it back and forth. "I guess I could have thrown it at him, but I throw like a girl, so I probably would have hit Dr. Wilmore instead."

Jake jerked his thumb back at the woman he had just brought in and cleared his throat. Dolores hurried to put her in a room and take her vitals.

"I've told Pepper," he muttered. "This clinic needs a panic button. This sort of thing worries me a lot. You all are pretty defenseless here, an easy target. There's cash and drugs here, too. Not to mention that some people are crazy."

"I think we have pepper spray somewhere, if you'll pardon the expression." Abby couldn't help but smile as she tried to focus herself.

"Pepper spray is not that great of an idea. Too hard to contain indoors—the person doing the spraying is likely to get sprayed as well. I'm going to talk to him again." Jake shook his head and pointed down at the report. "Severe blisters on feet, toes, heels, soles. Possible cellulitis, hard to tell. Probable dehydration, though I had her drink quite a bit for the last hour it took to get her up that final half mile of the Bright Angel Trail. Significant sunburn on face, shoulders, arms, hands, and in a halter-shaped pattern on her chest."

It was a common scenario. Despite warning signs posted in large letters all along the rim and at the trailheads, signs that predicted dire consequences for anyone starting down the path without ample water and sturdy footwear, tourists blew past the cautions all the time. On summer afternoons the full force of the brutal Arizona sun blasted temperatures to one hundred degrees or more, scorching hikers with a blazing heat that grew hotter and hotter as they descended. This woman had no hat, no sunscreen, and no water, only a Diet Coke, and flimsy flip-flops that looked like they came from a dollar store. Because the wide trail was easy to descend, she had quickly covered nearly two miles before her feet got so raw and blistered that she could hardly walk. Somehow missing the water station, she kept going even though her Coke was long gone. She had at least properly disposed the empty can in a recycle bin, Jake noted dryly. Crying and stumbling through the dust and over the rocks at snail-like speed, she labored out, assisted by Jake, who supplied her much encouragement and emergency fluids from his heavy backpack. Abby imagined that it would have been easier for him to toss the woman over his shoulder and haul her out.

It had been like this ever since the weather warmed up. People came into the clinic on their own or the rangers brought them in, overheated, exhausted, blistered, miserable. And when it was Jake, he always managed to stand close, his arm often touching her, leaving Abby both amused and annoyed. He was not her type, and she harbored no doubts he was like this with all women. Just be professional, she told herself. He would stop eventually if she didn't react.

In the meantime, Abby felt herself growing stronger. She was adjusting to the altitude and could jog several miles now without getting short of breath, and a few muscles showed in her legs, which used to be pale and shapeless. She ventured farther along the rim, and on her days off she began hiking down the South Kaibab trail, first just half a mile, then a mile. The return on that steep trail was brutal and made her muscles scream, but she was learning to distract herself, to ease into the effort by tuning in to the shifting play of shadows across the mesas, the raspy croak of ravens as they drifted through the giddy spaces, and the immense silence that filled the air like a solid presence.

As she was leaving at the end of the day, she found John Pepper in the office, scribbling his signature on invoices and sorting through the daily box of mail. He glanced up at her briefly, a harried scowl between his brows, his lips a thin line.

"Everything okay?" she asked. He looked like he needed a friend. That afternoon he had pulled Debbie from the front desk into the tiny office for ten minutes; their voices murmured quietly at first, then Debbie's rose abruptly. Seconds later she yanked the door open and left without a word to anyone, her long black hair swinging back and forth like the tail of an angry cat.

"I suppose so." He sighed. "I've got to start advertising for Debbie's position."

"So she was really that bad? I mean, bad enough to let her go?" Abby had acquired a perverse fondness for morose Debbie, a sad Eeyore kind of person, and was shocked that Pepper had fired her. There must be something else she didn't know about.

He eyed her a little irritably. "I think it's better that we don't talk about it. Some confidential stuff that probably needs to stay confidential."

"Okay, sure." Abby felt rebuffed.

"So — everything turned out all right with that guy who was causing trouble earlier today?"

"The Ritalin guy? Yes, Jake Peterson scared him away. Whew."

"Did you look him up on the pharmacy database?"

"Er, no. I was going to, but things happened very fast. Then I forgot to check later." Abby felt off balance. She should have checked to see if that patient had been getting prescriptions from other physicians, whether the state pharmacy database showed a pattern suspicious for abuse.

"Understandable." Pepper compressed his lips again; he didn't look all that understanding. His blue eyes cut back to his paperwork, frosty and remote.

"No, you're right. I'm sorry." Abby's words came in a rush. "I was going to do it right in the exam room on my tablet, but sometimes the internet server is so slow, and suddenly he was acting in this threatening way —"

Pepper reached out and touched her wrist with his long fingers. He smiled a genuinely warm smile. "No, I wasn't criticizing, really. I know I come across that way more than I mean to. I just have a lot on my mind. Peterson thinks we should install a panic button — what do you think?"

"I'm not sure I really have a feel for this place yet. Though I don't see how it could hurt, right?"

"Budget." He sighed again. "It's always about budget. But after this, maybe it's not a bad idea. It was just lucky Peterson happened along."

Abby changed the subject, wondering why she always felt slightly idiotic around him. But she realized that he was not having the best day, either. "Are you going to join everyone tonight? There seem to be plans for a pizza party."

"I might make it." He looked down at his pile of mail.

"Well, I hope you can." Abby hung up her white coat and shouldered her bag, turning to leave. She wanted to take a walk along the rim before supper. This time of year, the canyon was at its best mornings and evenings.

"By the way, I did look that guy up on the database," Pepper said, as if just remembering. "He's filled three prescriptions for Ritalin in the last week, in Tucson, Phoenix, and Prescott. And before that there were prescriptions in New Mexico. None of those docs must have checked. Hard to know if he's using them himself or selling them on the street. You can make pretty good money on it these days. Or maybe he's doing both."

"Well, I wasn't going to give him any meds anyway," she said defensively, chagrined. She should have known about that.

"Again, not a criticism. You're doing great. I just thought you'd like to know."

"Yeah. Thanks."

Not a criticism, like hell, she thought gloomily as she walked through the trees to the rim. She released her bun and let her hair loose, let it drift across her back and shoulders. But it was hard to stay glum as she approached the edge and the world fell away at her feet, that surreal gasp of space and shadow in every hue of red and orange and pink and purple, plummeting down through the earth's crust into secret blue crevices, the countless towers and mesas marching off into hazy distance. Abby gripped the nearby railing until her balance normalized; she always felt a moment of vertigo at the rim.

She moved around the rail and leaned against a large chunk of pale rock, enjoying the warm rough grip of limestone against her skin. Her breathing slowed, deep and steady, as she gazed across the panorama. This place was good for her. She felt more anchored, more solid, surrounded by all this stone and the stark display of eons, as if the planet had suddenly bared its soul and let strangers see its past. Her perspective zoomed out like a wide-angle lens, and she felt, comfortably, like a minuscule blip in the arc of eternity.

It was the same when she lost herself in the night sky — it felt good to be insignificant. To be assured that she mattered so little in the scheme of things, that her errors and failings, and even her minor triumphs, carried such marginal substance. If any at all.

A shadow moved alongside her as someone came up behind. Keep moving, she thought, having no inclination for small talk with tourists, and then a familiar hand gripped her elbow and pulled her away from her stone.

"Not actually the safest place to be," Jake Peterson said, releasing her once he was satisfied with her position back by the rail. He removed his sunglasses and studied her, his eyes drifting briefly down her frame. "When you see a railing like this one, it's there for a reason."

"I was just standing there." Abby started to rub her elbow but checked herself. She held on to the rail and looked out across the canyon.

"I know it's a gorgeous spot," Jake said, "but the footing is unstable and the drop over the edge here is tremendous."

"I guess this is my day to be an idiot." She might as well say it out loud since she'd been thinking it all afternoon. Jake made her feel light-headed, as if his solid body had a gravitational pull. Get a grip, she told herself.

"Hey, you have no idea." He shook his head. "A while back, no less than seven people died accidentally in one year. They just fell off the rim. Some were drunk, but most of them just took one step too many in the wrong direction, not looking, not thinking. Or they just tripped. Not paying attention, taking a photo. Things like that."

"You're kidding."

"I wish I was. It's horrible. And it's not exactly fun being part of the retrieval party either." He shrugged. "Hard to say why people get careless here, why they don't take it more seriously. How many warnings can you post?"

He moved behind her and took her shoulders, turning her body to face the vista toward the east. With his left hand resting on her shoulder, he pointed into the far distance with his right.

"See that lumpy blue smudge way out there on the horizon? The cloud with the fluffy white tips? Watch it for a sec."

They stood there silently, Abby aware of his hand on her shoulder and his thumb against the back of her neck, somehow underneath her hair. She heard a swish of tires and the rumble of a delivery truck out on the road. On the edge of her vision a squirrel flicked its downy tail and dove back out of sight. Then the blue smudge twitched, a tiny spritz of bright lightning forked the ground, and the little pile of cloud briefly glowed like a distant bulb.

Jake's hand squeezed her shoulder. "See?"

"That's so cool. I love it." She meant it. She probably would never have noticed the miniature storm so far away, too distracted by the canyon in the foreground.

"If we're lucky, that might come our way in a few hours. Have you been here in a big thunderstorm yet?"

"Not yet." His thumb was now ever so slightly rubbing the back of her neck, creating a static that ran down her spine like pale lightning itself. He shifted, bringing his hip against hers, and she felt a firm shape against her. She stiffened.

He leaned close to her ear and whispered. She felt his breath on her cheek, faintly scented with coffee and mint.

"Don't worry, ma'am," he said formally, officially. "It's just my flashlight."

Embarrassed and overtaken by impulse, she turned and smacked him on the arm. It was like slapping a chunk of granite. "You're terrible," she said.

"Yes, I am," he agreed, laughing. "Hey, it's good to see you smile. You've been so serious."

Abby straightened and tucked her hair off her face. She must not encourage him. She was frankly appalled that she had done that; too many years in medicine with so many men, too many off-color jibes and black humor, and nudging back had become second nature.

"Well, I'm a serious person," she said. "I'm trying to get things right."

"It's not Pepper, is it? Has he been giving you a hard time?" Jake's face tightened.

Abby shook her head, feeling suddenly protective of Pepper. Odd, since he'd just annoyed her significantly. "No, he's been very supportive, actually."

"Well, all right then. Hey, I've seen you hiking every now and then. Want to go with me someday? I can show you some other trails." His eyes lit up.

"Maybe . . ." She doubted that was a good idea.

"Come on. I'll get a few others to go with us, it'll be fun. Don't you have a day off coming up?"

How could he know her schedule? But it did sound fun, and she had been alone too much, she knew that, so she slowly agreed.

"All right. Next week?" He looked downright gleeful. They arranged a time and he set off toward Bright Angel Trail. "I've got the late shift," he explained. "Have to run down a ways and check for stragglers and anyone in trouble."

He walked away quickly, covering the ground in big strides.

She realized she was late for the pizza party. She stole another long glance at the faraway thunderhead, and was rewarded by a dancing prickle of lightning and another quick glow.

Then she hurried off to the party, which was in full swing, the noisy bar crowded with locals and tourists alike, a jovial rowdiness rising into the dark rafters. Ginger and Dolores were there, waving madly for her to join them, and she recognized three or four rangers and Tracy from the pharmacy. Ginger sat with her longtime boyfriend Diego, a dashing Hispanic man with a mop of black hair and a dazzling white smile that could stop a woman's heart. The contrast between his bronze complexion and Ginger's rosy freckled skin was striking as they twined together like a human yin and yang. Abby paused by the bar to pick up a club soda with a slice of lime, which she carried to the long table, sliding in next to Dolores, who was saving her a seat. Her husband was working that night.

"Have a beer!" Ginger crowed, starting to pour, but Abby raised her club soda in reply.

"I don't think there's much booze in that," Dolores laughed.

"Enough for me," Abby teased back. The good thing about club soda, or a plain Coke or a glass of cider, was that people couldn't really tell if she was drinking alcohol and she didn't need to say why she wasn't. She dodged offers of beer a few more times, but no one seemed to notice or care. It was nice to relax with friends, listen to their stories, poke a little fun. The pizza was hot and greasy and delicious, and she managed to burn the roof of her mouth and get a tomato stain on her shirt. She turned to look whenever the door whooshed open, but John Pepper did not appear.

It was a short walk home through the dark woods, car headlights swinging on the road, and every now and then the haunting low call of an owl, hunting its evening meal. She kept scanning the eastern sky for the thunderhead, but the heavens were clear and black, swarming with stars. No lightning, no storms, no drama. Probably just as well.

CHAPTER 3

Abby and Dr. Pepper were both at the clinic this morning, and the appointment schedule was packed. She covered routine visits while he managed the acute complaints, which meant that today Abby mostly saw the locals and Pepper mostly saw travelers. They traded the tasks back and forth.

"Guess this is sugar day for me," Abby announced to Dolores. Nearly half her patients were diabetic, and only a few had their sugars in line. Some were sheepish, some disappointed, some defiant, but no one was happy. "Has anyone ever tried having a diabetes group around here? Where everyone meets to learn about how to control their eating and how to motivate themselves to exercise? We could have a weigh-in, just like Weight Watchers. We would talk about calories, healthy recipes, how the medications work, you know."

"That's a great idea," said Dolores, studying the glucometer in her hand. "No one has ever done that, at least not that I can remember, and I've been here about six years. You should talk to Dr. Pepper about it." She patted her plump belly. "Heck, I would go to that."

"I didn't know you were diabetic."

"Not yet. But most people in my family are, so the writing's on the wall, right?"

"You're definitely at risk." Abby smiled. "But not doomed."

Her next diabetic patient was George Nutter, the portly chef from El Tovar. A swanky old hotel perched on the rim, El Tovar had been built from canyon limestone in 1905, and was now a National Historic Landmark. The gourmet dinners were delectable, with choices like roasted duck in sundried cherry merlot sauce, or rainbow trout amandine with rice pilaf. George brought her a huge square takeout box of blueberry cobbler left over from the night before, crusted with a crunchy butter topping, dusted with cinnamon sugar, and swimming in thick purple juice.

"Is this a bribe?" Abby asked. There was enough cobbler to share with all the staff. "Is this so I won't notice you've gained four pounds?"

"Lord, I hope so. Is it working?" He put on a shamed expression, but his eyes twinkled above his red cheeks. Add a white beard and he would be a dead ringer for Santa Claus.

"Unfortunately for you, I'm very good at multitasking, so I can enjoy your cobbler with one side of my mouth while I chastise you out the other side."

They talked about his weight, his lack of exercise other than running back and forth in the kitchen, his need to taste everything he prepared. Abby took her time to explain how his body's own insulin had become weak at regulating his sugar and now those high sugars ran through his bloodstream like an unruly gang of thugs, smashing up the cells in his kidneys and nerves, his heart and his retina. If he couldn't reverse it soon, he would need to start insulin injections to get the sugars under control and protect his organs.

"I never thought of it quite like that," he said.

Abby had an idea. "Listen, would you be interested in giving some volunteer classes in healthy cooking for other diabetics around here? We're thinking of starting a group."

He stared at her, mouth open. "You know what? I would love that. And I think it would help me too."

Abby was thrilled. They agreed to meet again to brainstorm.

Here came Priscilla, the new hire at the front desk, taking quick tiny steps down the hall in her tight miniskirt. Really, Abby thought. Priscilla was pretty, prim and proper, every blond hair perfectly in place as it fell past her creamy skin and curled against her shoulders, her lips pearly pink and her eyes green like a cat's. Abashed at her judgmental thoughts, Abby started to say something nice to her, but Priscilla breezed past and slid up next to Pepper, who had just emerged from an exam room.

"Dr. Pepper, I want to show you something." Her voice was low and crooning. She stood very close to him, murmuring quietly, pointing at a file. He had to bend his tall body to listen, and Abby saw Priscilla's pink lips near his ear, but she couldn't make out the words. Well, Pepper frequently complained about how loud everyone was and how they all needed to lower their voices to maintain patient confidentiality. Clearly, Priscilla had taken that to heart.

Abby turned away to finish writing up her notes on Chef Nutter. Pepper was a grown man, and he could take care of himself — after all, he was the one who had hired Priscilla. Who knew, maybe she was his type. What did Abby know about the mysterious John Pepper anyway? He never talked about his personal life. If you asked, he turned the conversation to something else; it had taken her a while to notice how he did that, every time. Maybe a messy divorce or a family scandal, maybe a wretched affair? Not that it was any of her business. Maybe he was gay and preferred to keep it quiet. Hah, take that, Priscilla.

Abby was in the tiny office checking emails when Pepper appeared in the doorway.

"If you're done, I could use some help with this next lot. Three patients from some kerfuffle up at the mule corral. Could you see one of them?" He ran his long fingers through his hair, which now stood mussed up on one side, and Abby could tell that he wished he didn't have to ask.

"Of course," she said, "but what the heck happened?"

"I don't know the details yet, but we've got a wrangler, a tourist, and a ranger with injuries." Pepper raked his fingers through his hair again, and it stood down. "Do you mind seeing the ranger? It's Peterson — you know, the one who's always bringing the broken hikers in to see you."

Abby looked up at him sharply, but he was already retreating. Her first reaction was to wonder what the hell he meant — had he implied that Peterson was singling her out? But that thought was immediately replaced by concern for Jake and what might have happened.

Dolores appeared briefly at the door. "He's ready."

Abby paused. This was a new challenge, providing medical care to someone she knew, and it felt peculiar. In a large city like Phoenix, they had a policy against it. There were many doctors, many offices and clinics, ample choices. Scholarly studies indicated that medical care often suffered when the physician knew the patient personally, and even more so if the patient was a family member. A physician was less likely to take a thorough history or ask the delicate questions. Less likely to perform a complete exam. More likely to overprescribe or undertreat. But in a small town or rural area, there might simply be no choice.

Jake sat propped up on the exam table, holding an ice pack over one eye. He turned toward her as the door opened, squinting at her with the other eye.

"We can make this quick," he growled, curling his lips in exasperation. Dust coated his back, his hat was missing, his hair disheveled, and he smelled distinctly horsey. "I told them I was fine, but they insisted I get checked out. Company rules or some garbage."

Relieved that he seemed relatively intact, Abby moved next to him and gently raised the ice pack. Jake winced and involuntarily grabbed her wrist.

"Easy now. That kinda smarts."

"No kidding." His eye was puffed nearly shut under a black-and-green swell of flesh. "What on earth happened?"

Jake sighed. "I'm usually pretty good at breaking up fights. Not this time. I think I caught an elbow. Knocked me flat."

"You *think* it was an elbow or you *know* it was an elbow?"

"It all happened pretty fast. One minute I'm pulling that tourist jerk off the wrangler — do you know that sweet old mule wrangler Pete Collins? — and the next minute I'm on the ground. I mean, who's drunk and fighting at eight in the morning? Over which mule he gets to ride?"

"Did you black out? Lose consciousness?"

"Nah. I was just stunned, you know? That big mule was hopping around, and everyone was shoving and yelling, and wham! down I go. I'm lucky I didn't get stepped on. And so that ornery old mule gets pissed off and lets out a kick, nails that guy in the ribs. Serves him right, and that mule knew exactly what he was doing. If a few of those ribs aren't broken, I'll eat my Smokey hat, wherever it is."

"Hang on." Abby wanted to hear the story, but she was having trouble getting Jake to focus. He was jumping back and forth, and she wondered about the clarity of his thoughts, worried that the mule might have kicked him or stepped on him, which could be a much more dangerous injury. "What was the fight about?"

Jake snorted. "This jerk decided he had to ride that big old pinto mule. It's all black-and-white-spotted, kind of flashy. For a mule. Guy got into a big argument with Pete over it, started pushing Pete away so he could get his foot in the stirrup. Pete pulled him off and the guy took a swing at him — hell, I don't know, I didn't come along till the last second. Just happened to be passing by."

There was a tap on the door, and a short, wiry older man in faded jeans poked his head into the room, his droopy gray moustache lifting in a smile when he saw Jake. He had a battered black cowboy hat smashed onto his head, and his leathery face bore a bright white bandage over one cheek where Pepper had just stitched up a small laceration.

"How ya doing, big guy?" the wrangler asked, after politely touching his hat brim in Abby's direction.

"I'm good, Pete." Jake grinned. "But I look a sight worse than you."

"Aw, your handsome mug won't hardly notice the difference. But a guy like me who ain't got much to begin with—I got to worry about my looks now. Helluva thing."

Abby shook her head, mildly amused, but wanting to get back to her examination. Still, she couldn't help but ask, "Why didn't you just let him ride the mule?"

Pete shook his head, removed the tattered hat and swiped back his salt-and-pepper hair, then replaced the hat carefully in precisely the same place. His eyes were startlingly blue under the brim. "Well, ma'am, it's like this. Old Idaho—we call him that on account of a big white patch on his haunch in the shape of Idaho—he don't like men. Once they've mounted up, he's likely to whip around and bite 'em in the leg. But he's partial to females, so we only let him carry the ladies. He don't look like it on account of his big blocky head, but he's a very sensitive mule."

They eventually got everyone sorted out, including the tourist with two broken ribs, who was arrested for assault. Jake's exam was reassuring and his X-rays were normal, though Abby continued to wonder about a slight haziness in his memory. She sent him home with ice packs and a prescription for pain pills, which he handed back to her. She explained that he might have a mild concussion and gave him head injury precautions, told him to take tomorrow off and return for follow-up the next afternoon.

The next afternoon came, but no Jake.

Priscilla minced back to Abby. She wore skinny black leggings that looked sprayed on, black stiletto heels, and a gauzy top which was thin enough to suggest a bright pink bra underneath. Next they'd be treating her for a sprained ankle in those heels, Abby thought. Where was Ginger anyway?

"It looks like this Peterson is a no-show," Priscilla announced. Today her lipstick was blood-red, a Marilyn Monroe sort of look. Her voice was plenty loud now that she wasn't talking to Pepper. "Should I send him a no-show letter?"

"No. I'll get hold of him. It's an on-the-job injury, so we really need to see him."

"Well, he's not answering his phone. I tried."

Now Abby was concerned. Maybe he had been kicked in the head after all and his injury was worse than she realized. Maybe he had deteriorated, maybe an artery had torn and bled inside his brain. He could be lying at home on the floor, unconscious.

Her breath caught, her pulse accelerated. She didn't trust her voice, so she nodded curtly at Priscilla and turned away, biting her lip to create a pain for concentration. It couldn't happen here — she had to deal with her panic immediately. She closed her eyes, pulled in an uneven breath and held it as long as she could, then exhaled very slowly, counting the seconds. Then again.

Trees, she thought, do it with trees. Start with A. With every indrawn breath she imagined a tree. A, for apple tree, thick with autumn fruit. Exhale. B for birch, a pale thin trunk swaying in the wind. Exhale. He probably just took a nap, forgot the time, he just — no, stop it. C for cottonwood, the leaves twirling and fluttering over a creek. Exhale. D. D? Nothing came to mind. Then E, eucalyptus, the sharp camphor scent of a crushed leaf. She held out her fingers and they were steady. Good. She was getting better at this.

Dolores emerged from an exam room and gave her an odd look. "Your last patient's ready."

"Great," Abby said brightly, moving quickly into the room.

It was a simple sore throat. Abby wrapped up the clinic loose ends and soon she was tramping through the woods to Jake's little house, having checked the address in his medical chart. It was a warm early evening, the air drifting with pollen and dust, and her emotions hopped back and forth like jackrabbits, fear then anger then dread then aggravation. She assumed it was his old pickup truck parked in front, but that meant nothing since they all walked most everywhere during the day. Stepping up on the cement stoop, without letting herself think about it, she knocked briskly on the door. Her heartbeat felt quick but not out of control. F, she thought, breathing deeply. Fir trees. She was surrounded by them.

No response. She knocked harder, then tilted her head to peer through the window, but the late low sun reflected a bright silver sky in the glass. She was about to cup her hands against the window and put her face to the pane when a touch on her shoulder made her gasp and jump sideways.

"Looking for someone?" Jake stood there in full uniform wearing his aviator sunglasses, which pretty much hid the injury around his eye. He grinned. "Is this a house call?"

Abby felt her foot teeter on the edge of the stoop, and then her ankle buckled and sent her tumbling sideways into a small pine tree growing next to the porch. A bright pain lanced her forearm and she toppled down to the hard dusty ground. As she struggled to get to her feet, Jake's strong hands lifted her and deposited her upright. Then he grabbed her arm and raised it over her head.

"What the heck?" she sputtered, pulling against his grasp. Her long hair had come loose and fallen across her face, half blinding her.

"Hold still," he commanded, gripping harder. "Your arm is bleeding. Quite a bit."

Abby stopped resisting. Apparently a sharp branch had pierced her out-flung forearm as she fell, and now she could feel the warm sticky blood trickling down toward her armpit.

"Are you okay? Can you stand here a sec and keep your arm up in the air while I run inside for a towel?" Jake's face was inches from hers.

She nodded. He was right: basic first aid for a bleeding extremity was to elevate the limb and let gravity help slow the flow of blood. Abby leaned against the doorjamb with her arm up, and Jake returned quickly with a small clean towel, pressed it against the wound, and led her inside to a chair.

"I'm fine," she said, self-conscious.

"Sure you are." He peeled back the towel, and they inspected her wound together, a jagged inch-long laceration, only oozing now. Darkening trails of dried blood ran up and down her arm. Jake reapplied the towel. "That might need a stitch or two."

"No way." Although Abby actually thought he was correct and a stitch would be the best treatment, she could not imagine calling John Pepper. Telling him she had fallen off Jake's front porch into a tree while trying to peek into his window. "Don't you have any butterfly bandages or Steri-Strips or anything?"

Jake's lips curved into a smile. "Sure I do. My first aid kit's out in my vehicle. Don't move."

It took him very little time to clean the laceration, pull the wound edges together with butterfly adhesives, and apply a thin film of antibiotic ointment.

"Nothing to it," he pronounced. "Now let's fix the rest of you."

"Excuse me?"

"Don't take this wrong, but you're kind of a mess." He disappeared into the kitchen, ran water, and returned with a fresh towel he had soaked in warm water. "Your face is filthy, you have twigs and pine needles in your hair, and in case you hadn't noticed, your arm is covered in blood."

He sat down knee-to-knee with her and swabbed off her arm from her wrist to her armpit. Then he put his left hand on top of her head, tilting it back, and softly wiped the dirt from her face, first one side and then the other. Abby briefly closed her eyes, feeling the warm strokes on her skin. It had been a long time since a man — since anyone — had touched her. Then her eyes flew open and she hastily pulled back.

"What happened to you today?" she demanded. "You had an appointment."

Jake put down the towel and gave her an exasperated look. "I felt fine this morning, so I went to work. Big deal."

"It's a workplace injury. You're required to follow up. There are reports that have to be completed," Abby said doggedly. She had to admit that his face looked remarkably better. The swelling was nearly gone, and his eye was wide open, with only the dark bruising surrounding it.

"So you came to my house? To fill out a report?"

"I —" She gathered her scattered thoughts, looking down at her arm, which had begun to burn. He should have come in so she wouldn't have been waiting and wondering. She raised her chin. "You should have at least called and cancelled. I was worried that I'd made a mistake. That you had been injured more seriously than I thought and that you might have passed out. But no, you were just being macho and going to work when you weren't supposed to."

Jake put his hand to his heart. "You were worried about me?"

Abby frowned. "I said I was worried about my judgment."

"About me." He batted his sandy lashes.

She rolled her eyes. "Get over yourself. If you —"

"Shh." He put his finger against her lips, held it there. "I'm sorry, okay?"

Abby stared at him, then she twisted her head away and stood up.

"I assume you're going home," he said. "I'll walk you back."

Abby moved briskly toward the door. "I'm quite capable of walking home by myself, thank you."

"You can't stop me," he remarked mildly as she stepped outside and he followed her onto the path. "I'll just walk behind you if you won't let me walk next to you."

The night was dark now. A full moon climbed through the trees, shining like a beacon and sending long black shadows streaming through the forest. Bars of light flashed back and forth across them as they walked. By the time they reached her house, their silence was almost companionable, because it was impossible for them not to remark on the shadows and feel a little hypnotized by that light-and-dark strobe from the vast brimming moon. At her door, Jake reached for her hair and his fingers ran through a strand, retrieving a sprig of pine needles, which he held up for her inspection before flicking it into the night.

"I think it's only fair to tell you." He paused to study her. "I'm not a very patient man."

Abby shook her head, frowning. "What are you talking about?"

"Nothing," he said, his expression now amused. "Nothing at all."

He turned and jogged back into the zebra-striped woods while the moon stared.

CHAPTER 4

Lucy was a hoot, and Lucy did not suffer fools gladly. A retired gynecologist in her late sixties, she stood a full five feet tall, with a stout body the shape and weight of a barrel of nails. She had a voice like rust and gravel from years of smoking. Her short iron-gray hair occasionally lay neatly combed around her head, but more often spiked out in all directions from her habit of twisting it around her fingers. Lucy had lost her medical license when she was drinking heavily before a difficult delivery and the baby died. Maybe it could have been saved, maybe not. It was impossible to know, for Lucy was in no condition to be making serious decisions that night. That was ten years ago. Once sober, she had never returned to her medical practice. She currently worked as a volunteer at a rape crisis center in Phoenix, and she was Abby's guide or friend or counselor or sponsor, depending on the day.

Because it was a rare rainy summer day at the canyon, the clinic had been very slow, and Pepper sent Abby home a few hours early. She curled up on her back porch to relax and savor the low cloudy sky, to watch the rain drip off the roof. Armed with a cup of tea, she called Lucy for the first time in several weeks.

Yes, everything was fine, Abby reported. She was managing her anxiety well with meditation and her relaxation techniques. Only a few minor episodes, which she had been able to quell. She felt better, felt mostly in control. Sometimes she couldn't even recognize the person she used to be when anxiety rushed through her every day like a runaway train and she started drinking every night to fall asleep. How had she come to that? Abby liked the relative simplicity of this new life, the smaller community, her spartan routine of work, exercise, and sound sleep.

"And you're not bored with that?" Lucy wanted to know.

"Surprisingly, no. Work has been very busy because of summer tourists. And I've been reading, mostly medicine but sometimes novels. I just —" Abby paused and Lucy waited. Lucy could wait a very long time.

"I've just lost my confidence," Abby said finally. "I feel like I constantly make little mistakes, little errors in judgment. I worry about making bigger mistakes. I worry that everyone thinks I'm not very good. I wonder if I'll ever feel right again."

"Maybe you won't. You may have to get used to this feeling. But maybe you weren't right before, you know? Maybe you need to find a new rightness."

"I know, I know. I mean, I clearly wasn't right. But I feel like I'm waiting for some other shoe to drop."

A long silence. The rained had stopped, and the trees were black with wet, branches drooping.

"Are you working with good people?"

"Yes, mostly."

"And you said you're working hard? Doing a pretty good job?"

"Yes, mostly."

More silence. Loud plopping drips from the trees. "Well, this confidence thing. It might take a while."

Abby heard a small metallic click, heard Lucy draw in a breath. "Aw, Lucy," she cried, "you said you quit smoking last month."

"And I did. Only I started up again."

"God, Lucy. Please stop."

"I'm working on it, honey. This is my first cigarette today."

"Oh, great. Now I'm driving you back to tobacco?"

"Get over yourself. I think better with a little nicotine, sweetheart. Because I'm addicted. If I get cancer, it's probably already inside me."

They sat quietly again. Abby knew she had to let it go for now. She counted twenty drips.

"There's something else," Abby said.

"I bet it's a guy."

"How did you know?" Abby was almost indignant. Was she that predictable?

"Because you're beautiful and adorable and there's probably a whole mess of guys who want to get in your pants."

Abby laughed. "No, I think just one. But I see him all the time at work, so that's awkward. And he's not my type, not at all. I don't even know why he likes me, or seems to like me, but he's persistent, even though I haven't encouraged him at all."

"Why isn't he your type? Is he super sexy?" Lucy had met Trevor, Abby's on-again off-again fiancé, and Lucy made it clear that she considered him good riddance. But Abby still sometimes missed the comfort of his subdued presence, his steady and methodical approach to things, the uncomplicated predictability of his lovemaking.

"Hey. That's not nice." Abby pretended to be offended.

"Just keeping it real, honey. So is he?"

"What?"

"Super sexy, you dimwit."

"All right, then. Yes, he is. And then some." Just saying it made Abby feel aroused, which made her seem shallow, frivolous. She wondered when she had become so weak. You're a basket case, she thought to herself.

"So what's stopping you?"

"Lucy. I told you. I work with him. It's awkward. Everyone watches everyone here—it's a small town. And I barely really know him. He's all macho and muscly, and I can't imagine why he's interested in me. I'm not even sure he *is* interested in me any more than he's interested in all women, sort of generically. It's like I'm a challenge, I think, or something like that."

"Seriously? You're right, honey, you do need some work on your self-esteem."

"We've never even had a real conversation."

"All right, I'll leave you alone. You'll have to figure it out, but—oh, there's the doorbell." Lucy's dog was barking madly, and she ended the call. "Later, hon."

The rain started up again, a steady patter through the woods. It was always good to talk with Lucy, even if the conversation hadn't accomplished much regarding Peterson. Abby picked up her book but couldn't concentrate. She laid her head back on the chair, focused on the raindrops, and began to drift into sleep.

Stupid men. Damn cigarettes.

CHAPTER 5

Abby stared down the beckoning sun-baked trail, then back at Jake, who shrugged and made a complicated face of chagrin and hope. He looked like a different man in civilian clothes, someone she hardly knew. Tan hiking shorts, a snug blue T-shirt outlining every muscle of his upper body, and a black baseball cap that accentuated the shadows under his high cheekbones. If she saw him walking down the street, she might have wondered what movie she'd seen him in.

"I'm sorry," he repeated earnestly, "but I didn't even know till late last night that everyone was going to back out."

"Everyone? How many 'everyones'?" She knew her tone was too sarcastic, but she couldn't help it.

"Two everyones. Look, I'll give you their names and you can ask them yourself. It just didn't work out." He swung his loaded pack off his shoulders and set it on the ground, sighing. "We don't have to go. I understand."

Abby shook her head. She knew she was being too dramatic. Maybe actually bitchy. The last twenty-four hours had been an emotional roller coaster, and she truly wanted to walk them off and clear her head. Even though it was still early morning, the heat was ramping up as the sun rose higher and sweat already dampened her neck under her ponytail.

She didn't know if she wanted to go with Jake regardless of whether he had made up imaginary friends, or if she didn't want to go because she was afraid of encouraging him. It all felt stupid, such convoluted quandaries. What on earth was wrong with her? Usually her decisions were coolly logical—even her poor decisions about her anxiety had made sense in a dysfunctional way—but now she had no clue in which direction logic pointed. The arrows were spinning.

"This is silly," she finally said, hoisting her own pack, her voice now carefully neutral. "I want to go. I had a disturbing day yesterday and I really want to go. So whatever."

Whatever? What was she, fourteen years old? But Jake didn't seem to notice.

"Listen," he said carefully as they started. As if he had to treat her delicately. "I'm not trying to be insulting or anything, but I can't help myself about this. Occupational hazard. Do you have enough water? It's already damn hot today, and it will get worse as we drop."

Abby allowed him a smile. "Yes, sir, over a gallon. Is that okay? We're going what—three or four miles total?"

"Yep, but it's steep. You'll need it."

Abby nodded. Jake had chosen a path too rugged and remote to attract average tourists, who would mostly be traveling the Bright Angel and South Kaibab trails in droves. Typically, she had arrived first at the trailhead, and entertained herself with the signs. Signs that many of her patients disregarded, much to their peril.

DOWN IS OPTIONAL. UP IS MANDATORY.
WARNING! FALLS FROM CLIFFS HAVE RESULTED IN DEATH.
HEAT KILLS. CARRY *AT LEAST* ONE GALLON OF WATER.

They tramped in silence for a long time, dropping rapidly down the path. The sky vaulted over them, a pale sun-washed blue, and puffs of soft white dust rose around their boots. Step by step, Abby felt her stress ease, felt the tug of long-past ages pulling at her like gravity every time she took a stride down. Her muscles warmed and stretched, and even with the heavy water sloshing in her pack, she felt her shoulders slacken and swing more freely. She began to regret her earlier behavior as she realized that Jake had no intention of saying another word until she spoke first.

"So, Mr. Ranger," she said in her best whining touristy voice, "is this what we call the Kaibab limestone layer?"

"Yes, ma'am," Jake laughed, clearly relieved. "A couple hundred million years old. Fossils and things."

"Fossils and *things*? That's all I get?"

"Hey. Just so you know, keeping all this geology straight is not my greatest talent. There's about a zillion little in-betweeny layers, so I just try to cover the main chunks of it. This rock was formed way back before the dinosaurs went belly up, I know that much."

Abby almost asked him what was his greatest talent, but caught herself in time.

They paused to let hikers pass them, going up. The three young men looked haggard and grim, their mouths gaping as they labored to breathe. Jake stopped with them briefly, chatting and making sure they still had water and some food, then waved them on.

As their footfalls faded, he and Abby gazed across the endless canyons and mesas, the colors starting to shimmer and melt in the heat. Rusty reds, ashen whites, dusty oranges, tarnished yellows. The distances and depths were impossible to gauge. Protectively, Jake touched her pack and pulled her back a few steps from the edge. He had told her before not to linger like that on a precipice, that a stumble or slip could be her last, but it was hard to be constantly vigilant when the precipices were everywhere.

"In-betweeny layers?" Abby asked after a moment.

"Yes, in-betweeny. That's a technical geological term." He hesitated. "Now listen, I don't share this with hardly anyone, but I have a system that I call my salad system. Kale and cheese, herbs and baby asparagus, and very old stuff." He laughed at the look on her face. "Kale is KL for Kaibab limestone, cheese is CS for Coconino sandstone. Herbs is HS for Hermit shale, and baby asparagus is BAS for Bright Angel shale. And the very old stuff is V for the Vishnu schist at the bottom, which is practically down at the center of the earth. Brilliant, right?"

"I'm speechless. Geology salad?"

"Quit laughing at me. It really works. And hey, it's nice to see you smile. I think I said that once before."

Abby sobered as it all came flooding back. Those dark bitter eyes.

"Tough day yesterday," she said briefly. She looked down at the gray-white dust thick on her hiking boots and legs, powder over two hundred million years old. Little bits of dried-up ancient fossils coating her skin, salt from ancient seas.

What difference did anything make, she thought, feeling hollow. Someday maybe flaky bits of her skeleton would be sandy grit on some future creature's skin, some human or semi-human descendant who would go home at the end of a long walk and shower her off its skin and wash her down the drain. Usually such thoughts made her smile, put her at peace to be a dusty particle in the perpetual track of time, but today something in her philosophy was missing, lost.

"What the hell happened?" Jake asked.

They sat on the warm rocks and sipped water, and Abby told him about the young woman they brought to the clinic, crisscrossed in scrapes and punctured with cactus spines, filthy with dirt and dried blood, her clothes torn and one sleeve missing. One sandal gone, the foot oozing blood and imbedded with sharp pebbles. Her injuries were extensive but not serious. The story unfolded from the rangers: at an overlook parking lot, she had revved her car wildly, aiming the little convertible toward the edge, a three-hundred-foot plunge, but she clipped someone's fender and her car slued against a barricade boulder, crumpling to a stop and throwing her out onto the pavement. Shaken but undaunted, she staggered to her feet and stumbled toward the edge to jump off, and would have succeeded, except that a nearby tourist who happened to be a vacationing firefighter managed to tackle her at the last moment, at considerable risk to his own health. They rolled and tussled into the underbrush until he subdued her, while bystanders called for backup. She tried once more before the rangers came, but her savior was quicker and tackled her again.

It was her utter despair and hate that had so disturbed Abby. Abby had talked with a fair number of suicidal people over the last five years, but no one like this, no one this venomous. The young woman, who was barely twenty-three according to the car rental papers from Las Vegas, would not talk, would not engage, would not relate what had driven her to such despondency. Even dirty and disheveled she was pretty, chin-length brown hair and an upturned nose, and her clothes looked expensive. The single delicate gold-strapped sandal was Bottega Veneta which, according to Priscilla who helped bag her few belongings, rang up at five hundred dollars a pair. They cleaned her wounds and plucked out cactus spines and she never winced, never flinched, lying woodenly on the exam table. Her dark downcast eyes flickered dimly like the depths of an abandoned cave in candlelight, as if she was already dying.

As they waited for the transport, Abby took her limp hand and tried to give her an opening to talk, and that's when those lethal eyes flared up at her, burning with hate and loathing—it was like a physical blow. Abby gave her back her hand, settling it softly in the woman's lap, and rolled her chair away a few feet to distance herself from the animosity radiating like a force field from that scraped and battered body, the unspeakable rage that she had not died. That she wasn't now a gruesome smear at the bottom of the cliff among the metallic shards of her car.

The drug screen came back positive for amphetamines and benzos, a wicked chemical mixture of uppers and downers.

"That damn movie," Jake growled. "I bet she watched it."

"Pepper told me, about what happened after it came out." Released to acclaim in 1991, *Thelma and Louise* told the story of two women who experienced one misadventure after another, pursued by the law across the West until they ended their predicament by driving their car off a canyon cliff to their deaths. Not exactly an inspiring message for women, he commented dryly.

Though the movie's climax was filmed in Utah, it was portrayed to have been at the Grand Canyon, and within a fairly short time after it played there were three drive-off-the-edge suicide deaths at the canyon.

As Pepper had finished telling Abby this grim chronicle, Priscilla sidled up to him, pressing the perfect pale moons of her nails to her rosy lips. She wore a very short red skirt with shimmery tights and suede boots adorned with gleaming little buckles. Hello, Abby thought, it's August.

"Dr. Pepper," Priscilla murmured in that low confidential tone, grasping his sleeve in a pleading, worried sort of way. "Do you think she'll try it again?"

Pepper bent to her and said something quietly. His hand patted her back reassuringly, and Priscilla nodded, dabbing at her eye with a tissue. Of course she'll try it again, Abby wanted to shout, did you see her eyes? If we'd turned away for a second she would have been out the door and over the rim. Do you have any idea how many people kill themselves every year? Thousands, tens of thousands. Because no one knows how to cope, how to ask for help. And no one bothers to listen, or knows how to listen. Because people try to solve their problems with alcohol and drugs. Because that young woman's health insurance, if she even had any, might not cover mental health problems, and once she left the hospital she might not have anywhere to go for good counseling, not to mention a stable place to live. Or she might just get lost to follow-up because the system was so fragile, so fragmented and disorganized, that she could simply disappear and no one would know. Or maybe even care. Abby felt like screaming at Priscilla, running from the clinic. Over and over, she saw those desolate, furious eyes.

Instead, she had turned her back on them and breathed slowly and thought of trees and running water. She had thought of how the moon runs steadily around the earth and how the earth journeys endlessly around the sun and how the unfathomable black holes pull them all into infinity.

"You okay?" Jake asked now, startling her.

"Yes. Sometimes all this crap is just hard to take. But this hike is helping. Let's keep going."

"You think you can walk back out? We've dropped a lot."

"Just a little farther, anyway."

He pulled her water bottle from her pack. "Then drink up some more. You're not drinking enough." He stood with his arms folded until she did.

They moved on and the dust turned deep red, as if they were walking through powdered rust. Herbs of the salad, Jake pointed out, Hermit Shale. Talking to him had helped; the haunted eyes were beginning to fade. After all, the woman wasn't dead, and she should have been. Maybe she would respond to counseling and treatment. At least she had a chance now. The sun beat down on Abby like a hammer and salt rimed her skin, and it felt good, exhausting and cleansing.

After they stopped for a snack in a wedge of purple shade, perched on the brink of the inner planet and surrounded by giddy miles of open air where croaking ravens scraped the sky with outstretched wings, Abby knew it was time to turn around. Twice as long to go up and get out, that was the rule of thumb. Shoulder to shoulder, they sat on a little crumbling shelf along the inside wall of the trail, leaning together to escape the searing sun. They shared peanuts and dried fruit, which tasted like a feast. Abby felt washed out, drained clean, both craving and dreading the hike out.

Then Jake turned and put his hand on her knee, and she jerked awake. She had been treating him like a friend, like a brother, not like the one-hundred-eighty-pound muscular mass who was now gripping her thigh. Unbidden waves of electricity surged up her inner leg.

"What do you want, Abigail Wilmore?" he asked somberly.

Her thoughts ran in all directions. What could he mean, what did she want? She wanted to be a good doctor, to take of herself and take care of others. She shook her head, doubting that was what he intended.

"Nothing. I don't want much," she said quietly, realizing as she spoke that it wasn't true. She wanted more, much more, to be wise and smart and funny and kind. She wanted a normal life, but she wanted something special too. Squinting up at him, she corrected herself. "No, that's not right. I want everything. At least, almost everything."

He stared at her, searching her face for clues. Abby froze, unblinking, like a startled deer at the water hole when it hears a sound, uncertain whether to flee.

"I want everything too," he breathed, and his hand slid behind her neck and his full lips covered hers, tasting salty and fruity and raw. Wait, Abby thought, and she was about to pull back when a visceral part of her veered, something primal and not quite human, and with a separate will of its own her mouth sought him, opened to him. A short moan escaped her. He responded eagerly, scooping her against him and pushing his tongue deep inside her. A low shudder passed through her and the sky turned crimson.

"No. Wait," she gasped, and put her hand to his chest. They were both panting, faces bright red and streaked with sweat and crusted with salt. "I'm sorry. I can't do this right now. I'm not ready."

He grinned at her, took a few breaths. "No offense, but you seem kind of ready."

"Clearly," she conceded with a dip of her head, "parts of me are ready." More ready than she could have imagined. Alarmingly so. "But I think my brain needs to catch up."

He cupped her chin and his thumb traced her mouth, slipped inside her lower lip, tugged. Shivers ran through every nerve and she drew a rough breath.

"Are you sure you're not overthinking this?" he said.

"Of course I'm overthinking it. It's what I do." She took his hand from her face and turned to look across the canyon. "There's something you should probably know about me. I'm kind of messed up."

He tilted his head, waiting. She tried to make it brief.

"I have this thing. An anxiety thing. Sometimes I panic and fall apart, and — long story short — I started treating myself with alcohol at night. Not drinking on the job, nothing that bad, but it wasn't good. It didn't affect my work, but it might have eventually. It ruined my relationship with my fiancé, and one time I called in sick to work because I hadn't slept. That scared me, and I talked with one of my partners and she helped me." Abby looked at her hands, twisting her fingers into complicated pretzels in her lap. She made herself stop and looked Jake in the eye. "I'm better now, and it's been over a year. I don't drink and I think I'm back on track, but I'm very unsure of myself. That's why I'm like this, questioning everything I do."

Jake's eyebrows raised. "But you seem okay now."

Abby shrugged. "I could have stayed in Phoenix, with that practice. They wanted me to stay. But . . . I felt uncomfortable. So here I am."

"Thanks for telling me. That explains a few things." He hesitated. "Maybe I shouldn't ask — just say so if it's not my business — but did something happen to you? Something horrible? Do you have, like, flashbacks or PTSD?"

"No, nothing like that. This kind of anxiety runs in my family, so I can blame genetics." Abby shook her head. "Some people are just wired wrong, you know? Their serotonin is messed up, and sometimes when they get anxious or nervous they can't make it stop — they can't stop the reaction from escalating. And then they have panic attacks." She shrugged again. "Anyway. I thought you should know. In case anything more happens between us."

"In case?"

"I told you, I wasn't ready." Abby backpedaled to safety.

"Yet. You said you weren't ready *yet*. You didn't say never."

"Jake. Please."

"Because I have to tell you, you kind of scare me."

"Scare you? I didn't think anything scared you."

"Just you. You scare the hell out of me." His eyes widened in mock terror.

"Right." Abby snorted.

He pulled off his hat and wiped his face. "You're so smart and serious and sort of funny, and I feel like a stupid idiot around you. And you're so pretty and so hot that you drive me insane. Especially since you don't seem to realize it, which makes me even crazier."

Abby rolled her eyes in disbelief.

"See? You really don't know. And even though you clearly think I'm perfect, I have a few problems of my own. As long as we're sharing." He glared darkly over the empty miles toward the North Rim. "About commitment. Long-term stuff. Not that we're talking about that. But sometimes I worry."

Abby stared at his profile and tried to think. She thought about her ex-fiancé and their staid relationship, how quickly he fled when she started to struggle. Not that she didn't deserve it.

She thought about the eons of time compressed in solid stone around her, the incredibly slow, ancient heartbeat of the planet, entire mountain ranges reduced to a thin band of rock and dirt. She thought about new beginnings, and about people who felt so hopeless that they tried to end themselves, even though human life was already unbearably brief. About men she thought she had loved and what love even was, if it even existed. She had no clear idea what she was doing or what she wanted or what she needed, and she knew that she should be careful.

And she knew she didn't want to be careful. She had been so careful for so long, over a year now. Watching and analyzing everything she said, everything she thought, every move she made. She felt wrapped in a cocoon, locked in a sterile room without a key.

"No one is talking about commitment," she said finally, matter-of-factly, squinting against the sun, which had moved along its path and nearly obliterated their sliver of shade. "The only thing that matters to me is honesty."

Jake nodded. He bent over and handed Abby her water bottle, took out his own. "Not to be rude and change the subject, but we need to get going before we fry to a crisp. So drink up and get started up the trail. I'll be along behind you in a minute. But first."

And before she could think anything else his mouth took hers again, more insistent this time. She moaned again, she couldn't control it, and he gripped her so hard that she nearly cried out. Then he released her abruptly and picked up her pack, helping her thread her arms through the straps and giving her a light push up the trail.

Abby took off quickly, too quickly, eager to escape his orbit, and soon she was gasping for air and had to slow down. Before long she heard the steady crunch of his steps as he adjusted his pace to hers, so she didn't stop.

She knew it must be monumentally frustrating for him to go so slowly, but her calves and thigh muscles ached, and she would pay the next day. They hardly spoke, stopping only to drink. When Jake paused to check on two backpackers who were heading down and planning to spend the night, Abby kept on trudging, knowing he would catch up easily.

She had plenty to think about. Her good friend Rebecca Cotton was coming to visit soon, and it would be a great distraction. Rebecca, now a general surgeon, was a high-spirited woman who had gone to medical school with Abby, and they had much to catch up on. They would laugh and hike and have a great time. That would slow things down with Jake, probably a good thing.

It was just a kiss, she told herself. Big deal. People kissed each other all the time. She could stop this whenever she wanted. Only she had learned unexpectedly that her brain and her hormones were not on the same page, not even in the same chapter, and that her hormones had teeth. Sharp teeth that bit down to the bone and shook her back and forth. Certainly no man had ever roused her like this.

On the other hand, so what? What was she worried about? Maybe for once in her life she should break out of her mold. So what if he wasn't her type — it wasn't like she'd been successful with her type, whatever that was. When had a handsome man like him ever wanted to make out with nerdy shy Abby, who had been tiptoeing around like a celibate recluse for so many months.

She pushed her weary legs the last few steps and found herself finally at the trailhead, Jake right behind.

"Not a bad pace for a novice hiker," he commented. He wasn't breathing hard, not even a little.

"That pace almost killed me," Abby said, trying to catch her breath, stretching her calves.

She started to slip off her pack, but he caught it and hoisted it into her trunk. Then he playfully grabbed her ponytail, pulling her against the car and tilting her head to his face. With his mouth an inch away, he spoke quietly in her ear.

"I'm going to be gone for the next few weeks for some backcountry training." His breath tickled her cheek and his lips brushed her ear and she felt the flick of his tongue. Part of her mind wondered how horrid she must taste, a terrible mix of sunscreen and dust and sweat, while the rest of her mind simply vaporized. "But when I get back, I hope to see more of you, Dr. Wilmore."

It was what he'd said that first day they met. Abby felt her face redden, a face that already seemed as red as it could possibly get from sun and exertion and arousal. She squirmed and tried to stamp on his foot, but his grip on her hair was like iron and she was trapped against the car. Knowing she was watching him, he let his eyes roam down her figure, taking his time with every inch until he reached the toes of her boots, then just as deliberately worked back up to her face again. Then he let go.

Abby could not even remember if she said anything in farewell.

That night, showered and composed, she told herself she needed more diversions than reading medical journals and beach books. Maybe she and Rebecca could take off, drive all the way around to the North Rim and camp there, get completely away from Jake and Pepper and Priscilla and everyone else who was complicating her life.

She needed a break.

CHAPTER 6

Abby couldn't believe it. For the last few weeks she had been looking forward to Rebecca's visit and to getting away for three days. She'd made a campground reservation at the North Rim and bought a new sleeping bag. Now, out of the blue, John Pepper told her he had changed the clinic schedule, and she no longer had the Friday off she had expected. Though the North Rim was only ten miles away in a straight line through thin air across the canyon, driving there from the South Rim involved a circuitous route of more than two hundred miles over empty desert and broken ravines on two-lane roads, and took almost five hours. For just two days, it wasn't worth it.

"I'm really sorry," Pepper said, "but I emailed you about this over a month ago. I asked if you had any concerns. I have to go to Phoenix to testify in court — I don't have any choice."

Abby had to admit that she had probably skimmed the email and deleted it. She had no plans back then, so what did it matter if he made a few changes to the schedule? One day was just like the next. Now it was already Wednesday, and tomorrow night Rebecca would arrive; she would have to kill all day Friday by herself while Abby worked.

"It's my fault," Abby said to Pepper, not completely convinced. He could have reminded her as the day grew closer. But she was an adult — why would he? She was so disappointed.

Dolores was sympathetic, though she had deeper worries on her mind, as she explained that day to Abby once Pepper had left.

"Ginger and I don't want him to go," she said, upset. Her mouth formed a grim line and her eyes flashed with fear. "That man was horrible. There was something really wrong with him. His poor wife, just a little bit of a thing, was lying here all blackened and bloody, barely conscious, and he was ranting up and down the hall about how two big Navajo men had attacked her and he had to fight them off. Of course there wasn't a scratch on him. I can't even repeat the horrible racist things he said, but that man was crazy. His eyes were jumping all over, he was yelling about revenge and getting his gun, and he even pushed Dr. Pepper. Pushed him! You'd better take care of her or else, he said. I don't know how Dr. Pepper stayed so calm."

"What was his name?" Abby asked for future reference.

"Luther Lubbock," Dolores and Ginger said together, with a simultaneous cringe. As if saying his name aloud was dangerous, like invoking Voldemort.

"Is he in jail now?"

"I think so," Ginger said. "But poor Dr. Pepper. He has to drive all the way to Phoenix and back, and he'll have to sit in the courtroom with him. And Lubbock will *know*. If he gets put away in prison—which better happen—he'll think Dr. Pepper is responsible." She shuddered, her normally pale face now ashen.

"He was so horrible, Dr. Wilmore. Her skull was fractured, and they say she still isn't quite right." Dolores shook her head. "I don't know why Dr. Pepper couldn't have just given a phone deposition. I think they offered him that. But he thought it would be more powerful if he was there in person. He said he wants to explain how Lubbock kept changing his story every few minutes."

Priscilla had been listening in the background. "He's so brave," she announced, her petite hand fluttering over her heart, a look of misty adoration on her face. "I hate to think of him there all alone."

"He'll visit his brother," Dolores said. "He won't be all alone."

"He's so brave," Priscilla repeated for emphasis, and that broke up the discussion.

So John Pepper had a brother in Phoenix, Abby mused. Who knew that the enigmatic Dr. Pepper had any siblings. He continued to deflect any discussion about his personal life.

Now it was Friday. Abby's friend Rebecca had planned to arrive late evening Thursday, leaving after work, but she was delayed by an unexpected urgent surgery and didn't get out of Phoenix until after midnight. She drove through the night, keeping herself awake with caffeine and chewing gum, and appeared on Abby's doorstep at six in the morning. Rebecca waved off Abby's apologies about the ruined camping plans, pointing out that she was exhausted and needed sleep more than anything. Abby silently agreed. Her friend's usual buoyancy had vanished, and dusky smudges of fatigue shadowed her eyes. She dragged herself onto the soft cushions of Abby's couch and threw her a faint smile.

"This is better," she said, yawning and pulling a magazine from her bag. "I just want sleep and relaxation. It's been one of those weeks where everyone's gallbladder or hernia or appendix simply did not want to stay inside their bodies. And I was okay with that, happy to help — who needs those silly little slimy things anyway? — but it's been relentless."

When Abby left the house for work, Rebecca was fast asleep.

With Pepper gone, the clinic was hectic. By midafternoon she had managed, among others, a skin infection, a broken clavicle, an asthma attack, a bad case of insomnia, a complex headache, dangerously high blood pressure in a tourist who'd forgotten his medications, a sprained ankle, a routine diabetic check, one case of constipation and one case of diarrhea, and a possible blood clot.

Then she'd treated a depressed man, an even more depressed woman, and two scruffy hikers who had been on the trail most of the night. They had made the common error of overestimating their fitness and starting out too late from Phantom Ranch at the bottom, yet at the same time they had made the uncommon error of actually drinking too much water, which dangerously lowered their sodium levels. Confused and nauseated, leg muscles weak and cramping, they were found staggering up the Bright Angel Trail a half mile below the top, having just drunk another large jug of water even though they were urinating colorless clear pee every twenty minutes.

Shortly after stabilizing them, Abby sent a fifty-six-year-old man off to Flagstaff with angina. He'd been troubled by heavy chest pressure off and on ever since arriving at the canyon's altitude the day before, and his alarmed wife finally convinced him to come in for a check. The landscape of hilly lines on his EKG rose and fell in a few of the wrong places, indicating how little circulation was getting to parts of his heart muscle. Before he left, Abby pulled a half-used pack of cigarettes from his shirt pocket.

"Okay if I get rid of these?" she asked.

"The worst thing is," he groaned, "that I really want one right now to deal with all this stress."

Abby nodded sympathetically and flipped them into the trash.

The rest of the afternoon was a little better. She diagnosed two more cases of chlamydia, which was on the rise in the state and seemed especially popular this month among the canyon workers, primarily the young temporary help. The clinic's sample drawer of free condoms was nearly empty, so Abby went up front with thirty dollars in her hand. Because the waiting room was now vacant, she asked Ginger and Priscilla if either of them wanted to take a break and make a pharmacy run to stock up.

"Wait. You're asking us to do what?" Priscilla's penciled eyebrows climbed high on her forehead.

"A rubber run," Ginger explained cheerfully, pushing her glasses up her nose. She had a new pair of stylish large eyeglasses and could not make them stay put. She looked sternly at Abby. "I bet that's your own money, Dr. Wilmore. The clinic should pay for it. And you should catch someone who's going to Flagstaff or Williams so they can get them at the dollar store. Much cheaper."

Abby kept a straight face. "So . . . you're saying I'll get more bang for my buck?"

Ginger broke into peals of laughter while Priscilla stared stonily at Abby. "I don't think you should ask us to do that," she said, haughtily patting a few invisible stray hairs into place. "What will those people at the pharmacy think? What would Dr. Pepper think?"

"The pharmacy will think we're stocking up on our samples, you silly goose," said Ginger, snatching the bills from Abby's hand and getting up. "And Dr. Pepper is the one who started this in the first place. I'd love a little break, and anyway I need to pick up some condoms for me and Diego. See you in a few." And she bounced out the door and down the walk.

The workday was over, just some labs to review and some notes to write. Abby thought of calling Rebecca but hated to wake her if she was still sleeping. Abby also began to wonder about Ranger Peterson, who was supposed to return from his training yesterday. No sooner had she registered these thoughts than here they both were, coming in the front door together, Jake stepping back and holding the door open for Rebecca.

"Please tell me," Abby said, giving Rebecca a little hug and nodding at Jake, "that this is just a coincidence and that you two don't know each other from a former life."

Rebecca looked like a different person. She was fresh and wide awake, her eyes snapping with mischief, and her outfit of tight jeans, cowboy boots, and a green satin blouse would make anyone look twice. Her hair stood out in a wavy dark mass around her face and spilled onto her shoulders. She had swiped on mascara, and her lips were shiny with gloss.

"We just met," Rebecca said, popping her gum and stepping back to stare at Jake appreciatively. "I say better late than never. But don't worry, he already told me he's yours."

"What?"

"I swear," Rebecca went on, "that has got to be the best sleep I've had in months! It's so nice and quiet up here. I slept all day and I am ready for action." She raised her fists in a boxing move.

"Well, it's a little late to go hiking tonight, but there's a lovely walk along the rim —"

Jake broke in. "I was telling her that a bunch of us were getting together tonight at the bar. You know, trying to class the place up a little. The tourist families are pretty much gone now that school started again, so it's a little less crowded." He never took his eyes off Abby. "You two should come."

Abby turned to Rebecca. "Is that what you want to do?"

"Absolutely. I'm starving, and I'd love a drink. Especially if Ranger Jake here has any friends who are half as good-looking as he is. I could use the eye candy. I'm tired of spending my days and nights with a bunch of uptight surgeons in scrubs. Booooring." She crossed her eyes and stuck out her tongue.

"We might be able to accommodate," Jake said, smiling.

"Hang on," Abby said, feeling left out of this exchange. "Rebecca, you always say you love operating, being inside someone's belly. What happened to that?"

"Yup, I still do. I'm happy as a clam when I'm up to my elbows in a patient's guts, but that doesn't mean I like hanging out with doctors all the time. Come on, let's go."

Abby glanced down at her paperwork. "You go ahead. Give me about twenty minutes and I'll join you. I need to change, too—I smell too much like betadine and heart attacks."

Rebecca laughed. "All right, then. But hurry up."

Jake left with her to show her the way, looking over his shoulder at Abby and shrugging. Abby couldn't help but smile. That's how Rebecca was, she just took over, but in such a good-natured way that no one ever minded.

By the time Abby finished her notes, checked the lab reports, and scurried home to change her clothes, it had been forty minutes. She wasn't worried, because Rebecca easily made friends. When she got to the bar, everyone was crowded around a table covered with food and drinks. Rebecca waved her fingers at Abby as she bit into a hamburger and reached to take a french fry from the man next to her. Ranger Tom Chance was beaming, sitting considerably closer to Rebecca than necessary, his arm on the back of her chair. Chance was a nice-looking happy-go-lucky guy, short and solid, with the look a scamp who was about to do something outrageous.

"Hey, Becky," he cried, "quit eating all my fries."

Becky? Never in her life had she known her friend to go by anything but Rebecca.

Jake shoved a chair up for Abby and handed her the club soda he had already ordered for her, which was turning flat. He looked great, darkly tanned, his hair sun-bleached and streaky. They all shared funny stories about the backcountry training exploits and tourist mishaps, and then Ginger proposed a toast to Dr. Pepper and his task in court.

Tom Chance had been in the clinic with Pepper that afternoon, and he confirmed how creepy Luther Lubbock was. "The kind of guy you wouldn't be surprised to hear had killed a few people. I mean, like, with his bare hands. He had these giant hands that were weirdly huge, like shovels. And he had crazy eyes, the kind that show a lot of white and jump all over the place like ping-pong balls."

Jake kept resting his hand on Abby's thigh under the table, sometimes squeezing lightly, just inches from her groin. Abby removed his hand more than once but soon it was back there again. She purposely didn't look at him or encourage him, but she also didn't stop him, partly because it felt good and partly because she was too distracted by what was happening across the table. She sipped her club soda and watched Rebecca, now leaning into Tom Chance as she tilted another beer to catch the last drops. His arm had moved around her shoulders, his fingers touching her hair and playing with it. Abby kept trying to catch his eye, but he either didn't notice her or was avoiding her. Avoiding her, she was pretty sure, and she knew why.

A few months ago she had tested and treated Tom Chance for chlamydia. He admitted to unprotected intercourse, which explained his burning urine. Abby dispensed antibiotics and a few condoms from the drawer, and reviewed with him the reporting protocol required by the state.

"Oh, man. Do you have to do that? Tell them my name and everything?" Tom was not happy. "Do you think you could just skip it this time? I mean, I don't really remember her last name, and she's not around here anymore."

Abby told him she had to report it by law, but she assured him that the state health department had far too few personnel to track down every case of chlamydia and all their contacts. The likelihood that they would be in touch with him was small. The health department went after the bigger concerns, the greater epidemiologic health risks, like HIV and syphilis.

"Which, by the way, you should get tested for," she recommended. "These infections travel together sometimes. If one of them finds you, another one might be along for the ride."

He declined the testing that day, being late for work, and Abby was pretty sure he had not returned for it. A few weeks later she was in the small local grocery store, throwing frozen corn into her shopping cart, when Tom came around the corner with a package of steak in one hand and a twelve-pack of beer under his arm.

"Hey, Doc," he greeted her, raising the steak in salutation. "Don't worry, I'm going to get those tests done. Right away. And just so you know, my symptoms cleared up really fast after those antibiotics. Thanks again!"

"Um, great," Abby had mumbled, glancing around and worried about privacy.

Now here she was tonight, knowing all this and seeing Tom and Rebecca heading rapidly down a path to an intimate destination. Bound by the rules of patient confidentiality, she could not tell Rebecca about Tom's diagnosis and treatment, but bound by the rules of decency and friendship, she had to do something. She didn't care if or with whom Rebecca decided to have a fling, but she did care if it wasn't safe.

Abby stood up and put her hand on Jake's shoulder. "I'll be back in a few minutes. Save my place." She grabbed her bag and left the table, and in seconds was on her way to the clinic, walking rapidly through the dark. If she hurried, maybe no one would notice she was gone a little too long for a trip to the bathroom. The night was chilly and she wished she had a jacket, but the cold hurried her along. There was no moon yet, and the stars stood huge and bright, spattering the black sky through the pines. She didn't bother to turn on the clinic lights, just hurried through the dim building to the newly stocked condom drawer and stuffed a few in her hip pocket. She was almost back to the bar when a hand shot out, grabbing her arm and pulling her behind a thick Ponderosa pine.

Abby nearly screamed before she realized it was Jake. "Good god," she gasped. "Don't you *ever* do that again."

"Sorry," he said, not sounding sorry. "Where'd you go? I started missing you." He wrapped his arms around her. "You're cold, you're shivering. Where's your jacket?"

She should have known he would notice she that she hadn't headed toward the bathroom. He never missed anything.

"I was getting supplies from the clinic. Something for Rebecca. Don't worry about it."

His hand slid down her back and into her hip pocket, lingered there cupping her rump and pulling her against him. "Hey!" she protested as he slipped the condoms out of her jeans and held them up for inspection.

"Yep, she may be needing these." He slid them back into her pocket, leaving his fingers there, pressing into her. "Awfully kind of you to worry about her contraception."

"Yeah. Well." Abby really couldn't say anything about Tom Chance without betraying confidentiality. She had to concentrate to not squirm against Jake's hand.

"I get it. Tom pretty much told everyone about his STD."

"Seriously?"

"Well, not in so many words. He kind of hinted a lot."

"Damn it, Jake. You know I can't talk about this." Abby started to pull away from him, but Jake grinned his impish grin, then scooped both hands under her butt and lifted her up. Reflexively, her legs wrapped around his waist, and the sudden pressure of her against him made her breath come short. He lightly kissed her lips, touching, teasing.

"I told you, I'm a scoundrel. Now you know. You should stay away from me."

"Put me down," Abby breathed, afraid to move, afraid to rub against him. Her groin felt hot, alive, not to be trusted, as if it had suddenly developed plans of its own.

"Mm. What if I don't?" He shifted her hips for a better grip, and heat flashed through her pelvis. His mouth was nuzzling her, brushing her cheeks, her nose, her jaw. "I'm just trying to warm you up."

"Jake." She was breathing hard for control, half hoping he would not let go. "I have to get back. I can't do this tonight. I can't do this while Rebecca is here."

"I hate to tell you, but I don't think you're going to see much of her tonight."

"You're probably right, but I need to be there in case something changes. It's a best girlfriend thing."

Jake sighed loudly. He loosened his grasp and let her slowly slide off him. She inhaled sharply at the friction, before her feet found solid ground. She dusted herself off, even though there was nothing to dust off except her discomposure.

"Thank you," she said rather formally. "I should hurry."

They headed back to the bar. Jake stopped her at the door, his face in shadow, his voice level. "I just want to remind you, again, that I'm not very patient. And you are seriously trying my patience. If you want out of this, you should tell me now."

Abby looked up at the half-shaded mask of his face. She thought of the playful abandon between Rebecca and Tom, and of the old forgotten stale feelings between herself and Trevor. Despite what he said, Jake had actually been fairly patient with her and her quirks. She looked past him to the burning stars, flaming back at her from thousands of light-years away, the cold distances extending back for billions of years and stretching ahead for billions more years to come.

"I don't think I want out of this."

"Good." He opened the door for her, and Abby was glad to see Rebecca still at the table, listening and nodding to a story Tom was telling while she forked into a piece of cobbler. Jake leaned in close. "Because just so you know, that wasn't my flashlight."

CHAPTER 7

Jake was right; Abby did not see much of Rebecca that night, but she did manage to follow her to the restroom and press the condoms into her hand.

"Trust me," she said.

Rebecca laughed, her eyes sparking. "Thanks, Mom. I was going to ask where I could buy some." She gave a funny shrug. "This wasn't exactly what I had in mind."

"You look like you're having fun."

"I'm having so much fun. No wonder you like it here — everyone's so friendly and outdoorsy and healthy, and everyone has such great stories. Mostly tall tales, I suspect. Are you sure you don't need a surgeon working here?"

"We might be able to rustle up about one case every week or two." Healthy? Abby thought about all the heart disease and diabetes and suicides and falls and chlamydia and heat injury, but this was hardly the moment to get into medical reality. She knew she had a unique and jaundiced view of the ups and downs of local health.

"And hey, do you mind if I go out with Tom tonight?" Rebecca looked suddenly unsure. "I mean, I know we had other plans originally."

Abby shook her head. "I can take care of myself."

Rebecca smiled slyly. "Yeah, I guess you do have someone you can call."

Abby gave her friend a hug, and they joined the group again until things broke up. Jake took Abby home and dropped her off, the perfect gentleman. She slept restlessly until Rebecca came in around 6:00 a.m.

"Everything good?" Abby called out.

Rebecca poked her head in the door and grinned. "Everything's good."

They both dropped into a deep sleep until afternoon, and spent the rest of the weekend together, taking long walks and catching up, sharing gossip and stories about old friends and teachers. When Abby asked if Rebecca planned to see Tom again, she waved her hand dismissively. "That wasn't me. That was someone named Becky. She's got some issues, I think."

Rebecca was stunned that Abby had not slept with Jake.

"What on earth are you waiting for, woman? Because if you're waiting for someone better-looking to come along, you might as well give up now. Is something wrong with him?"

"No. I mean, who knows? Probably not. I'm just afraid of making a mistake."

"But you're not afraid you're making a mistake by not getting involved with him?"

"Great. Now that you put it like that, I feel even worse." Abby began to wonder if she was really broken in some way.

After Rebecca left on Sunday, Abby half expected Jake to appear. As the evening wore on, she realized he was honoring her rules and waiting for her to make the next move. For a supposedly smart person, she thought to herself, you are remarkably dense. Only now it was late, too late to call, because he likely had the early shift tomorrow and was probably asleep. Instead she wrapped herself up in a heavy blanket and sat on her back porch and called Lucy.

Once assured that Abby was managing her anxiety, Lucy asked about Jake. Abby had to admit that at least on some level he was probably good for her, the way he encouraged her hiking and running, challenged her to be physically stronger and push herself. And it didn't hurt her ego to have a handsome man lusting after her.

"You mean you haven't slept with him yet?"

"Why does everyone keep asking me that?" Abby asked crossly.

"Yeah, why?"

"Because I don't want to regret it. I've had so many regrets the last year or so. And there's so much about him that feels strange."

"Like?"

"He's too handsome, too confident." It sounded ridiculous even to her. "Okay, I know that sounds absurd. But we have nothing in common. It's all . . . physical."

Lucy was silent.

"Come on, Lucy. I've already made some pretty big mistakes that nearly ruined me, so I think it makes sense that I'd be a little cautious."

"Sure." Lucy paused. "Listen, of course you need to have a normal degree of caution. I don't know this guy — maybe he's a player. Maybe he's a tool. Really handsome men sometimes are. Handsome women too, for that matter. Maybe your instincts are right and it's all animal attraction. Sometimes I think we forget that we're animals, though. Make a list, pros and cons. See how they balance out. But you can't be paralyzed either. I mean, you tell me. Are you too withdrawn? Is your caution normal, or overdone? You can't keep your life on hold forever."

"You're right," Abby said slowly. "I do feel paralyzed."

"And remember the six-month rule."

"The six-month rule?"

"You've got to date someone for at least six months before you really know who they are. Or have a relationship with them, or whatever you call it these days. So you really haven't even started. It takes that long to see how they behave in all sorts of situations, to see who they really are. It's pretty impossible to stay on good behavior for that long."

"Good point."

"And guess what else. I quit smoking again."

"Congratulations! Maybe this will be the time it sticks."

"Well, so far, so good. No promises."

Abby wished she could see Lucy, give her a hug, plant a kiss of encouragement on her wizened cheek. She suddenly felt very far from civilization. The pines stood thick around her, stretching for miles across the dark plateau, off on their own where no humans walked or drove or rode or spoke or dreamed or made blunders. A light wind stirred the branches, and the trees sighed along the distances and whispered the secrets that only trees know.

They said goodbye, and Abby pulled the blanket up to her chin against the chill. She sat for a long time with her eyes closed, listening to the trees and trying to decipher the message.

CHAPTER 8

Abby was worried about her first patient the next day.

Timothy James was a usually healthy sixty-year-old man who looked terrible. A retired schoolteacher with salty brown hair and moustache and wire-rimmed glasses, he had been working his way across the western states, taking his time to absorb out-of-the-way places, and had just spent several days in the Four Corners area, exploring a few of the more remote cliff dwellings on the reservation. Now staying at a canyon campground, he had suddenly become ill the night before with fever and chills and a roaring headache.

"Your blood tests are mostly normal," Abby told him, a line of worry creasing her forehead. "Just a slight elevation of your white count, which is too nonspecific to tell us much. It could be caused by something as simple as a cold, or by something more serious."

"So I should take two aspirin and call you in the morning?" he teased weakly. His face was pale and clammy with sweat.

"No. You should not take aspirin—too many side effects when you have a fever. Tylenol, naproxen or ibuprofen, yes. But I have to tell you, I don't like the way you look."

After a while in this business, you sometimes had a feeling, and Abby's alarm bells were ringing, yet she could find nothing to zero in on. There was the headache, but he had no signs of meningitis, no stiff neck. His neurological exam was perfect, all the reflexes jumping when tapped, all the muscles symmetric though weak. He had the slightest cough, but his lungs sounded clear through the stethoscope, and his chest X-ray was normal. She ran a full lab panel: urine, kidneys, liver, electrolytes. Nothing but the mildly elevated white cell count. "I have to be honest, I'm not very comfortable sending you back out to the campground by yourself. I'd like to have you go to Flagstaff for more testing, and maybe for observation."

"Is that really necessary? Can't we just see how I do for a day? Besides, I don't think I could drive myself to Flagstaff, not the way I feel right now. It's what, seventy-five miles? I just came through there yesterday." He lay back on the pillow, exhausted from talking, yet his oxygen level registered a normal 96%. "I don't think there's a cab."

Abby conferred with Dolores, who understood her concern, but it was difficult to justify an ambulance simply because someone traveling alone had a fever and weakness. She had no real medical evidence to justify calling it an emergency, so an ambulance ride would saddle him with a massive medical transport bill. And once he was better, he would need to find a way back to the canyon to get his car and his gear. If Abby had to guess, he was probably coming down with a bad virus, and in the next twenty-four hours would develop the classic symptoms of sinus congestion and cough. She reviewed his chart again uneasily. Though the Grand Canyon village was a center of bustle and activity, the place was still a remote outpost when it came to someone who might need all kinds of help.

Pepper was seeing patients, but Abby didn't think asking him would help. Besides, he had just returned from Phoenix and seemed even more distant than usual, a wintry chill in his eyes. Maybe Luther Lubbock did that to a person. When Abby asked him how things had gone, his face constricted, and he only said he was glad it was over. Fine, she thought, don't share anything—maybe after she'd been here a few decades he would open up to her a little bit.

Abby and Timothy finally settled on a plan, that he would return for reassessment at the end of the afternoon.

"Not too late," instructed Abby, "in case we decide to repeat your labs."

He waved a wan goodbye and shuffled out. Abby remained distressed over him as she typed up the encounter, looking for hidden clues in her own sentences. Maybe she should have kept him there in the clinic, let him rest in a back room where she could more closely monitor him—why hadn't she thought of that? She peered into the parking lot, ready to run out and pull him back in, but he was gone.

Between patients, she took out her phone and texted Jake. *Talk tonight?* Almost immediately, he replied with a thumbs-up image. Abby smiled, feeling better about trying to take hold of her own destiny. She had decided they needed to spend more time together, talk more, know each other better, so she would know what to do about him.

The rangers brought in a leery woman of about thirty who was found wandering the aisles at the store, alternately stuffing candy bars into her pockets and her mouth. Dressed in worn brown sweat pants and a ragged black sweater, her hair a matted nest, she was confused, hungry, and hostile. She shared her name—Shirley—but had no identification, and her pockets held only a five-dollar bill and the stub of a bus ticket from St. Louis.

Huddled on the exam room chair, knees drawn up to her stubbly chin, she glowered at everyone who came near and howled if anyone tried to touch her, smacking them away with her sticky hands. She kept picking up a torn backpack, mostly stuffed with tissues and empty water bottles, and consulting a tiny notebook filled with uneven writing. Then she would put it down and hug her knees again, frequently declaring, "They haven't found me yet." The rangers brought her to the clinic because they thought she might be using street drugs, but her drug screen was negative.

Dolores had been unsuccessful in getting a blood pressure.

"How did you get her here?" Abby asked one of the rangers.

"Bribed her with orange soda and a hot dog. I'm not saying I'm proud of it, but it worked."

It was impossible to know if her mental illness was acute or chronic. Abby suspected that an exhausted, embittered family had put her on a bus and turned their backs. She knew that if she turned Shirley out of the clinic, the woman would end up back in the store or out on the road or wandering the forest, or worse, wandering along the rim. You could still be drawn to that incredible panorama even if your brain wasn't right. It was October now, the days pleasantly warm, but the nights turned dark early and quickly went cold, and Shirley had no place to stay. They drew John Pepper into the conversation, but he had no good solutions either. Eventually everyone decided the best path was to arrest Shirley for shoplifting and take her to jail in Tusayan, just outside the national park. She would have food and shelter, and hopefully they could trace her family or get a social worker on her case.

Abby was sitting in the little office, completing her notes on Shirley so they could take her report along to Tusayan, when she heard a commotion of doors and rushing feet and a gurney rolling down the hall. She hurried out, afraid something had happened with Shirley, and saw Timothy James being pushed into the treatment room, with Dr. Pepper hovering over him and calling for an IV line.

"What happened?" she asked, joining Pepper and Dolores in the room. Timothy's skin was pasty gray, the color of cement, except for two bright red splotches on his cheeks. His glasses were askew, and there was an oozing abrasion on his forehead. For a moment his eyelids fluttered, then closed again.

"Mr. James?" Abby said, lightly taking his shoulder. His skin was overheated to her touch.

"Apparently he collapsed in the parking lot," Pepper said, turning to Dolores. "Open up that IV and get another ready, and get a chest X-ray as soon as you can. Oxygen, please, and — uh-oh."

Pepper stopped cold as he was palpating Timothy's abdomen. He motioned to Abby and showed her the swollen bulge under his hand, an ominous hump in the crease at the top of the right leg. Timothy winced as Pepper touched bulge, though his eyes didn't open.

"I'm assuming that wasn't there this morning," Pepper said, then rapidly, "Dolores, have Priscilla order a helicopter."

"No, there was nothing there," Abby said, feeling panicky. "His exam was normal except for the fever and weakness. Did you see his labs?" She reached out and gingerly palpated the tender lumpy lymph nodes, a growing dismay in her heart. "Do you think —"

"It's plague," Pepper said shortly, adjusting the IV and pulling on a medical face mask. "It advances incredibly fast sometimes. His blood pressure is in the basement—maybe septic shock. I can hear crackles in his chest too, so probably pneumonia. Dolores, are those antibiotics ready? And here, put these on." He handed both Dolores and Abby masks.

Abby slipped hers over her face, stunned and horrified. Not only that she had missed the diagnosis but that she hadn't even thought of it. Not even close. She'd thought of practically everything else, but not bubonic plague. She'd known that morning that her patient might have something bad, and she'd known that he had just camped in the Four Corners area. Low levels of plague-infested fleas had endured there for quite some time, but only a small handful of cases had ever been diagnosed, and few physicians had seen it.

As it was, Timothy James had a fair chance of dying from bubonic plague.

The IV fluids started to improve his blood pressure. His eyes opened, and a pale smile touched his lips when he saw Abby.

"Dr. Wilmore. Good thing you told me to come back."

Abby squeezed his hand. "Good thing you made it back."

"Thanks, Doctor."

Thanks? she wanted to scream. Thanks for missing a deadly disease that's about to kill you? She wanted to run and hide, she wanted to curl up and die. Her heart pulsed heavily in her neck.

"What can I do?" she asked Pepper, wanting to be busy with something, anything.

"Nothing. We've done what we can. He needs to be in the hospital ICU." Pepper's long face was creased in worry, his quick blue eyes scanning the labs and monitors.

They heard the deep thump of rotors as the helicopter arrived. In minutes, Timothy James was bundled up and out, Pepper giving a report to the transport medic as they moved him briskly into the copter. Then Pepper was back in the clinic on the phone, talking with the critical care doctors in Flagstaff.

Abby sat down weakly. Fortunately, all the patients were done, and somewhere along the way, the police had arrived and taken Shirley to Tusayan. Instead of slowing, though, her heart was racing faster, her breath coming quicker. No, not now. She could not have a panic attack now, not here at work. Take control. You know how. She made herself think of trees, flowing water, constellations, black holes, but nothing worked. She cast about for something to do, a note to finish, a phone call, a task, but everything was jumbled in her mind and she kept seeing the patient's gray, shuttered face. She had to get out of there. Now.

Pepper was still on the phone when she fled.

Abby ran through the twilight woods, half blind with anguish, tearing through branches and stumbling over rocks. She clambered up the stairs and through her front door, slamming it behind her and locking it, as if she could seal herself off from her demon. Now it took hold of her, her breaths coming in great whooping gasps that wouldn't stop. She fell to the floor, clutching herself, clapping her hands over her mouth, trying to force her lungs to slow down. Her ears screamed and her brain roared and she thought maybe this was it, maybe this one would really truly kill her. Her hands and feet and face went painfully numb from hyperventilation, tingling and burning as if stung by a million electric needles. Like a huge monster galloping inside her chest, her heart leaped and careened against her ribs as if it had become untethered, cutting off her air, filling her throat. She raised her head and began dragging herself toward the bathroom, where she kept her emergency medication, but her stomach convulsed and she bent double and vomited on the floor. Sobbing, wheezing, she curled up, afraid to move.

It went on and on. When it finally slowed, she had no sense of time. She might have been there hours — she wasn't certain if she had passed out. The house was cold and dark, the floorboards were hard and stunk of puke. She sat up weakly, afraid to stand, and pushed herself along to the bathroom with her feet. Fumbling in the cabinet under the sink, she found the case with a prescription bottle of pills, untouched since she moved here months ago. Her hands trembled so badly that she dropped it twice before opening the lid and shaking out one tablet of lorazepam. Such a tiny white pill, no larger than a grain of rice, yet it held all the relief she craved. Emptiness, dreamless sleep. She put the pill up on the counter rim and collapsed back against the wall.

Abby stared at the pill.

Just take it, she told herself. You're not a failure because you had one panic attack in months that you couldn't control. She stared at it until she shivered with cold from the bathroom tile, but at least her breathing was nearly normal and her heart had shrunk to almost its usual size. Tilting her head back against the wall, she counted backward from one hundred to zero, saying each number out loud with every slow breath. Then she stared at the pill and did the counting again.

Take it. Don't take it. Did her panic failure segue into some sort of success if she didn't take it? Or was she foolish for denying herself treatment? She had been feeling so solid about her ability to manage without medication. All those hours of cognitive training, all that careful attention to her thoughts and reactions, telling her brain and her nervous system where it could and shouldn't go.

Her cell phone was ringing. She pulled herself to her feet and walked unsteadily to the front room, where her bag lay spilled on the floor, the phone flashing. By the time she picked it up, it was silent again. Jake. It was his second call; she must not have heard the first. She had told him they should talk tonight, so he was doubtlessly wondering why she had vanished.

Surprisingly, there was also a call from John Pepper. She could count on one hand the number of times Pepper had called her outside the clinic. Maybe on one finger.

As she stood staring at the phone, slowly processing what to do, a text came through from Jake. It was a single symbol, a single question mark. She suddenly knew she needed to call him back, right away, or the next she heard from him might be at her front door. Definitely the kind of thing he would do. Abby moved into the kitchen, splashed water on her swollen, tear-blotched face, drank a sip of water. She pulled off a few squares of paper towel, wetted them, and wiped up the vomit on the floor. Then she took several more long steadying breaths and sat on the couch to call him.

"Hey," she said quietly, hoping her voice sounded better to him than it did to her.

"Hey yourself." His voice was hard. "Where the heck have you been?"

"I'm so sorry. I—I wasn't feeling well. I've got a sick stomach. I came home and fell asleep." She couldn't tell him about her panic attack, not right now. Her calm felt tenuous, and she feared slipping back into that whirling darkness. Better not to think about it, not to talk about it.

"I heard it was a tough day at the clinic. All kinds of nutty crap going on." He was more sympathetic now. "Are you better? Feeling okay now?"

"I think it's passing." He must hear the weariness in her voice. And did everyone know everything that happened at work? What the hell.

"Well, obviously, you need to rest tonight." An edge of frustration crept in. "Listen. Let's get out of this place. Sometimes I think your work makes you crazy. Let's go backpacking, overnight, really get away. I know just the place. You're off in a few days, right? Long weekend?"

Again with him knowing her schedule. But an escape felt right. Necessary. Crucial. She blocked her brain, refused to listen to her long complicated internal list of cautions. Only partly acknowledged to herself what this meant, camping overnight. She knew that if she allowed herself to think of even one precaution, the others would come tumbling behind, blocking the way, paralyzing her again.

"Yes." She barely paused. "Yes, let's do it."

"Awesome. I've got an extra frame backpack for you if you don't have one. I'll get all the supplies."

"That sounds good." Her conviction grew stronger. She had to do this. It had somehow become critical; she had to keep moving or become stuck here in this limbo with herself forever.

"Go back to bed. Get your rest. With what I've got planned, you're going to need it." And he hung up.

Whoa, quite a warning, Abby thought. Her lips curved into almost a smile, if only for a second.

What to do about Pepper's call. She really should not ignore it. Her greatest fear was that he'd called to tell her that Timothy James had died — in the helicopter, in the ER, in the ICU — somewhere far away, connected to a dozen tubes and lines, after a frantic prolonged resuscitation that failed. To tell her that sweet, gentle man had died because she missed the gravity of his symptoms, because she had forgotten about plague. That lovely man who thanked her for screwing things up.

But better to know than to wonder all night. Only it was getting borderline late to bother Pepper. They had just a working relationship; she had no idea when he retired for the night, how he felt about having his privacy interrupted. She pictured his chill dispassionate gaze and couldn't imagine he welcomed it. Choosing a middle road, she sent him a text. *Sorry I missed your call. Are you still up?*

The cool blue light of her phone glowed in her hands, lit up her lap with its ghostly sheen, then slowly faded out. She sat there waiting nearly an hour, trying to keep her mind empty and occasionally succeeding. Pepper never responded.

The untouched pill still perched on the edge of her sink. Finally she got up, put the pill back in its little amber bottle, banished it under the cabinet, and went to bed.

CHAPTER 9

After leaving her Phoenix practice, Abby had promised herself that she would never again miss work unless she was literally unable to walk. She rose in the morning after a long, restless night, where what little sleep she found gave her spasmodic dreams of running from plague-infested rats and fleas, scuttling away into deep twisting ochre canyons, lost in a maze of stone. Her face in the mirror still looked a trace swollen, her eyes sunken. So be it. She smudged on a little eye shadow to mask her reddish lids and trudged to the clinic. It was Pepper's day off, but she knew she could get the phone number for Flagstaff Medical Center. Only she wasn't sure she was prepared to hear what had happened with Timothy James. Dolores asked her once if she knew how he was doing, but Abby just shook her head.

The morning passed uneventfully, busy enough to keep her awake but not overly taxing. A few pointed discussions about why antibiotics will not work for a cold virus because antibiotics kill bacteria, not viruses. Stay home, rest, push fluids. Let the body's immune system do its thing and destroy the invaders. It will take a week to feel better if you don't take antibiotics; if you do, it will take seven days.

On a better day, she would have explained about antibiotic resistance, how taking unnecessary antibiotics made bacteria smarter and meaner, how someday all the antibiotics would quit working if they were used recklessly. How we were already there with some infections. How antibiotics could destroy the good, helpful bacteria inside the intestines and let the bad bacteria take over, causing terrible diarrhea. Today, she let it go and just gave them a handout instead of the personal discussion. There were no significant traumas.

Abby sat wearily in the little office at noon, eating a packet of cookies for a meager lunch. It was the first food she'd had since lunch the day before, she realized. She chewed slowly, her eyes closed in a sort of empty meditation as she focused on each bite, each swallow, until she gradually became aware that she was not alone.

"Are you okay?"

She opened her eyes, still chewing, and there stood John Pepper in the doorway, his face etched with concern, his pale eyes scrutinizing her. He wore those bull-rider jeans she remembered from her first day at work. He had the countenance of a young Roman noble, she thought, a high forehead mostly masked by his tousled brown hair, a slightly aquiline nose, a hollow to his cheeks. Abby swallowed her cookie and took a sip of water to wash it down.

"I'm fine." She looked at him quizzically. "Why are you here today? You're supposed to be off."

"I hope that's not your lunch," he commented critically, flicking his glance from the empty wrapper to Abby. Then he pushed himself off the doorframe and sat down. "I thought you'd want to know about your patient. I tried to call you last night, as you know. Now I've got the morning update from my friends in the ICU. He made it through the night, and they say he's better. He's going to be okay, they think."

A tidal wave of relief flooded through her, nearly swept her away.

"Thank you," she breathed. "Thank you so much for coming to tell me." She felt almost dizzy at the reprieve.

"You look exhausted."

"I didn't exactly sleep well last night." She could admit it now. "I thought I'd killed him."

Pepper tilted his head, his eyes softer. "Wait. You're not serious, are you? You know that you probably saved his life by having him come back the same day, don't you? Instead of seeing him the next day, like most doctors would have done."

"Oh, right. After I completely missed the diagnosis," Abby said bitterly, fatigue and the fear of her own incompetence threatening to swamp her. She felt sudden tears well up. No, no way would she cry now, in front of him. She sniffed hard and dashed her hand against her eyes, swiping the tears away.

"Allergies," she said.

Pepper stood abruptly and shut the door. He sat back down and bent forward, gripping her upper arms and giving her a little shake.

"Quit being so damned hard on yourself for once." He let go, then reached up, his thumb gently rubbing away the dampness on her cheek. He leaned back and shook his head. "No one would have guessed plague when that patient first came in. His presentation was too nonspecific. Do you think you're psychic or something?"

Abby shrugged, unconvinced. His unexpected touch lingered on her skin. She met his piercing eyes, then looked away.

"I thought you thought I'd missed it."

"Did I ever say that? What are you talking about?"

"Just the way you said it. *It's plague.* Like anyone would know. The way you looked, so upset."

"That's my fault—it's just the way I am. My face looks mad half the time." He smiled.

"I just wish I was better at all this. Maybe someday."

Pepper actually laughed. "You have no idea, do you? Do you realize how much good you've done here, how much everyone likes you? The staff would do anything for you, they'd turn cartwheels down the hall if you asked. The patients love coming to see you. Chef Nutter's sugars have never been better — you've saved him from insulin — and the diabetic group visits and cooking classes are the talk of the town. I know at least two smokers who quit after talking with you. The list goes on and on. Heaven knows you've taken a huge load off me. I finally have the time to think straight."

Abby blinked at him. "That's very nice of you to say. Though I know you're exaggerating."

"I don't exaggerate." He turned suddenly grave, his mouth a downward gash. "Listen. I know what it's like to miss something important. It haunts you, sometimes forever. It rips away a piece of you and you never get it back and the wound never heals, never quits aching. I know, believe me. And I know that's not what you did, not even close."

The silence stretched out. His jaw was hard, and his eyes were now a brittle arctic blue. Their roles had reversed.

"I'm sorry," she said simply.

"It was a long time ago." He was quickly back on keel. He got up and opened the door, ready to leave. "Just — be nicer to yourself. Don't always be wrapped up in your work. Try to get away every now and then."

Without thinking, she nodded and said, "Yes, it's already in the plans. I'm going backpacking for a few days this weekend."

"Not by yourself? Not down in the canyon?" Going alone was never a good idea. Too many people went for a solitary trip and never came back.

"No, I've got a companion." She felt self-conscious and wished she hadn't brought it up. Why did she feel so awkward?

"How nice. Who is it?" He was halfway out the door.

"Peterson."

"Oh." Pepper's face changed. "Well. I'm sure you'll have a great time."

"Yes," said Abby. "Thanks."

"By the way, I'm going back down to Phoenix later the next week. Helping my brother move. You okay if I'm gone a few days?"

Abby had no plans and no problem with his trip. Pepper was gone then, and the afternoon patients were waiting. Abby kept herself awake by imagining Priscilla turning cartwheels down the hall in her miniskirt and heels. She knew John Pepper was wrong about one thing: not all the staff would do anything for her.

CHAPTER 10

Not a good idea, Abby thought. She had no business hiking on the Hermit Trail. But Jake assured her she was more than ready, more than fit enough to tackle the remote, often unmaintained trail at the western end of the park. The sun shone cleanly, the air bright and warm but without the terrible blast of high summer. Flocks of woolly sheep clouds crowded the deep blue sky, sending patches of shadow slipping and sliding across the canyons.

"You'll be fine," he assured her. "You've been hiking and running up and down the trails for months. And it's not so horribly hot now."

He sorted efficiently through the gear and food, placing some of the items in her pack, some in his own. The lighter, bulkier things went into hers.

"You must be a little worried about my fitness," she noted dryly, "or you wouldn't be making your pack weigh ten times more than mine."

"Chivalry isn't dead," he replied, stuffing the last of the equipment away and tightening the straps. He stood and stretched his back.

Abby studied him. It felt downright surreal to be heading along this rugged path with this striking man. He wore his favorite black cap and his khaki shorts and a snug tee shirt that stretched over the thick muscles of his arms and shoulders. His sandy hair poked out from under the cap in golden wisps, catching the sun. His hazel eyes danced when he saw her watching him.

"You look ready," he remarked, smiling.

"Ready for what?" Abby felt utterly outside herself, playful, a little enticing, someone she hardly knew. Had she just taunted him? Was she out of her mind? Talk about playing with fire. But she felt enchanted by the brilliant sapphire sky full of puffy sheep, the light breeze that stirred her hair, the yawning tawny chasms at her feet, awaiting discovery. She knew she was still riding high, euphoric from the support and kind words of John Pepper and the recovery of Timothy James. It was the most joyful she'd felt in over a year. Two years. Maybe more.

"For what?" Jake gave her a fresh look and his voice turned husky. "Maybe there's time for a little preview before we take off."

And with that he took her by the waist and lifted her onto the hood of the car. He gave her a gentle peck, then his tongue thrust between her lips and greedily explored her mouth. She clutched at his shirt and he leaned into her between her thighs, pushing her down across the hood. Twisting to breathe, Abby writhed hard as he ran his open hand down her, a long stroke from throat to knee, grazing lightly along her breast, belly, and thigh. It was an odd gesture and nearly undid her.

"Jake." She could barely talk.

He leaned back, grinning, and pulled her up to a sitting position. "I know, I know. You're not ready yet. Like I said, a preview. Ready or not." He disappeared into the trailhead bathroom hut to give them both a moment to recover.

The campground was over seven miles down. The first two miles plummeted steeply, dropping two thousand feet, pounding her knees and feet with the slamming descent. With each step she felt the jarring bones of her legs, felt her femur thud against her tibia, felt the bashing impact on the cartilage pads between. Abby shifted to balance the weight of the pack and forced herself not think about the return trip up.

If there was one mantra she wished for this journey, it was simple and nearly impossible: quit thinking. Just go and explore, let go. Capture the moment, whatever it was. Be aware and alert, but don't project, don't analyze, don't regret.

Easy to say, but so unlike her usual approach to pretty much everything.

And lurking somewhere in the back of her brain was Pepper, with his acid words about making mistakes, his haunted face. Should she ask him what happened, or should she leave it alone? He probably wouldn't talk to her anyway. But now was not the time to think about that, and she thrust it from her mind.

The Hermit Trail had been built in the early 1900s as a path to reach a luxury campground deep in the canyon. When the camp was abandoned by mid-century, the trail fell into disrepair, ravaged by erosion and rockslides. In some places, it was barely a trail at all, just a jumble of stone blocks they had to pick their way around. Jake helped Abby through the rockfalls, guiding her around to return to the trail, moving easily up and down with his heavy pack like it was nothing. When they took a water break, Abby asked him about the tent strapped to his pack.

"Don't you want to sleep out under the stars?" She was excited by the prospect of seeing the night sky from deep in the canyon.

"Yes, and we can open the upper flaps for that, but I'm not so keen on waking up and finding a little friend sharing my bed. One that's shaped like a scorpion or rattlesnake."

Abby blanched. "That happens?"

"Not often, but it does happen. Once is one time too many. And until it gets much colder during the day, those critters are roaming around these cool nights, looking for warmth."

Abby tilted her face up, basking in the sunlight, following the cloud sheep.

"Beautiful," Jake said.

"Yes," Abby replied. "What a gorgeous day."

"No, you dimwit. You. You're beautiful."

Abby dismissed the compliment. "You sound like my sponsor. Lucy. She's always calling me names."

"You've got a sponsor? That sounds serious."

Abby shrugged. "Or you could call her my friend or my counsel or my surrogate mother or other things, depending on the day. Because it's serious stuff, you dimwit."

Jake laughed. "Fair enough. Isn't it weird, though? Having to check in with someone all the time?" He was playing with her ponytail now, braiding and unbraiding it, tugging it gently, putting the end across his upper lip like a moustache and wiggling his eyebrows, then across her upper lip, tickling her face with the tip of it, her ear, her neck, until she swatted him away.

"Not really. Because maybe I need that, you know? Maybe everyone needs that every now and then. And besides, I don't *have* to check in. I do it because I want to."

She thought of her mother, now living in Kansas City. Abby hadn't seen her for nearly a year, not since she re-married her second husband, an unfriendly man with a quick and sarcastic mouth. Abby didn't get it, but she knew her mom had difficulty being alone, being independent. Her mother had her own anxieties, and Abby backed away from being very critical. Though she was kind with Abby, they rarely had a meaningful conversation and drifted apart after Abby started college.

Thank heaven for scholarships. Abby's father was long gone, dead from a stroke at age fifty, when Abby was only twelve years old, because he didn't like doctors who tried to control what he ate and drank. He worried too much about medication side effects, worried about the motivations of physicians whose offices were filled with pharmaceutical samples and gifts.

So he didn't treat his blood pressure and filled himself instead with high-dose vitamins and bottles of unknown herbal supplements until he had the stroke. Abby still found traces of him in her behavior, pros and cons; she never talked to pharmaceutical representatives, and she never took vitamins.

Lucy was the one she would call for just about anything.

"What about your family?" she asked Jake.

"You mean my herd? I'm sixth out of nine. We pretty much raised each other most of the time, and the rest of the time we raised ourselves. Made the pope happy, though." Jake cast his eyes to the heavens and stood. "We should get going."

They encountered other hikers, but not many. People on the Hermit Trail for a day hike usually didn't go very far, often to a place called Dripping Springs, which often failed to drip or even be damp. Overnight campers needed permits, and the numbers were strictly controlled.

Finally they reached the campground, a cool oasis of creek and trees. Abby was footsore and tired, and when she closed her eyes, her retina glowed with an image of dull red cliffs and dazzling sky. Jake led her to the farthest, most secluded site, which was restricted by yellow caution tape and a small neat hand-written sign: Campsite Closed, Biohazard. Jake chuckled and pulled down the tape and sign, stuffing them into the trash pocket of his pack, which he dumped into the center of the space.

"What the heck?" Abby said. "Biohazard?"

"My buddies. Their idea of a joke. I asked them to save me this campsite. It pays to have friends in the right places."

He was all business then, setting up their camp. Abby wanted to help, so he gave her small jobs, but he quickly had the tent staked and the food hanging up, safe from varmints. When everything was stowed and hammered and arranged to his satisfaction, he sat on a rock and beckoned to her.

"Pull up a boulder," he said.

"Right. We need to talk." Abby felt clumsy, felt awkwardly naïve. It had been years since she had personally talked to a man about such things; giving advice to patients didn't count even though she did it every day. She had been with no one since tackling her anxiety, and she had been with her fiancé for four years before that. "So. Just so you know, a few weeks ago I dusted the cobwebs off my birth control pills and started taking them. Just in case."

His eyes lit up. "Just when I thought this couldn't get any better."

"Don't be juvenile."

"Good luck with that," he laughed.

Abby bit her lip. This felt so foreign, despite how many times she recommended that her patients get tested for sexually transmitted infections before starting a relationship, and that they ask their new partner to do the same. "The thing is, I don't have any testing. It's been over a year."

He stared at her and licked his lips. "We'll get back to that in a second." He fished into the bottom of his pack, extracting a slip of paper. "Knowing you and how you overthink everything — and I want to point out that those are your words, not mine — I brought you my STD report from Flagstaff."

Abby didn't look at it. "The fact that you brought it is good with me. And by the way, you were smart to get out of Dodge to have that done."

"Some of us value privacy more than others. But I brought condoms if you're more comfortable with that."

"So did I." Abby smiled.

"Come here."

He pulled her to him so that she stood in front of him where he sat on his rock. He shook the sandy hair from his eyes and looked up at her as she gazed down at him, her hands on his shoulders. He palmed the soft skin behind her knees, drawing her closer between his legs, and she felt a giddy twist of nerves deep inside herself.

"You'll have to correct me," he said, slowly caressing the backs of her knees, her thighs. "I thought I heard you say that it's been more than a year."

"It's true," she said softly. Her fingers were twisting in his shirt in response to his touch, but she held his gaze.

"So that explains why you've been so twitchy." His hands inched up beneath her shorts.

"Twitchy? What the heck does that mean? I'm not twitchy. Ooh." She gulped as he pressed his fingertips into her skin up high on her inner thighs. His hands were warm, his skin slightly roughened from hard work.

"Ha. You're so twitchy I can hardly stand it. All I have to do is breathe on you and you start getting hot."

"That is not true. So not true. You're just projecting your own macho testosteroney fantasies onto me. I'm always in perfect control of my . . . of my . . . ahh . . ." His fingers grazed the lower arcs of both her cheeks and her pelvic muscles constricted.

"Testosteroney?" He studied her face, his fingers sliding, toying.

"It's a . . . a medical . . . term . . ." Her legs were turning watery. Her hands kneaded wads of his shirt until she felt her fingernails scrape his skin.

Their eyes stayed locked, as if that was the point of this game, until he shifted his hands around forward so that his thumbs now rubbed the front inguinal creases at the top of her legs.

"I can't . . . I . . ." She was melting away, could barely focus on his face.

"Can't what?" His thumbs moved slowly back and forth, then he stopped.

Her eyes widened.

"Not here," he said. "Don't move."

As if.

Jake grabbed his sleeping bag out of the tent, took her hand, and pulled her after him. They stepped through a screen of foliage, prickly branches clawing their legs, but Jake pushed on till they emerged in a natural circle of pale red stones shadowed by the lacy branches of an old mesquite tree. Bees mumbled across the small clearing.

"So pretty," Abby managed to say before Jake's hungry mouth smothered hers, all his slow delicious teasing swept away. Now his hands were everywhere, grasping her face, her throat, seizing her breasts. Now her shirt was gone and his too, they were skin to skin and she cried out when her legs came apart and straddled his waist, and then his avid fingers slipped into her with an exquisite rough jolt of electricity. "You are so ready," he growled as he kicked open the sleeping bag and went down onto it with her under him. She tried to say something, find his name, but she had no language, just inarticulate sounds, and she cried out again when he sank inside her. She tried to wait, to prolong, but after only a few moments she lost herself, convulsing helplessly in spasms so violent that she took him with her over and over again.

They lay collapsed on the sleeping bag as their breathing gradually returned to normal. Jake shifted onto his side to watch her. She felt dreamy and lax.

"I was going to be all slow and romantic," he said, tracing his finger down her nose and around her mouth. "But that plan sort of didn't work."

Abby smiled faintly. Her chestnut hair rippled across her chest, splashed with sunlight, and he reached to brush it off her. The light contact made her rise and stiffen.

"Are you kidding me? You should be limp as a noodle right now." He repeated his lingering sweep across her, and she arched into his touch.

"Unbelievably twitchy," he murmured. She tried feebly to protest, but he slid his arm under her shoulders and drew her tightly against his chest as his other hand stroked firmly down her belly and into the fork of her, then back up. Once more, twice, and she buckled and fell apart all over again.

Later, he helped her into her scattered clothes and they made their way back to camp. The sun lay low, casting long lavender shadows.

"I recommend you take a little nap while I fix supper," he said, holding the tent flap open for her. "You're going to need your strength tonight."

They slept late the next morning, finally awakening when sunlight struck the tent and the temperature inside grew uncomfortably warm. The mighty Colorado River was less than two miles away, and they headed toward it, a short hike that now seemed like a stroll to Abby. Soon they stood by the bank, watching the heavy, muddy flow turn and roil, muscling its way past the canyon walls. Then it funneled into a smooth glassy tongue, deceptively peaceful, as it flowed straight into the roaring chaos of Hermit Rapid. A fine spray of water rose and hovered in the air over a line of big standing waves.

"Looks like chocolate milk," Abby said, nearly shouting to be heard over the river, which had heft and weight as it purled along, rubbing and pushing its way by. It looked more like pudding than water.

Jake agreed. "You might see it all sparkly blue or green every now and then, but mostly not. It's always full of soil and silt from erosion and runoff. 'Colorado' is Spanish for 'colored red.'" He squinted at her, smiling. "Guess I just went all ranger on you. But don't go thinking it's warm and toasty. That water's coming off the bottom of the dam, and it's really cold. It could kill you from hypothermia if you stupidly went swimming and stayed in too long. Not that you could survive the current anyway."

Abby stared at the formidable rushing water. "People have tried to swim here?"

"Yeah, and then they're found miles down the river, washed up somewhere, and I don't mean alive. If they're found at all. It happened right here not that long ago, a teenage boy." He suddenly pointed. "Hey! Our lucky day. Here they come."

A raft appeared at the top of the river. The rower stood in the central spot in the gray rubber raft, scanning the currents ahead as the boat skimmed through the calm upper water. Two riders sat perched in front for ballast, to keep the raft from flipping backwards in the waves, all hands white-knuckled around the rope rigging. They flew into the smooth silvery triangle of water that pointed into the rapids, the raft dancing and jigging up and down, knocked back and forth by the chop and current. Then it struck the first standing wave and threw up a huge gout of water that drenched the riders, then smashed into the second massive wave, rearing up in a colossal spray and completely disappearing from sight. For a horrified moment, Abby thought the raft had been swallowed whole by the river, but it reappeared intact on the other side, riders shouting and cheering in jubilation, faintly audible over the water's endless crashing clamor.

Abby and Jake watched the raft fade down the river and turned around to see the next raft enter the smooth tongue and bounce through a similar ride. A third raft appeared and raced past them into the watery mayhem, but swung sideways after the first wave, headed for certain capsizing disaster on the enormous second wave until the oarsman deftly dug in and at the last second completed the swing and entered the wave backwards. Again the tremendous crash of water and the raft disappeared, to reemerge unharmed, still backwards but triumphant. And on down the river. Abby and Jake cheered from their stone gallery. Such a delight to feel pure excited joy, Abby thought. She was actually doing it, living in the moment, suspending all her worries and fears. She barely recognized herself.

It was another nearly perfect day, warm sun and cool air. The flocks of cloud sheep were gone, leaving a landscape of empty blue sky and ruddy cliffs. Abby felt energetic and languorous at once, as if she could both scale mountains and curl up into a catnap. Jake showed her where the dark Vishnu schist lay exposed, the ancient basement rock of the canyon.

"Remember the V?" he said. "Very old stuff."

Abby touched the smooth black stone, held her hand against it with something like reverence, as if she were palpating the universe. "I know, I've been reading up on it. Nearly two billion years old."

"Whoa. Even older than I thought. Are you sure?"

"So they say. Not quite Big Bang old, but still."

"Well, I never was a Ranger Rick kind of guy. You know, the ones who know everything about nature. All the rocks and flowers and bugs and things."

Jake peeled off his tee-shirt and lay back on a large flat stone. Abby scooted next to him, forgetting about the earth's crust as she studied the muscled planes of his chest and arms, his streaky hair flipping up in the breeze. It still felt unreal to be with him, pulled into his trajectory by his potent gravity, but almost as if she were playing a part, a substitute for someone more suited than herself. Then she saw the red scratches marking his shoulders.

"I'm so sorry." She gently touched the welts she had left yesterday on his smooth skin. She was shocked she could have actually done that.

He shaded his eyes and smiled. "Badge of success. A very small price to pay, and well worth it."

"I've never . . ." Abby didn't know how to finish the sentence.

Jake had no trouble finishing it for her. "You've never been so turned on by such a manly man? Been so out of control? Had so much wild sex? Stop me when I get it right, because I can keep on going, but I'm guessing they're all pretty accurate." He stretched out and crossed his legs, hands behind his head and a smirk on his handsome face.

"I might have agreed, but now I'd have to say that I've never been with a man who's so unbelievably arrogant." Abby had removed her boots and socks, and she nudged him in the ribs with her bare toes. He turned, and his hand flashed down and grabbed her foot while his other hand started finger-walking up the inside of her leg. She twisted her leg, trying to break free, but it was like being caught in a steel trap.

"Hold still before you hurt yourself," he ordered as his fingers strolled up under her shorts.

Abby grabbed his hand, glancing at a few other hikers along the river. "Stop it, Jake! It's too public here."

"No one would notice if you weren't screeching and squirming around." She was pushing his wrist as hard as she could, but she was like a fly on his arm.

"I'm not screeching," she screeched in a whisper. Not that anything could be heard over the thunder of the river. His fingers reached the brim of her and stopped, marching in place for a moment, then slowly retreating. He released her ankle and watched her chest rise and fall.

"I'm just messing with you," he grinned. "Just keeping you in tune. Like a fine instrument."

"You're killing me. Taking years off my life."

"Someone needs to do it. Happy to oblige."

Abby moved her foot to nudge him again, then stopped herself. She felt physically out of her depth with him, that the slightest touch might set him off, his nearly insatiable hunger. She gave him a severe look instead and lay back next to him on the rock, soaking up the warmth of stone and listening to the deep roar of the river. Before she knew it, she fell asleep.

That night, they turned in at dusk. Abby was anxious about the hike out and wanted an early start, no matter how many times Jake insisted he could throw her over his pack and carry her up if she gave out. On the other hand, he conceded, getting to bed early meant more time in the sack.

"You have to let us get at least a little sleep," Abby said sternly. They lay sprawled on their backs, looking up at the inky sky, where a thin wisp of moon slipped through the night. Thousands of stars blazed across their slice of the heavens, framed by the canyon walls, and the Milky Way arched over them in a glowing silver path.

"Wouldn't it be great if a UFO landed here tonight?" Jake said, scanning the sky.

Abby laughed. "There is so much wrong with that statement."

"I suppose that means you don't believe in UFOs," he said in a wounded voice.

"Problem number one." Abby ticked it on her fingers. "Even if there was an intelligent life-form capable of space travel, why would they drop into this ridiculously deep and isolated canyon? Where there's only a few humans?"

"That's easy. Because we're clearly the most intelligent life they can find."

"Problem number two," she went on, ignoring him. "Until recently, we thought the nearest system able to support any sort of life was about fourteen light-years away. Now it looks like there might be an Earthy-like planet orbiting Proxima Centauri, only four light-years away. But a light year is almost six trillion miles. Even if we could travel a lot faster than we do now, it would still take us thousands of years to get there. Not very practical."

Jake raised himself up to study her. "I didn't know you were going to go all sciency on me. Are you secretly Mrs. Rogers?"

Abby made a face at him. "I didn't know you were going to go all science-fiction on me." She paused, not completely sure why she rarely shared this. It was one of those private things, the road not taken, and on some difficult days she wondered if she'd made the right decision. "I used to study astronomy. Thought about it as a career." She stared up at the distant burning suns, contemplated the incomprehensible distances from her to them, the impenetrable expanses between everything she saw and the tiny speck of her own planet hurtling through the cosmos.

"I don't know," Jake was saying, shaking his head. "No little green men? Don't you know about Area 51 in Nevada?"

Abby closed her eyes, starting drift off. "It's just too far to travel through space."

He placed his hand on her abdomen, moved it in a slow circle. "Don't you wonder about kinky Martian sex? Don't you wonder about what those little green men would want to do to you?"

Her eyes flew open. His hand was circling south, and he was making little high-pitched UFO beeping noises.

"Really?" she asked. Was there no end to his capacity for arousal? "What happened to trying to get some sleep?"

"It's not me," he apologized. "It's the aliens. They must have taken control of me. They insist on exploring everything. They're notorious for probing things."

"What? Wait, what are you doing? No, wait. Ooh . . ."

"Shh. You have to lie very still and let them investigate. They don't like loud noises."

CHAPTER 11

When Abby returned to work on Monday, it seemed she had been gone for a month. She knew she needed the escape, just not how much. Walking through the forest to the clinic, with an autumn chill in the morning air, she felt lighter, more engaged, and more energetic, despite her sore muscles from that crazy hike out. But she had done it, and she felt good about that too.

Jake announced Sunday night he would be away for the next three days on a trail patrol deep in the canyon. Abby confessed to herself she was a little bit relieved. She needed some rest.

Halfway through the morning, she saw Pepper at the nursing station.

"You look better," he observed neutrally.

"It was nice. Relaxing." Abby tried to sound casual. She felt his cool eyes check her sunburn, which had appeared down the back of her neck despite all the sunscreen she used because she usually forgot that spot, now exposed because she always pulled her hair back into a bun or ponytail at work. Her hair had lightened from the sun as well.

She glanced at his expression for hints of a smile or that I-know-what-you-did look, but there was nothing. Pepper was the master of the inscrutable face, to say the least. He would never show what he was thinking, though she suspected it wasn't charitable. Why she suspected that, she wasn't sure; why she cared, also not sure. Maybe he was a prude—who knew? Something she would think about. Later.

The lack of privacy was unnerving. Abby came from a large metropolis where anonymity was taken for granted. Now she realized everyone probably knew, from Jake's work buddies who had reserved the campsite to those who monitored the trail register, from Pepper to everyone at the clinic who asked her what she'd done over the weekend. Too late, she saw she should not have admitted to backpacking, since the next question was invariably with whom. Because if you camp overnight with a man, there is only one conclusion. She felt labeled and exposed, in a way she had never felt before.

Abby and Pepper both paused in their work to listen to Ginger talking with someone about a squirrel bite. Ginger and Priscilla were trained to register squirrel bites, which often presented multiple times each day. It was not good policy to ignore the bites in case one of them turned out to be serious or become infected. Despite myriad warning signs cluttering the rim, advising tourists to avoid squirrels and above all not to feed them, people seemed unable to control themselves. The signs cautioned that squirrels might carry fleas infested with plague or hantavirus, or they might harbor rabies—all potentially fatal diseases—but no one cared. It couldn't happen to them, they thought. Something about those cute pixie squirrels with their perky ears and bouncy bushy tails made people think of fuzzy little pets instead of little wild rodents with sharp teeth and highly-developed senses of self-preservation.

Priscilla did not like registering squirrel bites.

"Ick," she said once in Abby's hearing range, delicately wrinkling her perfect nose and glancing over to see if Pepper was paying attention from where he stood, just a few feet away. She shook out her blond hair and raised her chin, tugging her snug blue sweater smoothly over her chest.

"Vermin are disgusting. I like a man to handle these things. I think they're better equipped for it. Both mentally and physically," she emphasized, staring pointedly at Pepper, who smiled briefly at her and went on with his work.

Ick, thought Abby. It made her want to run outside and tackle squirrels with her bare hands, bring them back wriggling and shove them under that perky little nose.

Ginger, on the other hand, relished the squirrel reports and snatched them up when they came in. The clinic's squirrel-bite database logged only a few facts, since most bites were superficial nips. No squirrel in Arizona had ever tested positive for rabies, so rabies screening and treatment was not recommended, and there was nothing they could do about fleas on wild animals except discourage contact. The deeper, more concerning bites were seen by a physician, but otherwise the report merely gathered information about the patient's age and nationality, the location of the bite on the body and where it happened along the rim or in the canyon, and the circumstances of the "attack," which usually involved hand-feeding. The patient then received a handout on how to care for the wound and watch for infection.

After a while, Ginger started adding her own questions.

"What did the squirrel look like?" she asked with grave concern, pushing her glasses up her nose. And she proceeded to take detailed notes about the size, furriness, color variations, and facial expressions of each animal. People often added their own interpretations of the squirrels' personalities and motivations. Her log was impressive.

"It seemed so nice at first. Like it wanted to be my friend. Then it turned on me."

"It looked so darling. It reminded me of my granddaughter."

"I think it was angry. The bread was a little moldy and that really pissed it off."

"You're kidding, right? It looked like a squirrel. Aren't they all clones of each other?"

"It had scars all over it. It was really badass, like a gang squirrel or something."

"Furry, but not too furry. Dark brown mixed with light brown and a little bit of gray. I think it was a grandpa squirrel. It seemed wiser than you'd expect."

"There was a crazy light in its eyes. Like it was a wild animal or something."

Now Abby and Pepper listened to Ginger go through her list of questions and carefully record the details. They looked at each other and shared an amused smile before returning to work. It was a nice moment, which made Abby wonder why there weren't more of them.

That night she called Lucy. They had a lot to catch up on.

"So," Abby announced. "The suspense is over. Everyone can quit asking me when I'm going to sleep with him."

Lucy laughed. "I won't embarrass you by asking you much. That's what separates us women from the men and their tales of conquest. But do you feel okay about it?"

"Absolutely. Only thanks a lot, because now I have to imagine him telling all his friends."

"You bet you do. Getting you is quite a coup, I would imagine."

"Jeez, Lucy. It's not a battle." Abby felt embarrassed.

"Sure it is. Call it love if you want, but there's lots of strategy involved."

"I'm not calling it love," Abby said uncomfortably. "And I hate the lack of privacy. It's no one else's business. I feel like half the village sees me and says, 'There she goes, she's the one who's screwing Peterson.'"

"Or maybe they see him and say, 'There he goes, he's the one who's screwing that doctor.'"

"Are you determined to annoy me?" Abby pretended to be cross. "I have serious issues, sort of."

"Okay, I promise I'll stop. What's bothering you?" This was the time when Abby expected to hear the metallic rasp of Lucy's cigarette lighter, but nothing came. Maybe a good sign.

"Just one thing. No, maybe two." Abby hesitated. Lucy waited, gave her time to start. "I almost forgot to tell you. I almost didn't want to tell you. I had a horrible panic attack a few weeks ago, the first one in ages. I swear it nearly killed me. It was really bad, Lucy. Because I thought I'd killed a patient." Her voice had dropped, was barely audible.

"Were you alone?"

"Yes," Abby whispered. "It's better that way."

"Mm. And remind me. How often did you used to get them?"

"A lot. About every other day. Sometimes every day."

"Did you take a drink or anything? Take any of your meds?"

"No. Nothing."

They sat in silence for a while, until Lucy said, "Well. That sounds okay, then. I mean, you've done really well with this. You can't expect perfection, you know. Though it would have been okay to take your meds."

"Yeah, I guess. It's just—I thought maybe I was done with this. I want to control this, manage it, by myself, and I'd been doing so well." Abby sighed. "I just wanted you to know. In case it becomes a problem."

"Check. And promise me that you'll call me sooner if it does, okay? Is the patient all right?"

"Yes, thank heavens. And I promise, I will call sooner."

"What else?" Lucy prompted.

"Why do I feel like my boss—John Pepper—is judging me because of this thing with Jake?"

"Has he said something?"

"No. I mean, he always has kind of a judgy face anyway, so it's hard to tell. It's just that he seems . . . disappointed or something."

"Are you sure that's not coming from you? Are you judging yourself?"

"Heck no," Abby snorted. "I've never had such a good time in my life. I mean, not in bed. And Jake's actually kind of funny, kind of charming, in a macho way."

"Good for you. Then maybe this Pepper guy is jealous?"

Abby laughed. "Hah. I don't think so. I think he's got his eye on our slinky little blond receptionist with her tight sweaters and perfect fingernails. He's the one who hired her, so I'm guessing she's his type. She certainly has her eye on him, at any rate."

"Sounds like a regular soap opera up there."

Abby couldn't argue that.

By late in the week, Pepper had left for Phoenix to help his brother move and Jake was due back. Before leaving, Pepper motioned Abby into the little office.

"Listen," he said, his face serious. "I don't want you to go through anything like you did with that case of plague. Please call me if there's anything you want to discuss, if there's anything you're feeling unsure about. Any difficult situations. Even though you've been here a while now, this place has unique challenges. Trust me, it would be a welcome break from moving my brother's stuff from one crappy apartment to the next."

Abby raised her eyebrows and he sighed and went on. "My brother's a little troublesome sometimes. He doesn't often get along with people and he moves around a lot. He's found some new place that's under construction on the west edge of town and it won't have a very high occupancy for a while. Perfect for him."

Abby agreed to call him if she needed to, thinking to herself that it would be pretty much a last resort. His reactions to things were too unpredictable.

"Don't work too hard," she said, trying to be a nicer person after such thoughts. "We'll look forward to getting you back."

"I doubt you'll miss me much," he remarked cryptically. The corner of his mouth twisted, and his eyes had that winter chill as he left.

What the heck. *I doubt you'll miss me?* Did that mean he thought she was capable of functioning on her own, or was it a reference to her and Jake? Being around Pepper often felt like hard work, like trying to solve a puzzle that had no answer.

Dolores appeared with notes in her hand, her mouth grim. "We're getting a transport up from Phantom Ranch campground, Dr. Wilmore. A terrible thing."

Phantom Ranch nestled at the bottom of the canyon on the north side of the Colorado River, made up of a campground and a cluster of cabins. There were no roads to Phantom Ranch—it could only be reached via mule, foot, helicopter, or river. Hikers arrived there from the south by descending either the Bright Angel Trail or the shorter, steeper South Kaibab Trail, then crossing the suspension bridge. Or from the other side by the long North Kaibab Trail in the summer, but the North Rim closed up for the winter in late autumn.

Now the rangers were bringing up an adult male patient who displayed confusion, agitation, a rapid pulse, dilated pupils, low-grade fever, and intermittently combative behavior. A young couple discovered him wandering the campground, talking to trees, arguing with boulders. They summoned the rangers, who found his campsite and tent in great disarray, food and clothing strewn about. And inside the tent they found his female companion—dead. She must have succumbed during the night, for she had been deceased too long to for them to even attempt resuscitation, her body blue and cold.

A shiver ran up Abby's spine. "What are they thinking? Drugs? I'm guessing amphetamines. But probably a mix of stuff, with all those symptoms."

Dolores shook her head and made ready. Abby hurried to get the morning patients out, because clearly this would take all her attention. Soon two rangers arrived with a disheveled middle-aged man between them, struggling in their grip, throwing himself side to side as he tried to escape. His face was flushed unnaturally red, his dark eyes darted wildly. Clumps of long filthy gray-brown hair flew like snakes around his head, and he reeked of musk and urine.

"Keep them away from me," he cried frantically, reaching out, grasping at Dolores, who swayed back just in time to avoid him. "Did you see their teeth?"

"Easy now," Abby was starting to say, when he screamed, "They're going to eat me!" and flung himself on the floor in a terrified crouch, wrenching free of the rangers for a second before they pounced on him and held him down.

"Um, Doc," said one of them with exaggerated patience, sitting on the patient's flailing legs and planting one hand on his back, pinning him against the floor. "Do you think maybe we can give him something? This is really getting old. You don't even want to know what it was like having him in the helicopter."

Dolores was already drawing diazepam into a syringe. The patient howled during the injection, but soon he relaxed enough for them to pull him up onto an exam table.

"Don't you leave," Abby pleaded to the rangers as she began her evaluation. Fortunately, the patient suddenly sat up and announced that he had to pee, making it easy to get the urine for his drug screen. He didn't urinate much, but it was enough. Abby couldn't imagine trying to catheterize his bladder if he hadn't been able to produce the urine. His skin was hot and flushed, his pupils so dilated that she could barely see the rim of brown iris around them, and his heart raced like a terrified rabbit.

"Too bright, too bright," he kept saying to the overhead lights, so Abby dimmed them to give him relief.

"Hey, Walter," she said quietly, trying not to stimulate him. They had found his driver's license in a back pocket. Fifty-seven years old, from southern California. "What have you been taking? Any pills? Smoking anything?"

"No way, man. No way. I'm natural. Back to the earth, man, no chemicals for me." He shook his head back and forth, muzzy from the injection. "That stuff is bad for you. All I drink is tea."

"Any chest pain?" Abby studied his EKG, seeing some changes in the tracing lines that might indicate heart strain.

"Only where they bit me." He pulled at his dirty shirt, feeling his smooth skin for marks on his chest. "Long black teeth, so sharp. They've been biting me all night long. Over and over and over and over—" His voice rose but his words were slurred because of the diazepam.

"It's okay," Abby said soothingly. "We've got the doors locked. They can't get in."

Just in case, she put oxygen on him to support his heart, which still clipped along too fast. His urine drug screen was negative. What, then? Abby sat next to him, studying him, trying to think. His red flushed skin, dry and hot to the touch, a low-grade fever. His black dilated pupils with the slender circle of brown. The frightening hallucinations. A negative drug screen, so no amphetamine or cocaine or other stimulants. Then she felt the pieces fall into place in her brain, like a slow-motion video game where everything tumbles and turns until it fits neatly together. It was the perfect textbook presentation, just like the old saying: dry as a bone, red as a beet, hot as a hare, blind as a bat, and mad as a hatter. Every medical student learned it and it appeared on every exam. Anticholinergic poisoning. But from what?

Tea. He said tea.

Abby turned to the rangers. "Is there still any datura blooming in the canyon?"

They both nodded. They didn't even have to think about it.

Datura stramonium. Sacred datura, jimsonweed, devil's trumpet, moonflower. A beautiful, highly toxic plant common in the southwest deserts, used for centuries in Native American hallucinogenic rituals. Datura plants put out deep green vines with large white blooms, invitingly shaped into open funnels. Every single part of the plant was poisonous: leaves, stems, flowers, and seeds. Eating it or chewing it was highly dangerous; brewing it as tea was the most common method of ingestion, but brewing was tricky, for it was difficult to regulate or estimate the potency. Death came usually from heart collapse and cardiac arrest, likely what had happened to Walter's female friend.

After a few phone calls, one of the rangers at Phantom Ranch confirmed that datura plants had been found at the campsite.

Other than treating the agitation as they had, there was no safe treatment for datura unless the patient could be monitored in a hospital ICU.

"Nice work, Dr. Wilmore," Dolores said, patting her on the back after Walter was on his way. "You'd make a good detective."

"Some days more than others." Abby doubted she would ever completely recover from the experience with plague and Timothy James.

The afternoon was busy but uneventful. Abby found herself far behind in her charting because of the datura case, and planned to stay an extra hour in the clinic to put her tasks to rest. She was at the front desk checking messages as Priscilla, the last of the staff to leave, headed for the door.

Just then Jake appeared, back from his training, coming briskly up the walk. He pushed through the door, pulling off his sunglasses and dismissing Priscilla with barely a glance, smiling broadly at Abby. He looked great, windblown and tan, fit and hungry.

"Don't you forget to lock up," called Priscilla loudly, still standing in the doorway. Abby glimpsed half of her behind Jake, her elbow cocked, one hand on her skinny hip. She was never in a good mood when Pepper was gone, or when a man failed to give her a second look.

Jake advanced on Abby like a bear, sweeping an arm around her and bending her backward for a lusty kiss. By the time Abby found her feet again, Priscilla was gone.

"Did you miss me?" he asked, running his hands down her back, way down her back to her thighs and up again.

"Yes," she said quietly, feeling both aroused and suddenly shy and still trying to get Priscilla out of her head. She must have seen all that. Jake obviously didn't care.

"How about a house call?" Jake said as Abby locked the front door. He pulled her down the hall and helped her into her coat, pulled her to the back exit. Abby forgot completely about her charting and Priscilla and everything else that would just have to wait until tomorrow.

CHAPTER 12

Something had shifted.

Abby could not define it, but some lost part of her was awakening from a long sleep. As if something in her core had been drifting out in space, alone and frozen, bereft of oxygen, and that part was starting to thaw and breathe. Maybe it's just the sex, she told herself — a physical liberation. And Jake made sure she was liberated frequently, a heady pace. But it felt more encompassing than that, and she tackled her work and exercise with new energy.

Pepper returned from his trip to Phoenix, looking tired.

"How did it go with your brother?" Abby asked.

"Not great, not terrible," Pepper answered briefly, flicking a dispassionate glance her way.

"Well." Abby felt lame, disregarded. "Glad you're back."

"Um-hm." He was focused on the chart in front of him. Abby had been excited to tell him about the datura poisoning, how she had worked her way through the symptoms to the discovery, but this clearly was not the time. She felt frustrated and ignored. She couldn't believe she had actually contemplated trying to talk to him about that dreadful mistake he had mentioned from his past.

Then she remembered how Priscilla had watched her so coldly the day Jake returned and did his hungry-bear attack on Abby. Would Priscilla have talked to Pepper about that? Of course, which might explain Pepper's aloofness, his disapproval.

Abby imagined Priscilla pulling Pepper aside, touching his sleeve, imagined him leaning down to her crimson lips as she spoke softly into his ear: *I don't like to gossip, but I know how professional you are and I think you should know what happened right here in the lobby while you were gone . . .*

But there was nothing she could do about that. She would talk to Jake about public displays, for what it was worth.

Part of her awakening, Abby found, included a sudden rekindling of her passion for astronomy. In medical school, she had shoved the galaxies aside, blocked them out behind the masses of information she must learn, the mountains of memorization, the patterns of disease and the rhythms of the human body, trying to calculate the vagaries of the human brain instead of the distances and mysteries of the cosmos. She had nearly quit looking up at the skies, dim as they appeared in the bright glow of Phoenix. Now she started investigating places in northern Arizona where she might get a fix from the heavens.

"Hey," she said to Jake one evening, lying in his bed and consulting her computer tablet as he watched a basketball game. His window was always open despite the cold air, and she was layered in blankets. "There's evening programs at Lowell Observatory in Flag. You can use their telescopes. Want to go?"

"Mm?" Jake shifted against his pillow, his bare chest marbled in the low light from the television. He could have been a sculpture, one of those gods with perfect physique, chiseled from polished stone. Still surreal that she was here, Abby thought.

"Jake."

"What?" He turned to her and smiled, raising his eyebrows.

"Were you listening at all? Observatory, telescopes, stars?"

"Maybe . . ."

"There's also star parties every month at a state park east of Flagstaff."

"Stars? Like, with celebrities? At a state park?" He frowned skeptically.

Abby laughed. "No, you turkey. Pay attention. Star parties are where amateur astronomers get together with their telescopes at night."

"East of Flag? At Homolovi, then? That's a pretty far drive, about two hours. Kind of late to get home."

"Well, we could spend the night. That could be fun."

"Maybe . . ." Then the basketball game was forgotten and he was climbing under the blankets with her. "That's a lot of time to spend driving when we could be doing other things."

"Things like what?" she demanded, feigning innocence. "What could be better than a good telescope on a clear night and —"

"I think there's a heavenly body much closer, somewhere under here. It's so close I can almost taste it." And he threw the blankets over his head. The constellations and asteroids would have to wait.

The pace in the clinic had slowed a little with the season and the reduction of temporary summer help employed at the rim. There was still plenty of work, but Abby was pleased to have more time for the locals. Ada Cheshire, who had been one of Abby's first appointments on her very first day at work, came in to discuss the results of her abnormal mammogram.

"I knew I shouldn't have done this," Ada grumped, plopping heavily into the chair.

"Everything is likely fine," Abby told her, patting her plump hand. "This sort of finding on a mammogram usually turns out to be okay, about eighty percent of the time. That means only a twenty percent chance of cancer, which is pretty good odds. But we don't want to count on luck, so getting the biopsy is a wise idea. Just in case."

"Don't want it. I'll have to take time off work."

"Just one day. It's an outpatient procedure, and we can write you a medical excuse. Then it will take about a week to get the results."

"Can't I just put it off for a while?"

Abby felt bad for her. "I don't recommend waiting. If by chance it does turn out to be a breast cancer, we'll catch it early and you'll have a cure. Waiting longer might be risky."

Ada slumped, staring at the floor. "I'm scared, Dr. Wilmore."

Abby slid her chair next to Ada's and gave her a hug. "Of course you are. This is scary stuff. But remember, chances are good that it's probably not cancer, and even if it is, I'll be here to help you through it. It will be a really early cancer — if it's one at all — and you'll do well."

Ada returned the hug tightly. She smelled motherly, like baked bread and cinnamon. "Okay, let's get it scheduled before I back out."

Abby nodded. "We'll get it done as soon as possible. Less time to worry." She made two phone calls, and soon Ada's biopsy was scheduled for the next week. "But if more questions come up before then, or before the biopsy report comes back, just call me. And let me know if the stress keeps you from sleeping. We've got meds for that."

Ada laughed. "Nothing keeps me from sleeping. The way I react to stress is to sleep *more*."

The next patient was a young man just arrived from the campground at Indian Gardens. He was supposed to be Pepper's patient, but Pepper hadn't emerged from the exam room for over thirty minutes. Dolores and Abby waited a little while, their heads tipped toward the door, where they could hear a quiet conversation going on.

"I can knock and let him know he has an emergency," Dolores offered. "It's old Mrs. Fullerton from the gift shop in there with him. She doesn't have many medical problems. Maybe they're just visiting."

"No, I'll see the guy," said Abby. Whatever Pepper and Mrs. Fullerton were talking about was probably important. Abby couldn't imagine Pepper, the epitome of efficiency, sitting there chatting for so long when he knew there were other patients.

The new patient had slipped on the early morning ice at Indian Gardens, where he had camped with friends, about four and a half miles into the canyon and halfway to the river along the Bright Angel Trail. Now he couldn't walk, his ankle swollen and purple. The X-ray confirmed a fracture at the end of the fibula, the bone that ran like a strut along the outside of the lower leg. Abby explained the splint to him, stepping around his large backpack, which had been dumped in the middle of the room by the rangers.

"Let me just get this out of the way," she said, leaning over to grasp the straps. "I can't imagine why they put—" She hauled up on the pack and stopped short. Nothing moved, because it was like trying to lift a bag of cement. "What the heck?"

He ducked his head. "My friends brought too much stuff for our hike. Once they realized I'd be taking a helicopter ride to the top, they stuffed my pack with all the extra gear they didn't want to carry. It took two rangers to load and unload it."

Abby smiled. She could just see someone like Jake trying to carry it himself. "Please don't do that again. You'll give one of these rangers a hernia."

Pepper finally emerged from the other exam room.

"Everything okay?" Abby asked.

"I'm sorry. Thanks for seeing that last patient for me. I owe you one."

"It's nothing," Abby waved him off. She told him about the overloaded backpack and they shared a smile. Wow, she thought, having another pleasant moment with Pepper within a few weeks. Call the press.

"That woman I was seeing is seventy-two years old, and she's thinking of divorcing her husband of forty-five years." He shook his head. "She really needed to talk."

"Did you try to talk her out of it, or into it?" Abby asked, mostly teasing.

Pepper grimaced. "He's kind of a dick."

Abby's eyes widened. Regardless of how judgmental Pepper seemed, he rarely said anything specific, and usually never anything so crass.

"Dr. Pepper," she said in a stern voice.

He shrugged. "Sometimes you have to call it what it is. But you're right." He looked contrite then. "It was wrong to say that."

"I was kidding, you know. It's called humor."

"I guess my sense of humor has taken a beating lately. Keep reminding me." And he turned back to his work.

Talking with him was like threading your way through a field of land mines, Abby thought. Well, she seemed to be making a little progress. Dolores even mentioned it one day.

"I think you're good for him," she said. "He seems less stressed."

"Probably because he's not doing all the work by himself. Though I'm not sure how you can tell." Abby paused and glanced around. No one else was near. "What's his story, anyway?"

Dolores knitted her dark eyebrows, her expression careful. "How far back do you want to go? Not that I know it all. And not that it's my business."

"Of course. Don't tell me anything you shouldn't."

"Shouldn't? Who knows? Maybe I should." Dolores's mouth pursed as if in pain. "He was married. And then she died. I don't know the whole story, but I get the feeling he blames himself."

"Oh no. I'm so sorry." Abby felt like she had opened a door and found Pepper alone in the dark, distraught. She wanted to slam that door shut again, but it was too late. "I'm sorry I asked, Dolores."

"Don't be. I wanted to tell you." Dolores rubbed her face, as if trying to scrub off her emotions, then raised her chin resolutely. "I know sometimes he's hard to get along with, but he's a good man, Dr. Wilmore. And I do think you're good for him. He respects you."

Did he? Well, maybe he respected her medically, some of the time. Abby wasn't so sure what he thought about her personal life.

For the next few weeks, she tried hard to be kinder, even though Pepper had entirely reverted to his reserved self. And she had other things on her mind. She decided to go to the star party in Flagstaff, even though Jake said he already had plans with his buddies that night.

"It's okay to say so if you just don't want to go," Abby assured him, since she felt like that was the truth.

He never admitted he didn't want to go, yet he tried to talk her out of it. He was worried about the drive back to the canyon, the possibility of a winter storm. They'd had one storm following another lately, usually the fallout from a blizzard striking the Rockies, fluffy snowfalls that piled the ledges and branches with white frosting. Abby promised not to go if snow was forecast. Route 180 could be rough in bad weather, a two-lane road with more than its share of turns, blind hills, and skimpy shoulders, prone to fog and black ice. Abundant deer and elk roamed the woods, notoriously causing accidents.

Then Pepper tried to talk her out of it as well, citing his concerns about the road and wildlife at night.

"You're welcome to come along," Abby said crossly, tired of male micromanagement and insinuations about her driving competency. Neither man would have hesitated to make such a trip, but she clamped her lips and refrained from saying more and wasting her breath. Pepper gave her a sharp look that lasted a little too long. Then he politely declined, remarking that it wasn't a good time. Abby breathed an internal sigh of relief — what on earth was she thinking? What if he had actually said yes? How odd it would be to spend so much time with him, and who knew how Jake would react. She must not let herself retort to him, must not rise to his cynical remarks.

So Abby went alone and she loved it. Untethered from the canyon rim, her car sailed through the afternoon winter forest like a raven, slapped by the alternating shafts of shadow and sun between the trees. She sang in the car, she listened to talks, she even tuned in for a while to Navajo radio, the complicated cadence of mysterious syllables, like listening to a creek rushing through stones, carrying a clandestine message known only to a few.

The crowd at the telescopes was small because of the season and the cold evening, but there were a few dedicated adults and a handful of novices, and a nicely curious group of schoolchildren who showed up eager to learn. Abby met Dr. Bonnie Struthers, a quiet, intense astronomer whose focus of study included the behavior of long-period comets and the Oort Cloud.

"The Oort Cloud. Long-period comets," Abby repeated, joyfully tasting phrases she had not spoken aloud in years. "What's not to love?"

Bonnie laughed. Her pale platinum hair was pulled into pigtails under a warm ski hat, and her dangling turquoise-and-silver earrings caught the dim light.

"What solar system did you just come from?" she asked Abby.

Abby ended up helping her with the students, fielding what questions she could when Bonnie was busy talking with the adults. When the group finally broke up in the cold black night, Bonnie invited Abby to join her for a cup of coffee to keep her awake on her drive back.

"You should come more often," Bonnie said. She removed her rimless eyeglasses, foggy with steam from her mocha, wiped them on her sleeve, and replaced them on her slightly crooked nose. An old fracture there, Abby thought. "The people liked you — you're a natural at using the right lay vocabulary and not talking over anyone's head. Some of my colleagues can't seem to do that. And you know what you're talking about."

"I think I'd like that." Abby was eager for more. "But I do need to brush up. Some things have shifted."

"Dang universe. Or I should say, dang problems trying to understand the dang universe." Bonnie studied her visitor. "And why did you quit astronomy?"

Abby shook her head. "It was a little too mathy for me. I struggled with it. And . . . I needed people. Or I needed to be needed. People go into medicine for complicated reasons."

"Mathy?" Bonnie's eyebrows rose.

Abby smiled, a little embarrassed. "I have a bad habit of turning nouns into adjectives."

"I like it. But you're getting a little grammary for me."

They parted with plans for next month. Abby drove home at a sedate pace, high beams on most of the way, on the lookout for deer and elk. The forest enclosed her, ink-black with secrets under a moonless, star-splashed sky. She drove in silence, no radio, no music, just herself and far and endless spaces.

As she pulled up to her house, she realized that she had turned off her phone and forgotten about it. There was a missed call from Jake a while back, and a text message nearly an hour ago: *Let me know when you're home or I'll send out the highway patrol.* Knowing that he absolutely would, she quickly texted him and told him good night.

CHAPTER 13

Abby frowned. John Pepper was coughing again.

He insisted it was a virus, just a cold, but it had been almost a month and he was not better. If anything, he sounded worse. Frequently now Abby saw Priscilla hover about him between patients, offering him a chair and bending over him with a steaming mug of hot tea, tenderly expressing concern with her hand on his shoulder and her chest in his face, her hair drifting against him.

Both Ginger and Priscilla had left for the day, and Pepper was in the small office working on his charts as Dolores helped Abby finish up at the nursing station. The cough started again, harsh, repetitive. Abby and Dolores exchanged a worried look.

"Do something, Dr. Wilmore. He's really sick. He won't listen to me."

Abby nodded. She put down her work and went over to sit next to him. In the tiny office, they were nearly shoulder to shoulder.

"What's going on with that cough, John?" she asked. She hardly ever called him by his first name, but it seemed right now. "You sound worse."

"Stupid virus." His face was a little gaunt, his eyes deep. He briefly closed them as if to concentrate on not coughing.

"Have you lost weight? Because you look way too thin." Abby was rather alarmed now that she studied him closely. His clothes looked loose and his cheekbones stood out.

"Maybe a few pounds." He waved her off, taking several careful inhalations, catching his breath. "I'll be fine."

"Dolores," Abby called, "could you please bring us the pulse ox?"

"Hey, stop it. I said I'm fine," he protested, but Abby took his hand and held it still while Dolores clamped the device on his finger to check his oxygen level. He had the longest, most expressive hands and fingers. He started to resist, but Abby glared at him, daring him to pull away. He rolled his eyes and submitted.

"Only ninety," Dolores announced quietly. "Pretty low, Dr. Pepper."

"That's because I was just coughing," he said as the cough took him over again.

"Let's do this right," said Abby briskly, vaguely aware that she still clung to his hand, as if letting go might abandon him to his illness. "Dolores, can you please get his vital signs and a chest X-ray, then I'll see him in the exam room. We need to start a chart unless he already has one."

"Hello, I'm right here." He scowled at her, pulling his hand free. "You're not —"

"Yes, I am." Abby looked at him sternly. "I happen to be a doctor, and you need a doctor. If you can find another one anywhere around here, you're welcome to go see them instead. No? No one? Guess you're stuck with me." She smiled. "Your lucky day."

"Since when did you get so bossy?" he complained, reluctantly going with Dolores, who now had him firmly by the arm as if she expected him to escape.

"Since you started being so stubborn. And be sure to check his weight too, Dolores." Abby winced as he broke into a fresh fit of coughing. She had asked him about the cough a few times, but she had accepted his assessment that it was minor.

Her suspicions grew as she took his history. Exhaustion, partly because the cough kept him awake, partly from the body-draining fatigue of a serious sickness. Achy joints and mild headache. Low-grade fever. A slight pleurisy in the right chest, a sharp little stab with every cough and deep breath.

"Are you still taking those long walks every night?" Abby asked.

"What are you, a stalker? What makes you think that I walk at night?"

"I live right down the street from you, for heaven's sake. I'm not blind. Are you walking or not?"

There were several hundred houses on meandering streets scattered through the woods just south of the rim, where many of the people lived who worked at the canyon. By coincidence more than design, Abby and Pepper lived only a block apart. In the evening, she often saw his tall shadowy figure as he strode through the darkness and melted into the forest gloom. She sometimes saw him return much later, moving a little slower but still with purpose in his tread.

He hesitated, staring at her and looking very unhappy. His rumpled brown hair was longer than ever, curling below his ears and past his collar. He sighed, defeated. "No. I'm not."

"Shirt off, please," Abby said formally, feeling some discomfort for the first time. If you wanted to hear the lungs properly, it couldn't be done through fabric, because fabric fibers made their own scratchy noises against a stethoscope. She reminded herself that if she could examine Jake Peterson, she could examine Pepper. He slowly untucked and unbuttoned, sliding out of his shirt. He had a light dust of reddish brown hair on his chest, and his upper body was unexpectedly muscular. She couldn't help but ask, "What the heck, Pepper. Have you been working out?"

He gave her the ghost of a smile. "Used to, until lately. It's my stress therapy. That, and the evening walks. Which are more like hikes."

Abby kept talking, trying to dispel the vague awkwardness of being in a closed room with her half-dressed boss. "Hikes? At night? Where do you go?"

"Usually down the Bright Angel, a few miles and back."

"In the dark?"

"Well, yes. That's what happens at night. It gets dark, almost always."

Abby gave him a look. "That's a little crazy, isn't it?"

He shrugged and said nothing.

She slid the stethoscope along his chest. She had him inhale, then had to pause twice when his deeper breathing triggered the cough. Then she found what she suspected, a subtle crinkling noise with every breath near the bottom edge of his right chest.

Dolores tapped at the door when the X-ray was ready. Abby stood next to Pepper and they looked at the image together, where a fuzzy white cloud hovered low in his right lung.

"Ha," she announced. "There's your pneumonia—right lower infiltrate."

"I'll be damned," he said.

Abby stepped back and looked at him squarely. "I think you have cocci."

"What? No, I do not have cocci. There's no valley fever up here." He shook his head emphatically. "Why would you say that? That's ridiculous."

"You want to make a bet? I practiced in Phoenix, remember — I saw tons of cocci. I can even spell coccidioidomycosis if you'd like, and almost no one can do that. Your symptoms are classic, and you were in Phoenix last month. In a construction zone, where your brother moved to. Lots of dust, right?"

Pepper stared at her, and his jaw sagged. Coccidioidomycosis, cocci for short, better known as valley fever. Caused by a fungus that lay dormant in the desert soil until something stirred it up: a dust storm, digging, four-wheeling. Then the tiny spores floated on the air, drifted into someone's warm moist lung and started to grow. Most people contracted mild disease and recovered, and many had no symptoms at all. But a small percentage developed pneumonias and lung nodules. In a few, the infection spread — to bones, other organs, and even spinal fluid. In some of those cases, it could be fatal.

They discussed their strategy. Abby prescribed antibiotics in case she was wrong — it would take almost a week to get the blood test back. She gave him a potent cough syrup for nighttime so he could sleep. If the test showed positive for low-level cocci, he would recover on his own. If the cocci titer came back high, he would need antifungal medication for at least several months.

Pepper was shaken, she could see it. Not just because he probably had cocci, but also because he hadn't thought of it. Welcome to my world, Abby thought, remembering Timothy and the plague. Stupid medicine and all its confusing, furtive possibilities, all its labyrinthine prospects.

A mentor once told her that if you always feel uncertain, like you never know enough, get used to it. Because that feeling never goes away.

"You should take a week off," Abby recommended. "Get some rest. You look pretty awful, no offense. And you have to try to eat more."

"I can work," he insisted. "I'm not going to just sit at home."

"Then at least work a reduced schedule." Abby called for Dolores. "Can you set the computer, adjust the appointments so he only gets booked for every other patient?"

Pepper protested, but Dolores ignored him and fixed the scheduling as Abby requested.

"I know this is difficult," Abby sympathized. "Doctors are notoriously bad patients. Try to be a good one, just for a little bit."

From then on, Abby picked up his slack and found herself inundated with patients. Every day she arrived earlier in the morning and stayed later at night, trying to keep up with the endless charting and messages. All year she and Pepper had been taking turns having a day off, but now she no longer took it—she did not want to leave Pepper alone. Normally he would have called her out on that, but he seemed unaware.

There was some good news. Ada Cheshire's breast biopsy came back normal. When the report appeared on her desk one evening, Abby immediately called her. The next day, Ada arrived at the clinic with a box of chocolates for Abby, done up with a festive ribbon.

"That's for saving my life," Ada declared, planting a noisy kiss on Abby's cheek.

"It turned out that there was no cancer," Abby pointed out, "so no lives were in danger. So no lives were saved."

"Close enough," Ada said, squashing her with a hug.

In the meantime, Pepper got worse. His cocci test was positive, the titer high, and Abby started him on fluconazole. Lingering around ninety, his oxygen level was low enough that he got short of breath with exertion. Priscilla redoubled her solicitous hovering to the point where she was practically a fixture in the back office. Abby knew that Ginger was saddled with more than her share of the work, but she also imagined Ginger appreciated some peace and quiet. Apparently Priscilla carried on endlessly about Pepper and how he wasn't getting good enough medical care.

Then the morning came when Pepper did not show up for work or answer his phone. Abby felt anxiety rise in her chest as she repeatedly peered out the window. She counted her breaths, made herself slow down. Fresh snow dusted the ground, turning the forest frosty, sunlight sparkling in the branches. Neither she nor Dolores could leave because the exam rooms were full, so Abby gritted her teeth and went up front, where Ginger and Priscilla were verifying appointments.

"Someone needs to run over to Pepper's house and make sure he's okay," Abby said, looking at Ginger.

The moment the words were out of her mouth, she realized she could have called Jake or the nearest ranger, a much better approach. They could easily pick him up and bring him over if he needed help. But Priscilla had already leaped from her chair and was pulling on her downy coat. You're an idiot, Abby chided herself. Priscilla couldn't walk five steps in those absurdly high-heeled boots if she had to support someone.

"Call me right away and let me know," Abby instructed. Though worried for Pepper, she now felt really sorry that she had authorized Priscilla to invade his home. She looked pointedly at Priscilla. "Right away."

"Of course," Priscilla said haughtily, then whirled and was out the door.

Abby saw Ginger look at her and shook her head. "I didn't think that through. Maybe you should go too."

"Are you kidding?" Ginger put up her hands. "She would bite off my head. He probably just forgot to set his alarm. But we're all worried about him. When he turns sideways he disappears."

Abby saw three patients and made two phone calls to Phoenix in the privacy of her little office. She should have heard from Priscilla by now. She sat for several long moments, listening to the pine branches tap against the glass, the tiny drip outside the window as snow melted on the roof in the bright sunlight. She was picking up the phone to call Jake when Ginger appeared with a message.

"Priscilla says he's okay — he forgot to set his alarm and his cell phone was dead. He was still asleep . . . he's just exhausted." Ginger's eyes clouded with concern, then her face twitched. "She's fixing him some breakfast."

"Great. I owe him an apology. And I asked Priscilla to call me, not you." Abby would have to decide if this was a battle to pick. "Tell Priscilla to get back right away. I'll go see him during lunch. Please cancel all his appointments."

"You mean for today?"

"I mean all of them. Empty his schedule and block it. Until further notice."

Ginger hesitated. "What should I do with his patients, then?"

"Just double-book them with me if they need to be seen today. But warn them that they may need to wait longer than usual."

Priscilla was just leaving Pepper's house when Abby arrived.

"He's very sick. You need to make him better," she accused, her lips a thin line as she carefully placed her feet on the ice-crusted walk. "He hardly ate anything."

"I'm working on it," Abby said shortly. She watched the small frosty clouds of her own breaths, counting each exhale to collect herself, until Priscilla was off down the road. Then she tapped on the door.

"It's open," Pepper called. "More like a revolving door these days, anyway." He sat on the couch propped with pillows, haggard and pale. The day-old beard on his face looked rugged and helped mask the wan color of his skin.

"I'm really sorry about that," Abby began. "We were just so busy and so worried when you didn't show, and she was the only one who could come over. I should have called the rangers." She didn't have the courage to ask him if he'd wanted Priscilla to come by. Too personal.

"It's fine." He wearily closed his eyes. "I screwed up."

"No, I screwed up. You never should have tried to keep working, and I knew it." Abby paused, then plunged ahead. "You're clearly not getting better, which I imagine you've noticed. You're losing weight you can't afford to lose. So I've made you an appointment with Dr. Bloom, my favorite pulmonary doc in Phoenix. In two days. He's excellent, and he's a cocci expert."

Pepper looked dully at her, shook his head. "I don't think I can drive down to Phoenix. I mean, I can't even stay awake for more than an hour. I've been falling asleep at work, all the time."

"Isn't there someone who can take you? If there's not, I swear I'll close the clinic and drive you myself. I've always got people to visit there." She realized how nice it would be to see Lucy.

"You can't do that." He was appalled.

"Well, we have to do something." She felt annoyed at his dodging. "We could always ask Priscilla, but she'd probably jump your bones before you made it ten miles down the road. And you'd be too weak to fight her off."

Pepper started to throw her a dark look then he burst out laughing, which promptly triggered another round of coughing. It took him a while to stop and catch his breath.

"Are you trying to kill me?" he finally gasped.

Abby smiled, but she knew when to change the subject. "What about your brother?"

Pepper looked thoughtful. "You know, he might just want to do that. He's between jobs again, and he likes to drive. In fact, he loves being on the road."

"Check with him and let me know. You might be more comfortable at a lower altitude for a little while anyway. You'd have more oxygen to breathe."

"Will you be okay? Managing the clinic by yourself?" He laid his head back against the pillows. He looked fragile, breakable.

"Of course. You're not much help right now anyway." Inside, Abby quailed a little. It would be strange having no medical backup. A few days was one thing, but this could be weeks, possibly even months if the infection had spread. He looked so terribly ill. She forced away her anxiety about him and tried to be reassuring. "I can always call you if I have trouble or need something. You can be my long-distance consultant. And I've always got Ginger and Dolores to help me."

"You forgot Priscilla."

"No, I didn't. And here." From her bag, she pulled out the chocolates Ada Cheshire had given her. "Eat something with lots of calories. A patient gave me these, but I don't need them." She saw him hesitate. "Don't worry, it was a nice patient. A normal person. Not anyone crazy."

He smiled and took the chocolates.

Pepper was no fool. At this point, he knew he needed help. Within an hour, he let Abby know that his brother was willing to come get him immediately.

CHAPTER 14

Jake invited Abby for supper. She truly appreciated it, for she had been grabbing sandwiches and eating oatmeal or canned soup for supper all week, and the thought of home cooking made her mouth water. She also needed Jake and his zany abandon. Between the patients and the administrative workload at the clinic, Abby felt overwhelmed by invoices and forms, authorizations and reports, paychecks and budgets. She quickly formed a new appreciation for what Pepper did every day—no wonder he always looked aggravated.

That night she pulled on her jeans and puffy jacket, threw a folder of papers into her backpack, and tramped through the frosty woods to Jake's house. It was late February, and a cold spell held the air in thrall, the sky velvet black and utterly still, stars sprinkled thickly through the trees. Like sugar spilled on a dark tablecloth, she thought. Not a branch moved, not a pine needle stirred, and her footsteps crunched loudly through the forest. She could hear cars whine way out on the road, and somewhere a dog was barking, over and over. She took a moment to stand motionless and stare upward, trying to feel the planet, sense the long distant tow from the sun, holding the solar system together as it careened through space. She smiled and reminded herself that the next astronomy event was coming up.

The good news from Phoenix was that Dr. Bloom had reviewed all of Pepper's tests, including the new labs and scans he'd ordered, and found no signs that the cocci infection had spread beyond his lung. Though the pneumonia lingered, the X-ray was no worse. For now, he thought Pepper mostly needed time to rest and fight off the fungus. And he recommended staying in Phoenix at a lower altitude.

When Abby came in the door at Jake's, stamping dirt from her feet, he turned off the stove, threw her backpack to the floor, and dragged her into the bedroom. "First things first," he announced, and proceeded to show her exactly how much he had missed her that week. When they had tried getting together at her place a few days earlier, Abby had apparently fallen asleep on him, for she awoke in the middle of the night, all tucked in by Jake, who was gone by then. She still felt bad about that.

Jake's stew was delicious, fragrant and spicy, tender chunks of pork and vegetables. Abby sighed with pleasure, sipping her tea as Jake declared her off duty and cleared the dishes himself. She wore a flannel robe she kept there, and Jake came up behind her and started massaging her neck.

"Mm. That feels great." She leaned back into him, eyes closed.

"You're really tight here," he said, working his thumbs on her muscles. "When's Pepper getting back? It's been almost three weeks."

"Don't know yet, but probably not for a while. He's been so sick." She took a breath, tried to focus. "I maybe should call him tonight and see how he's doing. That, and finish a few reports and some Medicare paperwork. Then I'm all yours." She tipped her head toward her backpack. "It's all over there. My portable office."

"Maybe. Not sure that's on the agenda."

"Excuse me?"

"You're kind of obsessed with all this. Can't it wait till tomorrow?"

"Possibly . . . but tomorrow there's a clinic full of patients." She felt tense just thinking about it.

"Seems like some of this could just wait till he gets back. You could use a break, you know."

"I hate to do that to him, leave him all the paperwork. And it puts the clinic so far behind —"

"The hell with the clinic. And the hell with him. Look at you. You're too obsessive. You're not sleeping well, and all you can talk about is work and Pepper. He's a big boy — he can manage for himself. Have you seen the circles under your eyes? And you're eating a bunch of crap, not even taking time to fix a meal. I think you've lost weight." He looked down at her from above, tipping her head back. Then his eyes lit up. "Hey. You want some weed?"

Abby frowned at him upside down. "Jake. You know I can't do that."

"It's not like it's addictive. You could just mellow out a little."

"It's not happening."

"I don't get it. I thought you were just avoiding addictive things."

"Jake. I'm avoiding everything that alters my brain in a chemical way. No uppers, no downers. I want to manage things without help, so to speak. Manage them myself." Abby realized it had been a while since she talked with Lucy. Add that phone call to the list of things to do — soon.

"You drink coffee and Cokes," he challenged. "Those are caffeine uppers. And caffeine is addicting."

Abby nodded. "You're sort of right. It's all relative, isn't it? Caffeine seems pretty safe, but I'm not going to deny it's a slippery slope."

"Fine. You just don't seem like someone with a drinking problem to me," he said, already tired of the subject.

"Maybe I am, maybe I'm not. It doesn't matter, because this is how I'm handling things."

"Fine," he repeated. Then his impish grin appeared. "But I'm still going to try to save you from yourself. And that means I'll just have to take matters into my own hands. Literally."

"Just let me do a few things first." She started to get up, but he held her there.

"Nope, I'm abducting you." With one hand clamped on her shoulder, he snatched up her blankets from the couch. Then he pulled her up and began wrapping the blankets around her.

"Jake, stop it." Abby laughed, partly serious. Her arms and legs were pinned, and she felt like a mummy. He stood back to admire his work, then pushed her back into the chair so he could pull her socks and furry boots onto her feet. He added a warm hat and nodded.

"Perfect," he said.

"It's too hot," Abby protested, trying to wiggle free. "I'm starting to sweat in here."

"Good. I like you all sweaty. But you won't stay hot for long." He stooped and lifted her in his arms and carried her out the door to his truck, ignoring her struggles. "Stop it. Hold still so I don't drop you."

"Jake—come on! I'm not really wearing anything, for heaven's sake." She kept her voice down, glancing at the lighted windows around the neighborhood.

"I know," he said, his eyes dancing. "That's what makes it so good."

He deposited her on the bench seat and solicitously strapped on her seatbelt. Abby fumed, annoyed and amused. He climbed behind the wheel and drove them to an empty parking lot at a secluded overlook, pulling as close to the edge as possible and turning off the engine.

The truck's wide windshield faced across the dark canyon, all the mesas and gorges faintly illuminated by starlight, endless hues of black and gray that fell into the invisible depths. She couldn't see it but she could feel it, the vast sunken space, the empty dark air. The sky was jammed with stars, glittering and twinkling and shining.

"Magnificent," Abby breathed, caught up in the display.

"Sometimes you need to get away from the trees for a good look." He swept his arm across the view as if he had personally arranged it for her. "And sometimes you need to just get away."

"Thank you, Jake. I know I've been difficult to —"

"Shh. You just sit there and enjoy the sight while I see if I can find something else for us to do, as long as we're out here." He started loosening the blankets and reaching under the folds. "I know what you're thinking. You're all worried, that someone will come by on patrol, but you can relax, because they all know my truck and they'll leave us alone. Trust me."

"It's too cold," she objected.

"You've got on your boots and hat — which makes you adorable, by the way — so I can't imagine what else you would need to keep you warm except me. And right now you seem pretty hot to me," was the last thing she remembered him saying for a long time.

She never did get her tasks done that night, which left her twice as much work the next day. And Pepper had to wait another day. Abby did feel bad about that, but what made her think he cared or even noticed if she called to check on him? Maybe he wished she would leave him alone. Pepper still seemed annoyed about her interference, or pretended to be annoyed, even though he once admitted she'd done the right thing. Maybe she could have handled it better.

And that was the last good night with Jake for a while. Some nights he worked late, most times it was Abby. Always preoccupied and tired, she called patients in the evening when she couldn't get to them during the day. She apologized to Jake constantly, promising things would get better soon. She talked with Pepper every few days.

"I'm a little better," he ventured cautiously. "Not quite as short of breath."

"Thank heavens. How's your cough?" She wasn't convinced.

"A little better."

Abby wondered if he was just saying that. "Please tell me you haven't lost more weight."

"No. You'll be pleased to hear that I gained a whole entire pound. Sixteen ounces, in case you're counting. Happy?"

Abby informed him she was immune to sarcasm. Overall, he was not very communicative. She wondered if he'd kept that beard, which she rather liked on him, and she worried that the isolation was not good for him. She thought of his long walks and his working out "for stress," which he was no longer able to do, and wished they had talked more about that. Maybe she should bring it up, but she wasn't certain where the line got drawn between being a friend or colleague and becoming the analyzer, the treatment. It felt like a delicate boundary marked by a thread, easily broken, difficult to repair. They did not really teach these things in medical school.

When they talked, she always had a list of questions about inventory and bills, sometimes about a certain patient or case. What she did not expect, and didn't tell him, was the nebulous loneliness she felt knowing he would not be joining her the next day to discuss a diagnosis, evaluate a situation, share the occasional laugh. Okay, those laughs were uncommon, but she still missed the possibility, especially when she heard Ginger take a squirrel history.

"It was the scariest damn squirrel you ever saw. I swear it had these sharp little teeth like fangs. Is there such a thing as a vampire squirrel, like a vampire bat?"

Abby smiled. Listening in the hallway, she studied the pencil drawings hanging on the walls, intricate trees and shadowy canyons, the skies teeming with complicated cumulus clouds and delicate cirrus. The pencil lines were careful, exquisite.

Dolores saw her. "Dr. Pepper made those."

"Really? When on earth does he have time for that?"

"He seems to keep himself busy."

No kidding.

Jake came in to tell them about the metallic wreckage sighted that morning, strewn hundreds of feet down the side of the canyon. They were organizing a helicopter crew to investigate, a tricky proposition in canyon updrafts near the cliffs. Everyone assumed it was a drive-off suicide, but even with binoculars no one could see a body. Abby mentally crossed her fingers and hoped that the woman she had treated months earlier hadn't come back to finish the job. Then she felt bad for hoping that someone else was dead. You couldn't win on this one.

In the meantime, Priscilla's mood grew more and more foul without Pepper around. She started coming in slightly late to work, just five or ten minutes, barely enough to notice but nearly every day. Pepper always insisted on punctuality, and Abby understood her lateness as a challenge to Abby's personal authority. And Priscilla started dressing more seductively, if such a thing was possible. Now she rarely left the front desk, and Abby could hear her flirting with male patients and rangers.

"I can't believe you did that. You must be incredibly strong," she would say, listening with rapt attention, her finger poised against her gleaming lips. Abby tortured herself with doubt, wondering if she should say something or let it go and wait for a worse transgression. She had no management skills and was the first to admit it; she just wanted to do her work. But if Priscilla kept it up much longer, or if it got worse, they would need to talk.

The suicide driver turned out to be a middle-aged man, a grim recovery mission. There was not much left of him. The car was a rental from Flagstaff, not unusual, as people seemed oddly reluctant to destroy their own vehicles in their hectic journey to destroy themselves. That evening Abby walked along the rim and peered down at the wreckage where the fragments caught the late sunlight along the nearly sheer stone. It would take more aerial trips and a heavy-duty helicopter to clear out the mess, risking danger to others like Jake in the process. Which was maddening at a whole different level. The sky smoldered dull yellow in the west, fading upward into a deep mint blue so clear and clean you could almost taste it. Abby knew that the waning moon would not rise until far into the night; the stars should be stunning until then. She tried to imagine the sensation of being that driver, the last seconds of acceleration, the bulky car leaving ground and taking clumsy flight, soaring through that long downward arc, perhaps an airy feeling of weightlessness and abandoned worries, just before the slamming lethal impact. She shuddered.

The astronomy event was in a few days, unfortunately one of the only nights that week when Jake was free. He was already unhappy about her plans to go, instead of being with him, and this time she hadn't suggested he accompany her because she wanted to visit with Bonnie Struthers. Not that he brought it up either; he obviously wasn't interested.

A storm was gathering across the Colorado plateau, mostly cold rain, and she expected him to forbid her to go. Which didn't matter, because she planned to go anyway. Abby understood that Jake was controlling and liked to dominate her, that he didn't really comprehend her need for independence. She figured it went with his work, being an authority, being an enforcer. She recognized that these were the sort of conflicts that they had to work on.

"You can't go," he said flatly over the phone that day. "It's too dangerous. That road will be slick with ice."

"It may not even rain. I saw the forecast, and the precipitation is iffy. I'll be fine."

"That's just ridiculous. You can't be out there by yourself in the middle of the night."

"Jake, I'm going. I've promised to help. And it's not the middle of the night," Abby insisted mildly, then tried to be funny. "You're not the boss of me, you know."

"Oh, that's mature." He sounded really upset.

"Jake. I have to go. I promised to help. I'll start back as early as possible, and I'll let you know where I am all along the way. Okay? The sky is clear now, but if the storm slides this far south, there won't be any stars to watch anyway. Just clouds."

By the time Abby got there, the sky was thickening with a sullen gray overcast and the temperature had dropped.

"You'd never know that spring was just around the corner," Bonnie said. They were both disappointed, but such was the lot of sky watchers, who must be philosophical about being marooned on a planet with so much atmosphere.

Instead they put together a demonstration of space and solar system distances by placing the people who showed up in strategic spots around the parking lot, in roughly planetoid positions, though the huge lot was still not nearly large enough. The young father who was Earth, with his small daughter as the moon, took fifteen steps from the smiling gray-haired woman who was the sun, and the teenager who was Saturn had to move beyond the parking lot at nearly one hundred fifty steps from the sun. Because Neptune would have been across the road and three blocks further away at nearly six hundred steps, no volunteered because the wind had picked up and the rain started spitting.

They called the session off, and Bonnie and Abby had dinner together, planning their next meeting. They were talking about a possible star program at the South Rim when Abby realized with a jolt that she needed to be on her way. Bonnie invited her to spend the night, and Abby would have agreed except that with Pepper gone she needed to be up early for the clinic. Besides, the road might actually be worse in the morning after a long freezing night.

She texted Jake that she was on her way. *About time,* he replied. She drove carefully through the night as sleet whispered against the car, its slanting lines in the headlights making her slightly vertiginous.

Then as she came down a slope around a curve, a deer suddenly floated across the road in front of her with an eerie flare of reflected eyes. Although the deer was gone before the car reached it, Abby could not control her foot's quick reflex tramp on the brake and then the car was gliding sideways, starting to circle on its own. Turn into it, turn into it, her mind shouted, and after what seemed like many hours she moved the wheel in the right direction, that counterintuitive bend. The car quit sailing unmoored—she felt the tires grip the road and come to a stop, angled and facing the opposite direction, with one back tire off the pavement.

Abby's heart banged in her chest and her hands shook on the wheel as adrenaline gushed through her. The headlight beams shone into the forest, throwing ghostly tree shadows far up the slope, shiny with rain. With a clunk her brain started working again, telling her she was sideways on a bend in the middle of the highway. She threw the car into reverse and backed around until she could turn in the right direction, then pulled over on the crumbling shoulder to recover.

Still miles to go. Abby waited until her heart subsided, then sent Jake a message that she was getting closer. *You'd better not be texting and driving,* he sent back. She could hear the growl in his voice, which made her smile. And this time, she admitted to herself, he'd been right. She took a long time to drive the rest of the way, calling him briefly halfway there and again once she arrived.

Needless to say, that skid was not a thing she ever told him about.

CHAPTER 15

Pepper was coming back. Everyone at the clinic pitched in to arrange his welcome home party, and Abby heaved a sigh of relief. She could hardly imagine what it must have been like for him during the last few years, being the only physician, with the nearest professional support so far away at Flagstaff Medical Center, over seventy miles away. All the traumas, all the heart attacks and heat strokes, all the local care, had been completely on his shoulders. It was a wonder he stayed here, Abby thought. Then she remembered his unspoken mistake and what sometimes drives a person to retreat to a remote place. Here she was, after all.

Pepper came through the door looking considerably better, though not completely back to his normal self. He had indeed put on a few pounds, and his color was better, though a hollow delicacy in his face made Abby wonder if he should have waited a little longer. She filed a mental note to call Dr. Bloom. A new haircut made Pepper look younger, and the beard was gone. He only coughed, briefly, once or twice. He made his rounds, hugging Dolores and Ginger first. Priscilla, waiting coyly, practically jumped into his arms and deposited a quick kiss on his cheek, leaving a shiny scarlet rime like a wound. Pepper didn't miss a beat, turning to Abby and wrapping his arms around her in a surprisingly strong embrace, even slightly lifting her off her feet. Yep, she thought, he's been by himself too long.

She smiled and offered him a slice of cake. "Nice to have you back, John Pepper. Now we're going to fatten you up." She was pleased to see that he seemed hungry and ate the entire piece. "But I have to tell you, I miss the beard."

"Really? I thought women didn't like facial hair."

"So you're an expert on this subject?" Abby teased.

"I guess not." His cool eyes caught hers, quizzical, and she quickly looked away.

He was not pleased that he had no patients scheduled.

"You can handle all the administrative stuff this week," Abby told him. "That would be the most wonderful thing. We're not going to rush you back into this, so you can just be mad about it if you want, but it's not going to change."

Dolores stood next to her and crossed her arms as if they were erecting a barricade. He knew when to give up, though he was heard muttering something about who was in charge around here.

Pete Collins, the mule wrangler, arrived at the clinic with a rattlesnake bite. He had been riding a new mule down the trail, testing its composure on the hairpin turns and steep drops, when he had to dismount in an open stretch to pry a stone from its hoof. Accidentally dropping his hoof pick, he reached into the grass and barely heard the low warning trill before the snake struck halfway up his right forearm. A passing hiker had applied a tourniquet above the elbow and quickly helped bring him in.

"I damn sure hope it's a dry bite," he said, anxiously scrutinizing the fang marks. The skin of his forearm was swollen and bruised around the bite.

"I don't think you're that lucky." Abby released the tourniquet while Dolores started an IV line. "We don't use tourniquets anymore because they might keep the poison in one place, where it can cause more tissue damage."

"Oh." He looked slightly greenish with fear. His cowboy hat sat next to him on the counter, his bright blue eyes glittering beneath a pale forehead that probably hadn't seen sunlight in years.

"The bruising and swelling are signs that you're probably envenomated," Abby said. "Do you think the bruising has spread?"

"Yes . . ." He stared at his arm.

"Well, we're going to go ahead and give you the antivenom. It's not worth the risk of not doing it." His pulse was rapid, but that could be from fright as well as from the snake venom, and at least his blood pressure had not dropped. "Are you feeling nauseated?"

"Yeah. In fact, you all better keep a bucket near me just in case."

"This will have to do," Dolores said with a smile, handing him a small plastic basin.

Abby talked to him while Dolores prepared the antivenom. "You'll probably be fine. Your blood pressure is good, and that's a great sign. We'll have your clotting tests back soon, and that will tell us more. But you'll probably need to go to Flag for observation for a day. In case your blood pressure drops."

Pete nodded and lay back, closing his eyes. Pepper had heard about the case and poked his head in the door. Everyone was fond of Pete.

"Found a snake for us?" Pepper asked him.

"Yeah," Pete joked weakly, "but it got away. You hankering for a new pet? 'Cause I can try to get you another one."

Abby and Pepper looked at the lab report, which showed a low platelet count. Platelets helped blood coagulate, and rattlesnake venom could alter that function, causing bruising and internal hemorrhage. Not what they hoped to see. They gave him more antivenom and packed him off to Flagstaff, where he could be watched overnight in the ICU.

"You'll be back soon," Abby reassured him as he was wheeled out. She turned to Pepper. "Thanks for helping."

"Helping? I didn't do a damn thing." He looked frustrated. "Look. Do you think I can actually start working again? Since you're apparently the boss now and since you've got the rest of the staff under your power."

"I'm not sure, John." Abby looked at him impatiently, suddenly remembering. "Guess who I talked to earlier today."

"As if I would know." He looked guilty, though.

"Yeah. Well, it was your pulmonary doctor, Robert Bloom. Apparently you didn't quite understand what he said, because it seems he told you it would be best if you waited a few more weeks to return to work, or maybe a month, especially to return to altitude. Something about your lung capacity. And I've noticed that sometimes you have to stop speaking to catch your breath."

Pepper dodged. "And why is he talking to you about my personal medication condition? Isn't that some sort of a breach of confidentiality?"

"Except that I'm the referring physician, so that lets me in. What were you thinking?"

"I had to get out of there," he said simply, looking away. "I love my brother, but a little of him goes a long way. And a little of Phoenix goes a long way too."

"Give me a break." Abby remembered the dreamy spring days and enchanted twilights this time of year. The desert hills would be dotted and dancing with the yellow flowers of brittlebush and poppies, globe mallow with its long stems carrying delicate orange cups, and soon large creamy blossoms would crown the arms of saguaro cacti. Quail would be running through the sand, trailing their tiny broods on whirring feet. "Phoenix is just about perfect right now."

Pepper shrugged. "I needed my place. And my people. I'll be fine."

What could she say? She knew she would feel the same.

So Pepper started seeing a few patients a day. They were also about to get a new staff member for a month, a medical student from the University of Arizona on an elective rotation, who would study with them and see patients under their supervision. Abby thought it would be good for Pepper to dedicate some time to teaching her, which would also reduce his schedule. They knew that this student was trying to decide between emergency medicine and family medicine for her career. "So it's up to you," Abby told Pepper, "to convince her how great it is to be a family doc." To which he said, "Yes sir, ma'am," and saluted her, and Abby threw a pen at his head. He caught it in the air, tucked it in his pocket, and walked away with a wounded air.

Pete Collins returned from Flagstaff in good shape except for the weeping wound on his arm, which would take a good while to heal.

"Good thing I just put my arm in the grass, and not my face, like a mule woulda done," he observed. A few years ago, a mule bitten on the nose had died.

It was April now, still cool at the rim but warming up inside the canyon. As Pepper took up his work, Abby and Jake fell back together with more consistency although Jake was busier now as summer approached, and things between them were not quite so intense. Abby knew that was normal — how could they have kept up the pace? The park service had suffered more cutbacks and did not have the funds to hire as much summer help this year, but Jake managed to stop by the clinic often, with or without patients, to share his stories and see Abby. He liked to stand close to her, lean against her, make sure he touched her, a possessive sort of thing. She noticed this especially if Pepper was nearby, though Pepper seemed oblivious.

Men.

Jake also referred frequently to a project he was trying to start with one of the new hotel managers, which had him rather excited.

"We want to step up the game, something beyond ranger talks and guided walks," he explained enthusiastically, a spark in his eyes. "You know, something in addition to the same old lectures. Juliette thinks the concession could hire experts, expand topics, and charge a small fee for them. Do something a little different than what the park service offers, make some money."

"Juliette?"

"Juliette Powers. From the concession company. She used to be here a few years ago, but she got promoted to another site back east. And now she's back. She's really excited about these new ideas." He paused and looked closely at Abby. "You probably should know. We used to date each other."

"Okay." How did she follow that? The last thing she wanted to be was the jealous girlfriend. "I guess we've all had a past."

Though Jake's past was undoubtedly more colorful than hers.

Shortly after that, Abby met Juliette during a noon walk. Since Pepper's return, Abby tried to get away most days during lunch, even if only for a short stroll, to refresh her energy and prepare to tackle the afternoon. On her way back, she saw Jake and a woman in the parking lot gesturing at the sun-filled forest, drawing lines in the air, talking animatedly. A large red SUV stood at the curb. When Jake spotted Abby, he waved her over and introduced them.

"I've heard so much about you," Juliette said, giving Abby a rock-hard handshake that she felt in her fingers for minutes after. Tall and sleek, Juliette had a fit runner's body and seemed a little older than Jake. She sported a spunky bob of yellow hair in a slightly unnatural shade of gold. With her long, graceful limbs and her toned muscles, she looked like she could polish off a marathon before breakfast. Her grin was slightly off-center and engaging.

Jake pointed to the woods, sketched a frame with his fingers. "We're trying to figure a place for a new amphitheater."

"Jake tells me you know a great deal of astronomy," Juliette said. She had a forceful way of talking, as if each sentence was packed with weight and meaning. "That's something I might really want to consider. He says you know people at Lowell Observatory in Flag."

As Abby was giving her Bonnie's name and number, Juliette grabbed her arm.

"And medical stuff!" she exclaimed. "There could be talks and demos about medical topics, like heatstroke and frostbite. And sunburn! What else?"

"Snakebites?" Abby ventured.

"Snakebites! Perfect," enthused Juliette. "This feels really big."

Abby smiled and hurried back to the clinic, leaving them to their schemes.

That afternoon she saw George Nutter for his diabetic follow-up visit. His gradual transformation had been impressive, and was still underway. He had lost weight every month since last summer, and was now down by fifteen pounds; his face was thinner, and he was developing a waist.

"Look at you," said Abby. "You look great. What's your secret, because I need to pass it along."

"Focus and inspiration," he said without hesitation. "Ever since we started that cooking class and focused on nutrition, I've just been inspired to keep it going. Even my cobblers have fewer calories now, but you can't taste the difference. It's a great challenge to find the right ingredients that work. I can't thank you enough for suggesting that."

Abby laughed. "I've got lots of ideas. It's just that nobody ever thought they were any good until this one."

His sugars were low enough that it was time to cut back on his medications. As he was turning to go, he paused and turned back to her.

"Listen," he said. "This is awkward and I probably shouldn't do it, so just ignore me if you want, but my family's going to be spending a few weeks here with me soon. I have a super nice nephew about your age — he's a great guy, and I was wondering, er, if you might be interested in doing stuff with him. You know, kind of hanging out or something . . ." His voice trailed away.

"Are you trying to arrange a blind date?" Abby asked, smiling.

"I guess . . . That's not very appropriate, is it? Just forget it." He reddened.

"No, it's fine. But I'm already involved with someone, you know. Ranger Peterson."

"Oh." He seemed surprised. "I thought he — never mind. I'm sorry."

"That's fine," Abby reassured him. "And thanks for thinking of me. That's very sweet."

George recovered quickly. "Don't say sweet. Just the word itself makes me gain weight."

CHAPTER 16

The medical student, Emily Weeks, fit in almost immediately. Slightly plump, with wavy dark hair that bounced on her shoulders and framed a round face, she was smart and a bit shy, eager to learn and serious about her patients. She reminded Abby a little of herself at that stage. She was conscientious to a fault, looking up the evidence on every condition and illness, constantly sitting with her face in a book or studying the computer, carefully preparing each presentation she made to Pepper as she saw patients with him. Although it was April, they were experiencing a late influenza epidemic at the canyon and in Arizona, which kept everyone busy and provided plenty of cases for her.

Abby often heard Pepper gently grilling her about her knowledge.

"I'm pretty sure it's influenza," she told him earnestly. "He's got all the classic symptoms."

"Which are?" asked Pepper.

"Sudden onset. Severe muscle pains and headache. Even his hair hurts! High fever and chills. And a terrible cough. We've got his rapid flu test coming back any minute now."

"Good. And if it's positive, will you treat him?"

Emily paused, the tip of her tongue showing between her lips — something she did when she was concentrating. "I don't think so. He's been sick for four days, and all the studies show that you need to start taking medication like oseltamivir in under seventy-two hours to make any difference at all. Twenty-four hours is better."

"Excellent. Except what circumstances might make you want to treat him anyway?"

Emily squinted her eyes shut to think. "Um. If he had any other debilitating conditions, such as poorly controlled diabetes. Or if he was immunocompromised, like if he had cancer or was taking chemotherapy or had AIDS. Things like that."

"Good, good," Pepper encouraged her. "Or if . . ."

"Wait, wait. Let me think." She nearly bounced in place. "I know! If he had pneumonia from the influenza and he was really really sick.

"Good job. So will you treat him?"

"No," she said. "It's been too long. And he's always been healthy and he's fairly young, so he should probably start getting better in a few more days. Otherwise we'll need to see him again."

"Perfect," said Pepper. "Let's go examine him together and we'll make a plan with him."

Abby smiled. Working with Emily seemed good for him, kept him engaged, kept him from slipping back into the gloom where he was prone to go. He seemed fully recovered now, and was back in charge. It was a relief, and she was more than happy to relinquish control. Not that she ever truly felt she was in control. But that was another issue.

That afternoon, Abby gradually became aware of Priscilla's presence. Priscilla no longer had the excuse of checking on Pepper to keep her coming back from the front desk, so something else was on her mind. And she seemed to be trying to catch Abby's attention, a rare event indeed. After her third trip up and down the hallway with the short quick steps that were all her constricting pencil skirt would allow, Abby finally looked up. She had to admit she had developed a habit of not making eye contact with Priscilla.

"Are you looking for something?" Abby asked.

"Oh, no, Dr. Wilmore. Just stretching my legs. How are you today?" Priscilla sidled up to her, licking her blood-red lips.

Abby immediately felt on guard. So unnatural for Priscilla to approach her, to make small talk.

"Fine," she said neutrally. "Just fine. And you?"

"Oh, I'm perfect, thanks." Priscilla shifted her gaze up and down the hall, which was empty at the moment. Her eyes were deeply masked in coal-black liner and shadow. "I was just wondering how you were doing, that's all."

"What do you mean?" Abby felt like she was moving toward a trap but was powerless to change direction.

"Oh, you know. With that Jake Peterson. I heard you'd broken up." Her lips pursed into a sad pout.

"Excuse me? Where on earth did you hear that? We haven't broken up."

"Oh." Priscilla's mouth made a surprised round O. "I guess I was wrong. I just saw them last night — him and that blond concessions woman — eating dinner at El Tovar."

Abby did a quick mental check, remembering that Jake had mentioned he had plans last night, though he hadn't said what. "That's not unusual. He and Ms. Powers are developing some new educational programs around here."

"I see." Priscilla smiled tightly and arched her penciled eyebrows. "Well. You might want to know that they were sharing bites, but then maybe the food is part of the deal. For the new programs."

Abby felt a dull flush. "I'm sure it is. I wouldn't worry about it."

"I'm not worried if you're not worried," Priscilla said with a pitying glance. "We girls just need to stick together, that's all." And she minced back up the hall, pushing through the door to the front desk with a tiny flounce.

Abby wanted to run after her and tackle her to the ground. What the hell was that? Then Dolores appeared, needing to discuss a patient, and Pepper and Emily came into the office to look something up. Abby shoved the Priscilla encounter distastefully away, but could not shed a lurking unease, a creeping vine of apprehension curling and crawling along her subconscious. Late in the afternoon she took a moment to send Jake a text: *Can I see you tonight?* It wasn't until she was home several hours later that he finally responded. *How about tomorrow instead? 6:30 pm?*

Abby kept herself busy. Reading didn't work because she couldn't concentrate, so she put on music and cleaned her little house. Once she got into it, she let it take her over, a working meditation. She changed the sheets and did her laundry, inhaling the clean soapy scent of fresh cotton. She scrubbed the bathroom and wiped down all the counters till they shone like mirrors. She mopped the wood floor, admiring the warm gleam, until the whole house smelled of lemon polish. She didn't think, didn't project. It was nearly ten o'clock by the time she was done. Too late to call Lucy, which had been on her list. But Abby was wide awake and knew that sleep was a distant hope. She looked out the window and startled, because there went Pepper, already past her house and walking back to his place, his head down in thought.

Maybe that's what she should try, a long walk, especially now that there was no likelihood of running into Pepper. She tightened her sneakers and slipped into a jacket and started out briskly without any plan for where she would go. Not down any trails into the canyon, that was for sure. The sky crawled with tattered clouds, lit up by a perfect half moon that slid in and out, playing hide-and-seek. Without thinking, she found herself headed for Jake's.

Maybe that was okay. Maybe she should surprise him — he just might like that. Abby knew she was not very spontaneous with him, mostly because he himself was so over-the-top impulsive that he always had her worn out before she had a chance to think. The minute they were together, he took over. Sometimes endearing, sometimes annoying, usually creative.

Nearing his house, Abby paused as headlights swung suddenly along the curved road, probing the woods. She stepped behind a tree, not wanting to spook a driver who would not expect to see a human out wandering this time of night. The big vehicle moved past her, turned in a smooth arc, and pulled up in front of Jake's place behind his old green truck. A red SUV, Juliette's car. Kind of late, Abby thought, but what the heck. The two of them had been obsessed with their crazy ideas and couldn't seem to stop talking about them. She would wait for Juliette to drop him off, and then she would go to him.

Juliette turned off the car and the lights. They didn't get out immediately. Come on already, Abby thought, quit yakking. She couldn't see into the vehicle.

The passenger door finally opened and Jake slid out, but instead of moving toward his house he walked around the SUV and opened Juliette's door to help her out.

She laughed and stumbled slightly and said she'd had too much to drink, and he said he liked her tipsy and pushed her against the car and kissed her for a long time. Then they fell in side by side and Jake led her into the house. She was a little unsteady and clung to his arm. Abby heard her laugh again and saw the door shut. The lights never came on.

Stunned.

Blank.

Abby stared and stared, her brain empty and unbelieving. Clearly there was some mistake, a trick of the moon and clouds, a defect of her vision in the dark. Then something broke loose inside her and all the wheels started spinning at once. Putting her off until tomorrow. Priscilla. Nutter. Abby paced up and down the road as if shifting her angle on the scene would make it different, create a different conclusion. She felt the cogs and gears of her thoughts heating and smoking, and suddenly fury flashed through her like wildfire, unbearably hot and quick. Her hands shook and she could barely see. Casting about, she picked up a heavy branch, hefted it, swung it like a cudgel though the air, nearly roared an oath like a berserk warrior. She imagined smashing it into the vehicles, crumpling fenders and splintering glass.

Then, just as quickly as it had come, it passed through her and she dropped the branch. She felt consumed, devoured by flames, charred to the bone.

You knew, Abby told herself violently, feeling sick to her stomach and feverish and numb. She stepped back into the woods and sank down in the pine needles, staring at the SUV. You knew, and you didn't want to know, and this is how it came to you. He was not right, you were not right with him. You knew, and everyone else knew too. Chef Nutter knew, even Priscilla knew.

Abby couldn't quit saying it, like a brand-new mantra: you knew, you knew, you knew. The SUV lurked massively in the dark like a military tank, like some obvious hulking metaphor she had failed to comprehend for a very long time. She sat and stared until her eyes turned gritty from not blinking and her mouth hung open, dry as sand. She wasn't sure how she would rise again.

The moon rode unevenly across the sky, weaving through the ragged clouds. Abby finally had to move because her feet and legs were tingling painfully. Bracing against a tree, she pushed herself up and turned her back on him and walked slowly home along the same path as on that first night when he followed her and said what she had almost forgotten. *I'm not a patient man.* He had said it many times. And she had given him much to be impatient about, at least in his view of their world.

By morning, after an endless night watching the moonlight shift across her bedroom, Abby felt empty enough to face the day. She had not wept. She knew that there was no excuse for his deception and dishonesty and that they would have to talk about it that night, before she never saw him again. But she also felt fundamentally defective, profoundly naïve, staggeringly devoid of insight. She felt so intensely a fool.

The day was a blur, robotic, a smear in her memory. She must have talked with people, and she knew she wrote notes and made diagnoses and prescribed treatments, because the charts were there with her words in them. A few times Dolores or Pepper asked her if she was okay, and she simply said she was tired, had a headache, and that took care of things. Everyone was busy, everyone had their own problems, everyone had to get through the day. They hoped she wasn't coming down with something, like influenza? Abby shook her head no and drank cup after cup of coffee and ate nothing, and before long she truly did have a headache.

Exactly at six-thirty that evening, Jake came bounding up her porch and pushed open her door. He was still in uniform, pulling off his Smokey hat and sunglasses as he came in, giving off a warm scent of dust and leather, trees and sun. The gleam in his eyes quickly faded when he saw Abby's face.

"What's wrong?" he asked cautiously.

Abby took a slow breath, looked away, looked back at him. She had rehearsed this a thousand times but could not remember anything she meant to say. She wished now she had just sent him a text and ended it there. She had no desire to see him, talk with him.

"I know about her," she said quietly, and immediately hated herself for sounding like a trashy country song. She didn't care anything about Juliette, only what Jake had done.

"What do you mean?" He had not moved, his face was stone.

"Jake. Please. Can you just be honest with me?" Abby felt so distant she could be in Alaska. In China. Some place far on the other side of the world where no one spoke a language she could understand.

Jake sat down across from her, still holding his hat and sunglasses. He rubbed his face with his free hand, his features creased and troubled. The old part of her, which she had not realized had not quite left, longed to reach out and take his hand. He compressed his lips and finally looked straight into her eyes.

"I'm sorry. I should have said something. But you're always so busy." A little defiant.

"Really? That's the best you've got? That I'm busy?"

His eyes were flinty now. "We never said we were exclusive with each other."

"And that was my mistake, I suppose," Abby said softly. She felt even farther away, off the planet, beyond the atmosphere. Out with the asteroids, a dull tumbling chunk of riddled stone. "I just assumed."

Jake stood up, paced back and forth. He took one step toward her and stopped, sat back down. "I'm sorry. I didn't plan for this to happen. We just sort of fell back into old habits."

Abby shook her head, felt her brain float like a balloon. She knew she was too tired and her thoughts were untethered, random. She hadn't slept in over thirty-six hours, and she wished he would leave. "So now I guess I'm the old habit. That's nice."

"Listen, Abby." He leaned forward. "I thought you didn't care that much anymore. You've been so wrapped up in your work, not very available, not very interested. Tell me if I'm wrong."

A laugh escaped her, short and bitter. "Life gets complicated and messy and people go through things. People have ups and downs. And sometimes you can't put yourself first. Why didn't you say something?"

"I thought I did."

They stared at each other through a long raw silence. Abby thought of her astronomy trips and Jake's attempts to distract her, to talk her out of it, how she fell asleep on him. Hell, maybe it was mostly her. But she had never been deceitful.

"So tell me," she said, even though she didn't want to know, wasn't sure why she was asking. Why it was even important now, but for some reason it was and she couldn't stop herself. "That whole time before we started really seeing each other, before we slept together. When we were getting close, making out, all that. Were you involved with anyone else at the same time?"

He waited too long to answer.

"This is getting us nowhere," Abby finally said, defeated, exhausted. "You should go."

Jake stood abruptly. "I don't like us ending like this."

She could actually see distress in his face, which made her angry and confused. "I'm sorry too, Jake. But I don't see how there's any other way for it to end."

He stared at her, a muscle moving in his jaw. Once again he took a step toward her and stopped. Then he jammed his hat on his head, turned and left.

The door slapped shut.

CHAPTER 17

Everyone knew, of course. Abby said nothing and was never certain how, but within a day or two the local gossip machinery turned its wheels and accomplished the task. Everyone knew that she and Jake were no longer together.

She didn't care. She made sure she didn't care about anything, in fact. She put her head down and buried herself in work, taking on extra patients, crowding her schedule with urgent cases, making phone calls that were usually left to the staff, even cleaning up the exam rooms before Dolores could get to it. She doggedly attacked the pile of unread medical journals and devoured the contents as if those research articles contained the very secrets of civilization. Her chart notes became elaborate, elegant discussions of symptoms and possible diagnoses and potential treatments, long treatises on the nature of humanity itself. By filling every waking moment with work and patients and duties and chores, she kept from thinking about herself much at all. At night, she fell into sleep as if anesthetized. Most of the time she felt she was managing, though despair and irritation struck unexpectedly.

The late influenza epidemic continued to take its toll. Businesses and schools operated shorthanded as employees and children fell suddenly ill, often out of commission for a week or two, shivering and sweating at home, wracked with cough and high fever. Fortunately the vaccine was a good match this year, so those who received it were spared. The clinic had signs shouting from every wall: *Stay Well! Get Your Flu Shot!*

Cora Dunkin, head of housekeeping at the Thunderbird Lodge, came in one morning for a bladder infection. She was a smoker and had not been vaccinated.

"You really, really should get a flu shot," Abby said in her best persuasive voice. She had already tried to talk to her about quitting smoking, but Cora would have nothing to do with that conversation. "Don't waste your breath," Cora had hissed.

"Especially as a smoker, you're at a higher risk of pneumonia and complications if you catch influenza. Can we do that today?" Abby cajoled.

Cora sat bolt upright, stretching her thin neck. "No way. Those shots have terrible complications. People have died from them."

Abby smiled, clenching her teeth. "No, they really haven't. Whatever you do, don't believe what you read about this on the internet—it's full of untruthful paranoid stuff. What actually happens is that a small percentage of people feel a little achy or tired for a day or so after the vaccine, but most people don't notice a thing. Influenza is miserable, you know, and you are around lots of people at work. And you have two grandchildren, so your exposure is really high. I'd hate to see you get it."

"My cousin got a flu shot last year, and within a month she developed diabetes. And now she has kidney failure and she's on dialysis. You can't tell me that didn't happen." Cora put her fists on her hips and scowled at Abby.

One more effort, Abby thought wearily, and she would let it go. "Really, Mrs. Dunkin. That was a coincidence, believe me. If you would just try getting it once, I think you would find that—"

"What is it with you doctors?" Cora spat. "You must be making a lot of money on this or you wouldn't be harassing me so much. Of course, no one would tell me, even if that was true."

"Nothing of the sort. We barely break even on flu shots. We might even lose money on them. If you—"

"You listen to me." The woman shook her finger at Abby. "I don't trust doctors. I don't trust flu shots. I've never caught the flu, so I don't see any reason to get a flu shot."

"Then you've been lucky," Abby said with uncharacteristic force.

Cora right now reminded Abby of her father, refusing medication for his high blood pressure until the stroke killed him. That same righteous tone, that same defiance, as if physicians were white-coated fiends with diabolical schemes who wished them harm. As if doctors only worried about profit and cared nothing about the risks. Her brain flared and her voice rose.

"Does this mean you're going to wait until you're in a car accident before you start wearing a seatbelt?" Abby couldn't stop herself, felt her mind flooding with analogies. "Are you going to wait until you get skin cancer to start using sunscreen? I bet you've never had a tetanus infection, but I see you got your tetanus shot last year—what on earth made you decide to do that?"

Cora Dunkin pulled back, eyes wide.

"I'm just saying," Abby finished primly, back in control. She realized she may have gone a little too far, but she didn't especially care at that moment. "You should think about it, that's all I'm saying. It just makes sense. Dolores will be here in a minute with your prescription for your bladder. Let me know if you're not better within twenty-four hours. And call sooner if you develop a fever or get worse."

Abby left the room and quietly shut the door behind her, then looked up to see Pepper, Emily, and Dolores standing at the nursing desk, all staring at her in mute concern. Clearly, they had heard her tirade.

"I'm just saying," Abby repeated calmly, and went into the office to write up her notes.

But that incident was unusual. Mostly Abby was subdued and kept to herself. She always left the clinic now at lunch, always walked along the rim, far from the houses and cabins in the woods, and barely made it back in time for her afternoon patients. She craved the peace and avoided lunchtime talk.

A few days later, Pepper caught her as she was exiting the back door at noon.

"Mind if I walk with you?" He asked pleasantly, but his eyes were a pale cold blue.

"You really don't want to do that. I'm not much company these days," she replied dismissively.

"That makes two of us," he said, joining her anyway.

Abby was annoyed — this was the last thing she wanted. They paced along in silence until they reached the path along the rim. The day had turned blustery, a cold wind kicking up across the canyon, the colored striations muted. The chasms looked oddly depthless without shadows, like a backdrop to a scene. Low rough clouds scudded across a pewter sky, putting the world in an uneasy mood and sending tourists back on the road.

"Bench," Pepper announced, pointing.

"No, I'd rather walk."

"Come on and sit for a second." Pepper dropped himself down and gestured at the space beside him.

"What's this about?" Abby said, impatient, still standing. Her hair was trying to come undone in the wind, and she tucked it back.

"Call it a job review. Come on, sit." Now it was more of a command.

Abby perched on the other end of the bench and crossed her legs. "Yessir."

Pepper suppressed a smile. "Where's your food? When do you eat lunch?"

"I'm not very hungry. I've got a granola bar at the clinic." Abby folded her arms and she half turned her back on him, watching a raven hang stiffly in the wind.

"That's certainly a meal."

"If you wanted to criticize me, you could have done it without coming out here."

"Okay. Instead let's talk about how you saw a patient of mine for a simple case of cellulitis on his finger and then you wrote a note that was two pages long." She turned her head to look at him, vexed, as he went on. "For a visit that could have been less than half a page. I felt like I was reading a Victorian novel."

"I've decided to be more thorough," she said with starch. "I should think that's something you would approve."

Pepper shook his head and slid toward her. His eyes were kinder now. "Look. You can build whatever great big wall you want around yourself. Make it as high and as thick as you want. Cover it with broken glass and barbed wire. I don't care, whatever works for you. But I will check in with you every now and then, like right now, and ask if you're okay."

Abby stared at him. His brown hair was growing long again, ruffling in the breeze, and his mouth was stiff with concern. She knew he was being considerate and she felt badly about it, but she couldn't meet him there. He was right about the wall.

"I don't think I can talk about it."

He nodded. "You don't have to tell me a damn thing." He made a little flourish with his graceful hand. "I'm just offering the opportunity."

Abby looked away across the empty miles, layer stacked on layer of prehistoric time dropping into the chasms. An unseen raven croaked, a raw sound, and unexpectedly her breath caught in her throat. She swallowed hard.

"I just feel so stupid." She couldn't look at him. What could she possibly say? She had been swept off her feet like a silly adolescent girl by a handsome seductive man, a man with whom she had nothing in common. He was dominating, controlling, often selfish, ultimately dishonest. Yes, he could be inventive and fun, but those traits felt insubstantial now because everything was always on his terms. It didn't matter; she barely even blamed him at this point. The disappointment was all in herself, how long it took her to realize, her brainless obliviousness.

Pepper let her words blow away in the wind.

"Guess what? It happens. We all make mistakes. Some are worse than others." Now he gazed away. Then his eyes jumped back at hers, that brittle blue.

Abby felt something stir outside herself for the first time in days. She examined his face, which had turned wary. She meant to be more careful, but she still felt aggrieved at losing her noon solitude, and her words came out bluntly.

"What happened to you, anyway?"

He put his elbows on his knees and pressed his long fingers into his face. Abby was beginning to think he would never move when he straightened and leaned back, glancing over at her then out across the mesas.

"I'm only telling you this because maybe it will help. It probably won't, and I'm pretty sure I'm going to regret it. Maybe I just want you to know, just get it over with. I'll give you the short version." His eyes closed briefly before he went on. "I got married young, too young. Looking back, I was practically a boy, at least emotionally. You know how that is, honor student, always studying, socially clumsy. But she was a cute sexy nurse and we had a great time together. I was crazy about her and she pulled me out of my shell."

He paused for a long time.

"Sounds like it was good," Abby prompted.

"It wasn't, not for long. I worked long hours, lots of extra night and weekend shifts in urgent care to make more money and pay off my school loans, besides working during the day at my practice. She didn't mind the extra money, but pretty soon she got tired of me, and tired of waiting for me, and tired of me being tired, and she started running around, having affairs. She wasn't even very discreet. When I tried to get us into counseling, tried to talk to her about it, offered to slow down my work and spend more time with her, she just laughed and told me to grow up. If I persisted, she suddenly had a migraine, or her back was bothering her, or she was coming down with something. Then I'd take care of her and she'd be grateful, and then it would start all over again. It was dysfunctional and sick. Finally I couldn't take it anymore. I'd had enough of it and I filed for divorce. She didn't want that, tried to resist it. Then she started complaining of abdominal pains, and I just laughed. She kept wanting me to check her stomach, see what was wrong, but I wasn't about to be manipulated again. Yeah, I was too smart for that."

Abby waited. He was breathing heavier, staring at the low clouds.

"Turns out she had ovarian cancer. Advanced. You know how that story goes. She died three months later." He turned to her with an acid smile. "And that's the end of my little story."

Abby shook her head. "Except that it isn't. Because you're still blaming yourself, which isn't fair."

"The hell it isn't. And you're damn right I blame myself."

"John. I'm really sorry. But you know it wouldn't have made any difference. By the time she had symptoms, it was already too late."

"Yeah, I tell myself that all the time. Every now and then I try to believe it. But this isn't about me—I shouldn't have done that. I never meant to do that today. It was wrong and selfish, and I apologize. I just want to be sure you're okay. That you're not having any weird thoughts."

"Weird?"

"Destructive. Self-destructive. Suicidal. I'm not terribly worried, you know. But you can be a little hard to read. And the only way to know is to ask."

Abby studied him. "No one's harder to read than you, let me point out. But no, I'm not having any so-called weird thoughts." Then it dawned on her. "Did you? Think those things?"

"For a while. I had no one to talk with. That's why I'm offering. So please come talk to me if you need to." He had visibly recovered. "I'll leave you alone now. But here."

He leaned over and scooped up a handful of pebbles and dirt. He took her hand and placed it on his thigh so that the palm faced up. It was strangely provoking. He trickled the rubble into her palm and curled her hand into a tight fist around it until the pebbles bit into her skin. Abby watched him and didn't move. A thick strand of her hair came loose and blew across her face.

"That's Kaibab limestone," he said, finally letting go. "It's two hundred fifty million years old. Compared to this, we're nothing, not even a blink. Our lives are so absurdly short—all we can do is try our best. And try to do better when we get the next chance." He reached up, caught the drifting wayward strand of her hair and slid it behind her ear. Then he stood and started back to the clinic. "Don't be too long. Dolores gets cranky if we're late."

Abby sat for a long time with the dirt in her hand, rubbing her fingers against the grit, knowing she touched tiny flakes of ancient mollusks and corals, remnants of an unimaginable undersea life that was now stranded high on this edge of the earth's upthrust crust. She felt the deposits below her, sinking a mile into the planet, down to the stained river that rubbed endlessly away at black schist two billion years old. She felt young and ludicrous and bitter and aged all at the same time; she felt that she would never know any more than she knew now and she also felt that she had not yet lived her life at all.

She sat for so long that she was slightly late, despite Pepper's warning, but no one noticed. News had just reached the clinic that Luther Lubbock, the man with the domestic violence conviction, the man Pepper had testified against, had escaped from prison. According to his cellmates, he was obsessed with revenge.

CHAPTER 18

This day was apparently never going to end. They found out that Luther Lubbock had managed to escape by disguising himself as a gardener and slipping out when a row of half-dead eucalyptus trees was removed from the prison grounds, tucking himself under the pungent branches and clippings as they were carted away in trucks. The police came to the clinic and talked with Pepper, and they put up a photo of Lubbock by the front desk for Ginger and Priscilla. The photo had already been placed at all the entrance stations to the park. His mug shot showed a stubbled man with close-set eyes, slabby lips, and wispy orange hair floating above his head in a faint cloud. His face was pasty, thick and pocked. He stared into the camera with unnerving hostility, as if the lens itself were his enemy.

Everything ran late and everyone was on edge.

Abby typed up her final entry and closed her computer, thinking she was the last one in the clinic. She startled at the tap on the office door, even though it was open. Emily appeared.

"Still here?" Abby asked, surprised. Tomorrow was Emily's last day, and they would miss her. She was upbeat and dedicated, and she had already promised to return for another elective rotation. Then she saw Emily's face, her grimly clamped lips, her distressed eyes, red at the edges. Concerned, Abby pulled her into the other chair and handed her a tissue, which she took gratefully and dabbed at her nose.

"What's wrong? What happened?" Abby asked.

"Oh, Dr. Wilmore. I've made a terrible mistake." Her breath caught in a small sob, but she cut it off and lifted her chin. Abby knew you didn't get this far in medicine as a woman without learning how to snip your emotions off.

"With which patient?" All of Emily's work was supervised, so nothing could be that far amiss. "I'm sure we can fix anything—"

"Not with a patient," she moaned. "It's so embarrassing. I didn't know who else to talk to."

"Of course," Abby assured her, having no idea. "Just tell me."

Emily gulped, then let it out in a rush. "Last night. I had too much to drink. I don't know why! I don't even like alcohol. But some people I've met were giving me a little farewell party and passing around tequila shots, and everyone was hoping I'd come back soon, and everyone was being so nice and especially that cute helicopter pilot who's been taking me on some of those paramedic runs into the canyon and I really like him a lot and he's really funny you know and he always makes me laugh and the next thing I know I'm at his place because the bar had closed and things got really exciting and then we were in his bed even though I didn't really mean to do that and then we had sex and I don't really know anything about him and I'm not using birth control and we didn't use any protection and I can't believe I let this happen because I should be smarter and and—" Her voice was rising to a howl when Abby grabbed her hand and shushed her.

"Emily. Shh. Listen to me for a second." Emily nodded and looked at her lap, silent now. "This is important. Did you want to, or did he force you? Was it consensual?"

Emily groaned. "He didn't force me. He's actually really nice. I could have stopped it, but I didn't. Why didn't I?"

Abby squeezed her hand. "I don't know — because it felt good? And because you were disinhibited by the booze, and because you like him?"

Emily took a deep breath. "Maybe . . ."

"Those are a lot of good and bad reasons, depending on your angle. If you had used some protection, would you feel the same way right now?"

Emily considered, and then her expression softened, a little less agonized. "I guess not. Not so much anyway."

"There's nothing else messing this up? No one else, no boyfriend back home?"

"No. I haven't even had a real boyfriend since college. And barely then."

Abby nodded. Emily was socially young for her age, as was common in many medical women who spent their weekends in the library instead of a bar, who volunteered at the homeless clinic instead of taking up a sport. Many medical men, too. Abby thought fleetingly of Pepper's story. His vulnerability, even though he would never use that word. "And you're not a nun? So you haven't broken any vows?"

Emily actually laughed, then sobered immediately. "But Dr. Wilmore. What if I'm pregnant? It wasn't the best time of month for this. I thought I'd figured out last night that I'd be okay, but I had the dates wrong. I realized it this morning."

"If you want, there's always a thing called the morning-after pill."

"I haven't learned much about it," Emily admitted.

"You can buy it at the drugstore, the sooner the better. You've got up to three days to take it, but it works best if you take it right away. And it might make you vomit."

Abby thought about the nearby pharmacy, still open, but it might be old Ralph working this shift. He was about to retire, and he had been known to rail at young women who sought the medication. "Or I can give you a prescription for birth control pills and show you how to take them so it's the same thing. Two tablets now, then two tablets twelve hours later. If you really don't want anyone to know."

Emily's lips quivered. "Could you?"

Abby wrote the prescription and sent her off before the pharmacy closed. Emily was so grateful that Abby practically had to shove her out the door. Then she punched up the computer again, made a very short chart on Emily for the clinic files, briefly outlining the situation and prescription, and went home.

It was far past time to talk with Lucy. Abby dreaded it, mostly because she just didn't want to repeat the whole sordid Jake story again. As long as she kept busy, she could almost be herself. Once she started thinking about Jake, her emotions raced hot and cold, cycling through anger and disappointment, doubt and self-deprecation. And the worst, most disturbing reaction was that sometimes she actually missed him, missed his silly antics, missed the sizzling sex. He would be a hard act to follow, and she suspected he had ruined her for the rest of her life regarding *that*. She was lonely, and she physically ached for his touch no matter how much she intellectually loathed the very thought of him caressing her again. It was as if her brain and body had become disconnected, belonging to two separate people who despised each other. And clearly this was not something she could talk about with Pepper.

Lucy listened quietly, occasionally asking questions, until Abby exhausted herself.

"I'm sorry, honey," Lucy said then. "That just really sucks."

"Yeah."

"So. What do you think now? I mean, about yourself."

"I don't know, Lucy. I think I make bad decisions. That I don't think things through. That I don't see what's happening under my nose."

"Worse than the average person?"

"I don't know." Abby sighed. "I'd like to think I can do better than average. I mean, I take a little pride in my deductive abilities. But maybe I shouldn't. I sure didn't use much reasoning with this."

They talked for a long time. With Lucy's encouragement, Abby told her everything: about Pepper and their talk and about Emily, about the tension over Luther Lubbock, about her patients and her walks and reading all the medical journals and even about her long chart notes. How she hated Jake for being so fickle and false and yet how she still missed him at times, the confusing juxtaposition of her wrath and her cravings. It grew late, and at last she was too tired to go on.

"Just let me ask you something before we hang up," Lucy said.

"Sure." Abby sagged, emptied out. It would all come rushing back tomorrow, she knew, but at least for right now, talking to Lucy had helped.

"During all this craziness, did you ever think about needing a drink? Or taking your pills?"

"No, I didn't." It hadn't occurred to her, even when she couldn't sleep.

"Did you have any anxiety, have a panic attack?"

"No, I didn't." Abby sat up, wide awake.

"Huh. Isn't that interesting." It was a statement, not a question.

"Huh," Abby echoed. Her mind quickly replayed every incident, every troubled moment. It wasn't there.

"Okay then. Good for you. And at the risk of being an unoriginal copycat and stealing your lines, let me ask you one more thing. Something else that you might want to think about."

"All right . . ."

"Are you a nun? Did you break any vows?"

For just a moment, Abby smiled.

CHAPTER 19

Luther Lubbock's trail had gone cold. A security camera caught a grainy video of him stealing a car from a convenience store near Casa Grande, but the car was found abandoned in the desert a day later. One rumor had him walking across the border into Mexico at Nogales in disguise. Another rumor had him crossing at the small town of Naco during the annual spring Wallyball Tournament, when American citizens on the north side and Mexican citizens on the south played volleyball across the border wall. As the weeks went by with no further sightings, real or imagined, the clinic staff began to relax. They figured he was probably halfway to South America by now.

Considering how often Jake used to appear in the clinic, Abby found it odd that she never saw him now. Another thing he was good at controlling, she thought. Then she heard the gossip, that he was leaving the canyon next month, quitting his job to join Juliette and the concession company, moving to another state. Though surprised, she had to admit she felt relieved. The sensation never left her that he might turn up around the next corner, reach out from behind a tree. She saw him once, driving down the road too fast, looking preoccupied. He didn't see her.

Abby was glad it was summer, thankful for the busy days that left little time for introspection. A new male medical student was starting next week, one who would mostly work with her this time. Pepper's free time was occupied with a new research project about sodium levels in hikers, collaborating with a team from the medical school.

Late one afternoon after seeing his patients, Pepper ran home to grab some supper before returning to the clinic for an evening conference call about the project. Abby waited for him because she wanted to discuss a patient with an abnormal calcium level.

She also wanted to thank him for the drawing. It wasn't all that special, because he'd drawn little pictures of everyone on staff at one time or another. Priscilla had a full-length sketch of herself, complete with tall heeled boots and miniskirt, a determined expression on her face. She loved it and made him sign it in the corner, then framed it and kept it at her work space.

Abby found the drawing he'd made for her that morning under her pile of mail, a small pencil sketch of her face. The nose wasn't quite right, a little too long, but the mouth was pretty good and the eyes were nearly perfect. He'd given her a faraway look, pensive, not exactly sad but serious. Wisps of hair drifted across her cheek, and thick clouds filled the background sky.

She was touched and wanted to reciprocate. Since her artistic skills were nonexistent, she tore a piece of computer paper in half and made a childish cartoon with puffy clouds and a shining sun, its rays shooting out across the page. Then she drew a stick-figure Pepper, his eyes and mouth tilted down in a frown. She had him posed with one stick hand on his hip and the other pointing at a rectangle, with "Bench!" in a word bubble floating over his round head. A small stick-figure Abby stood across from him, hands on her hips, saying "No!" She left it propped on the phone in the little office where he would be sure to see it that night.

Abby checked her watch, five thirty-five, hoping Pepper would be back soon. As usual, Dolores was restocking the exam rooms for the next day, and Ginger and Priscilla were submitting the billing. Abby heard the front door open, heard Ginger politely telling someone that the clinic had closed for the day and could they possibly come back tomorrow? Yes, Dr. Pepper would be here in the morning. Then Abby startled at a heavy bump against the wall, like someone falling, and unexpectedly the door flew open.

Abby jumped up as Ginger stumbled into the nursing station, propelled by a fleshy man wearing a bulky dark coat and an oversized baseball cap. Abby reached out for Ginger's hand, to catch her and balance her, but the man grabbed Ginger roughly and yanked her into the crook of his arm, shoving Abby aside. Ginger cried out and flailed her arms, knocking off his hat, and then his right hand came across and pushed the muzzle of a gun to her face.

"Where's Pepper?" he shouted out, whirling around, dragging Ginger with him. His head swiveled back and forth and his eyes flew up and down the hallway, and then he twisted his thick neck and yelled at Abby, who came up close behind him.

"Get the hell away from me!" His eyes bulged and spittle flew from his mouth, and a stench of rancid sweat radiated from his filthy clothes. Abby could smell the sharp chemical odor of hair dye oozing from his stringy black hair. He raised his elbow toward Abby to fend her off and called out again. "Pepper! Get out here!"

"He's not here," Abby cried, frantically trying to think. Thank heaven Pepper hadn't returned. "Please let her go and talk to me. I'm the other doctor. You can talk to me. Tell me what you need. Let me help you." Abby's mouth kept speaking, a trail of nonsense, but she somehow found time to think *Why Ginger? Why not Priscilla?* and then to be utterly appalled at herself for thinking it. "Luther. That's your name, right? Let her go, Luther. She doesn't know where Pepper is."

"Get me Pepper!" He tightened his hold on Ginger and advanced on Dolores, who stood frozen in an exam room doorway. His hands were huge, mottled red and gray like old meat and the gun was nearly engulfed in his right hand, but Abby could still see the dark metallic gleam against Ginger's face. He pulled up and his eyes bounced back and forth from Abby to Dolores to Ginger, wild and white, then again he glared up and down the hall.

"Pepper!" he roared. "Where the hell are you hiding? Come out here like a man!"

"Luther. Listen to me," Abby pleaded, sidling, trying desperately to get into his vision, trying to get him to look at her, to somehow connect. But his eyes slid past her, leaping toward Dolores as Abby kept talking. "Pepper left. I promise you I'm telling you the truth. Let her go and we can go find him. Please don't hurt her. She didn't do anything. Please."

He flashed his eyes at Dolores and snarled, moving toward her, dragging Ginger along. "I remember you! You're his nurse. You know where he is, don't you?"

Dolores shrank back, raising her hands and shaking her head no.

"She doesn't know where he is," Abby cried, edging forward and trying to draw him away from Dolores. Ginger's fingers fluttered toward Abby, her eyes wide with shock and Abby reached for her, moving still closer. "But I know where he is," Abby said. She heard a ring of conviction rise in her own voice, as if she believed it herself. "Listen to me, Luther. Look at me. *Look at me.* Let's go get him. Let her go and take me with you. I know where he is. Really."

"Oh yeah?" He turned and shifted the gun toward Abby, his face twitching, sweat beading and trickling down his pitted cheeks. His eyes finally jerked and jolted onto her, as if seeing her for the first time.

"Drop the gun! Right now!"

Jake's voice, deep with authority. He and another ranger crouched in the hall by the back entrance, their guns drawn and pointing straight at Luther, who spun and clutched Ginger before him like a shield.

"You can't get out of here," Jake shouted. "Just put down the gun and let her go. You can't get away."

Abby could see Jake trying to sight his gun, could see that Ginger was too close to Luther to risk it. Ginger pinched her eyes shut, and Abby grasped her outflung hand.

"Abby. Move away. Right now," Jake ordered, glowering briefly at her. But Abby couldn't. Her fingers were entwined with Ginger's now and she couldn't let go, couldn't abandon her.

"Luther," Abby implored once more, trying again to break through. "Luther, listen to me. Pepper isn't here, but you can talk to me. Really. Let go of her, she's just in the way. Let's—"

Something altered, a small sound, a shift in the air.

Everyone felt it and they all turned their heads toward the front to see Pepper standing there rigidly, his arms angled out and his hands carefully away from his body. His jeans clung to his hips and even without a weapon he looked like a gunslinger, about to draw. Abby could see every detail of him, his chest rising and falling as he breathed, his fine lips curled and nose flared, his eyes searing.

"Here I am, Lubbock," he said slowly, each word loaded, an unmistakable offering. A sacrifice, utterly exposed. Abby stared in dread; she felt like her heart had stopped. He lifted his chin and braced his feet, ready. "I'm the one you want. You let her go."

Luther gave a low chortle, as if he couldn't believe his luck. His dark eyes lit up, and his gun hand pulled away from Ginger's face and started to move in Pepper's direction, started to extend. Without thinking, without planning, with simple sheer reflex Abby wrenched Ginger's hand as hard as she could, heaving Ginger toward her and jerking Luther off his aim. Enraged, he bellowed and swung round at Abby in a powerful arc, smashing the gun against her face.

Pain burst in her forehead and a bright light exploded as she tumbled backward. She did not see Pepper charge at Luther and into the line of fire, but she heard the sharp cracks of revolvers as she and Ginger fell to the floor.

The place erupted. Rangers and personnel poured in, dragging Luther onto a gurney as scarlet blood spilled from two gunshot wounds. Still partly tangled beneath Ginger, Abby raised herself to look for Pepper and make sure he was unhurt, and she exclaimed as her left wrist buckled under, skewered with pain.

Then she saw Pepper, his shirt stained red, but he was standing across the way, his face ferocious as he pointed straight at her, calling out orders, his other hand on Lubbock. She tried again to rise, but hands held her now, helped cradle her left wrist, which had crumpled under the combined weights of herself and Ginger when they went down. Someone pressed something against her forehead where sticky blood ran down, gumming up her eye and trickling across her cheek and lips. Then Ginger was smoothing Abby's hair out of the way, her fingers smeared red, her hands shaking. Someone shined a light in Abby's eyes, first one then the other, making her wince, and a voice was instructing her to squeeze her hands, move her feet. Abby resisted, trying to see, wanting to find Pepper again to be sure he was safe and that the blood on his shirt was not his own.

Somewhere in the background she was aware of Priscilla parading back and forth, explaining again and again in a shrill overwrought voice how she had been the one who pressed the newly installed panic button.

Jake appeared above her, blocking out the chaos. He slid his arms under her, lifted her from the floor. So warm and familiar, such a comforting déjà vu, that Abby leaned her head against his chest and hooked her arm around his neck, taking a deep stuttering breath. He clutched her protectively and carried her out of the commotion into the treatment room, releasing her gently onto the table, propped up in a half-sitting position.

"You okay?" he asked gruffly, putting a pillow under her head. Dolores and Ginger were with them, pulling supplies out of cabinets, setting up the metal tray.

"Sure." She waved loosely at her injured arm and face. "So to speak." Her head and wrist hurt fiercely and she desperately wanted someone to dim the bright overhead lights. She felt stunned and hyperalert at the same time.

Everyone paused while her arm was X-rayed, but no one left the room, defying the radiation rules. Then she heard Pepper's voice out there and tried to get up.

"Is he okay?" Apprehensive, straining to look, Abby twisted around, swung her legs and started to move off the table. "Did someone check on Pepper? There was blood —"

"Whoa there." Jake planted his hand on her chest and pushed her back. "Just stay put. Pepper's fine. He's crazy as hell, but he's fine."

She sat again, but she must not have looked convinced because Jake moved his hand to her shoulder and didn't yet let go, as if he didn't trust her to remain. With his other hand he carefully lifted the bloody dressing off her forehead and frowned. "Ouch. That's getting a few stitches for sure."

Dolores gave him a somber look and took the dressing from him, replacing it with fresh gauze.

Abby turned her head to Dolores. "Don't they need you out there with Lubbock?"

"The hell with him," Dolores snapped, twisting open a new bottle of peroxide and swabbing maternally at Abby's face to clean away the blood. "Close your eyes, sweetheart, so I don't get this peroxide in them."

"Listen here," Jake said to Abby when she opened her eyes again. His face was flinty. "If enforcement personnel tell you to move, you should damn well move, understand? Between you and Pepper, I'm not sure who was trying hardest to get themselves killed." Then he abruptly changed gears and bent closer, and right in front of Dolores and Ginger he touched her face softly. "I'm really sorry, Abby. About how bad I handled things. If I could do it better, do it over again, I would. I mean it."

Abby could only stare at him.

They heard a cart roll down the hall — Luther being hurried away, bristling with tubes and IVs, to be loaded onto a helicopter under heavy escort. No one thought he would make it, but his only chance was in Flagstaff, not at an outpatient clinic on the edge of the Grand Canyon.

Pepper came in then and Jake turned to leave without another word to her. On his way out the door, though, he grabbed Pepper's elbow and punched him hard in the upper arm. "Don't ever pull a stunt like that again," he growled. "You crazy bastard."

"Ow." Pepper rubbed his arm, pretending to be offended. "What the hell? That's going to leave a bruise."

Jake laughed, and then he lowered his voice and squinted over at Abby, and she knew they were talking about her. She couldn't see their faces, but it felt so odd seeing them together. Then Jake was gone and Pepper stood next to her, murmuring something reassuring as he removed the gauze to examine her wound. He quit talking and she saw his mouth tighten, saw his lips go white and his eyes turn arctic. Dolores saw it too, for she placed her hand on his arm as if to calm him, and Abby thought it was a good thing that Lubbock had been taken away. Ginger busied herself with washing out the sticky strands of Abby's hair. She ran a basin full of clean water and rinsed away the blood, turning the water rusty red.

"Are you all right?" Abby asked her. Ginger nodded vigorously, her face streaming silent tears that dripped off her chin into the basin. Moments later, Diego arrived in a rush, gathered her in a long embrace, and whisked her away.

Dolores stayed next to her and Abby heard people come and go, talking in the hall, for what seemed like a long time. She closed her eyes and wondered what she looked like, then decided she didn't want to know. There was nothing she could do about it. Pepper went out and returned several times; someone kept calling him out to discuss something, but Abby couldn't make out the words.

Then he was back and he asked Dolores for a suture kit, shucking off his stained shirt as she handed him a clean scrub top. They paused to look at the X-ray, which showed a small crack in the radius just above the wrist, nondisplaced. It would heal with a simple splint, which Dolores strapped on. Her wrist felt better immediately and Abby sighed with relief. Then while he washed his hands, Dolores started cutting off Abby's blood-spattered top.

"Not much privacy around here," Abby muttered as Dolores stuffed her shirt in the trash, briefly leaving Abby in her bra.

"He's a doctor," Dolores reminded her, holding up a cotton gown and sliding it over her arms. "He's seen it all before."

"Let's just check on your brain first," Pepper said. He smiled at her momentarily, on and off again, then clicked on his penlight and flashed it into her eyes to check her pupils. "How bad does your head hurt? You might have a concussion."

"I don't have a concussion," she said testily, turning her face away. She felt like she'd had enough and she didn't want to do this; she didn't want him examining her or hovering over her or making diagnoses or doing anything at all. She knew he needed to stitch her up and almost resented it, and if she could she would have done it herself. She felt self-conscious and tired and impatient, she wanted to stand up and leave, and she wanted everyone to go away and for no one to look at her. "He didn't hit me that hard. Besides, someone already did my neuro checks."

"Get used to it, because it's going to keep happening. And just so you know, since you don't seem to realize, he hit you very hard. Now, how bad does your head hurt?"

"So hard that it made a *sound*," Dolores put in.

"All right, all right. My head hurts medium." Abby closed her eyes because it actually hurt worse than medium, but she couldn't bring herself to say so because she wanted Pepper to leave her alone. She felt sick and damaged and longed to crawl into her bed at home and pull the covers over her head.

"Medium? That's not very scientific. What happened to the one-to-ten scale?" He tapped her reflexes and tested her strength, he asked her the year and the date and who was president. Abby quit answering and insisted she was fine. She saw he still had a smear of Lubbock's blood along his jaw.

"Hold still a minute, Dr. Pepper," Dolores said as he lowered the table and sat down at Abby's head. She swiped his face with alcohol and said darkly, "They better test that man for a few things since everyone's been exposed to his blood."

"Hang on now, this is going to sting pretty badly," Pepper said to Abby, taking the syringe of lidocaine from Dolores and injecting the tattered edges of the wound. The lidocaine burned sharply and Abby's face muscles flinched but she kept her head still, and then he instructed her to close her eyelids while he sutured so he didn't accidentally poke her in the eye. He worked quickly and quietly but it still took a long time, and the one time she cracked open her lids and glanced at him, his expression was savage, and she knew he was thinking about Lubbock. When she tried to empty her mind, she could smell blood and Pepper's sweat and his antiseptic soap, could hear the metallic clicks of the needle holder and felt the tugging on her skin as he drew the suture through, could feel the smooth rubber of his glove against her face.

He tied the final knot and sat back, snapping off his gloves.

"I'm not happy with this. It's a crooked laceration, and it's deep and it goes against the skin lines. It's going to leave a scar, especially where it runs into your eyebrow, I'm afraid. The edges were crushed and it's not very smooth — some of those tissues may not be viable. You may need to go to plastics."

That was the least of her concerns. Abby felt shaky and spent, hungry and nauseated. She'd had nothing to eat or drink for many hours. She must have looked as pale as she felt, because Pepper checked her pulse and brought her a cup of water. He sat with her while she sipped it and Dolores cleaned up the tray and a crew clattered in the hall, trying to manage the mess out there.

"I think you're pretty dry," Pepper said, fingers on her pulse again. His face was softer now. "You're still tachycardic. Maybe some IV fluids?"

"Heck no," Abby protested weakly. "I can drink my fluids, just get me home. It's been kind of a long day." Then she hiccupped and her stomach tilted and she leaned over and retched onto the floor.

"Adrenaline," Pepper muttered as Dolores wiped Abby's face with a towel. Abby kept apologizing to Dolores, who cleaned up the watery bile and told her kindly to be quiet. Pepper went to the cabinets and pulled out an IV set-up; he threw Abby a strict look and picked up her right arm and she knew better than to say anything else. It took nearly an hour more to give her the IV fluids and pack her up. Dolores helped her into a scrub shirt before they left.

Pepper dropped Dolores off at her place first, then drove Abby home and walked her into her house. A full moon blasted like a searchlight through the trees and a breeze swung the branches, casting looming shadows that ran swiftly at them, up and down the front walk. Abby startled and cowered, and Pepper threw his arm around her. "Easy now," he said quietly, and they stood there for a moment until she recovered.

"Thanks," she said inside, wearily, wanting nothing more than to lie down in her own bed. "I'll see you tomorrow."

"Yeah, and you'll see me tonight. I'm not leaving. I'll fix you some soup, and you're going to get neuro checks every few hours all night. Unless you'd rather I drive you to Flagstaff right now to get a head scan."

Abby protested, and Pepper accused her of being a bad patient, refusing to leave when she ordered him to go. Sitting in bed, she ate only four spoonfuls of the chicken soup he'd heated up, and could not stomach more. He studied her critically for a moment and she wondered what she'd done now.

"You can't sleep in your slacks," he said at last. "Do you have some sweat pants or something?"

Abby pointed to her dresser, then looked doubtfully at the cumbersome wrist splint, which barely allowed her fingers to move. "I'll have to take this off . . ."

"Just let me help," he insisted. "I promise I won't look at you. Stand up."

Abby stood and closed her eyes, feeling awkward and acutely embarrassed as he unzipped her slacks and slid them down. He fetched the sweat pants, helped her step into them, pulled them up for her, the entire time discreetly turning his face away. She reminded herself that it wasn't the worst thing that had happened that evening.

He set his phone alarm, told her to fall asleep, and flopped onto her couch. Her bedroom door stood open, and she could see his long legs dangling over the end. She was wide awake and sleep was impossible, unbearable. The scenes replayed in her head over and over, Lubbock's stench, his leering lips, Ginger's fluttering fingers, Pepper's sacrificial appearance. She made herself count her breaths backwards from one hundred, but she was too jittery to make it past ninety, even after three attempts.

She wondered if Pepper was asleep, and just then he was standing at her door. He leaned against the frame and told her a funny story about one of her patients earlier that day, then he told her another story about a friend who had taken the wrong hiking trail and then tried a shortcut and misplaced the trail altogether and nearly got lost forever inside the canyon until he remembered he was carrying a special GPS that could show him the way out. Abby managed to summon a smile and he talked about something else that she couldn't really focus on, but she began to unwind.

"Close your eyes. Please just try."

Abby nodded and obeyed. The next thing she knew, the phone alarm was sounding and he came in and quickly went through the neuro checks and orientation questions. She fell back asleep then found herself bolt upright and terrified, electrified by her own leaping heart and an ugly voice in the dark shouting *Where's Pepper?* and Abby cried out begging "Please don't hurt her, please don't!" and then Pepper was there, hushing her and shaking her lightly and telling her that it was a bad dream and she was safe. Abby gulped and stammered as she tried to climb out of the nightmare, and he pulled her up and held onto her until she could finally draw a full breath.

"I'm sorry," she said, straightening, self-conscious. "I didn't see that coming."

"Sorry? Are you kidding me?" He left for the kitchen, returning with an ice pack that he placed on her forehead. "You're developing some prize-winning bruises, let me tell you. Championship stuff. Don't look in a mirror in the morning."

He nudged her over in the bed and sat next to her on top of the covers, pushing off his shoes with his toes. She drew in his clinically comforting scent of antiseptic and shampoo, though she couldn't think when he'd had a chance to shower. She tried to breathe evenly, but every now and then her throat caught and a tremor ran through her from head to toe. Pepper pressed his shoulder against her.

"Tell me about the moon," he said, pointing at the window where a white square of light blazed through a thin curtain. The moon's bleached head floated in the sky.

"What?"

"Tell me about the moon. You're the astronomy expert. I want to know more about the moon."

"Okay." Abby gave him a sidelong glance. "What do you want to know?"

"Everything you know. How big is it? Where did it come from? What's it made of?" He leaned against her as she shivered again.

"What are you, four years old? Besides, I'm not a moon expert."

"Do your best," he insisted.

So Abby told him about the moon, 239,000 miles away but sometimes nearer and sometimes farther, because the moon does not follow a predictable circular orbit but wanders a little on its own. She told him how the moon is not really round, not perfect, but eccentric and shaped more like an egg, and how we never see a third of its surface because it likes to hide something for itself. How the moon is not completely cold and dead but has a small hot core and experiences tiny little moonquakes. The way the moon's gravity sloshes the earth's seas night and day, tugging the ocean tides away and then giving them back. That the moon is actually leaving us, moving steadily away from Earth at an inch and a half a year, that when it first was formed from an impact against Earth it was only 14,000 miles away.

How only a few humans have ever been there. How lonely it must be up there, and how lonely the earth would be without it.

He kept her going, prodding her when she paused. As her words slowed and she began to drift back to sleep, Pepper repeated her neuro checks. Drowsy, Abby deliberately answered incorrectly, murmuring that her mind was clear as a bell and that the president was Leonardo da Vinci and the year was 2325. He told her she had a warped sense of humor and let her sleep. The next time, it was 2005 BC and the president was William Shakespeare. Pepper was not amused, and she made a face at him, told him to quit pestering her. She fell back into a restless sleep, then awoke on her own with a full bladder, finally hydrated enough to pee. It was awkward with the splint, but she managed, though it took a while to do everything with one hand. She followed his advice and did not turn on the light or look in the mirror.

Coming back from the bathroom, she paused to watch him sleep. He had slumped sideways, one leg dangling to the floor, breathing deeply through his slightly open mouth. His blue scrub top was scrunched up, showing a few inches of his flat stomach, and a folded piece of paper protruded from the breast pocket, about to fall out. Abby gently pushed the paper back in place and saw that it was her cartoon drawing. Which meant he had discovered it and tucked it in his pocket sometime after Lubbock. He stirred at her touch, mumbled, his eyebrows lowering in a grimace, his face grave and troubled. Abby slid back into her bed and found her eyes wet with tears.

Early in the morning, which according to Abby at her dawn interrogation was in the year WD40 under President Frodo Baggins, Pepper pronounced her brain to be hopelessly damaged. He gave her a fresh ice pack and went home to get ready for work, but not before forbidding her to show her face in the clinic for a week.

CHAPTER 20

Abby finally faced the mirror. Blackish purple bruises spread over her left forehead and down across her left eye and cheek, where blood had crept beneath the skin from all the crushed capillaries that oozed and seeped before coagulation worked its wonders and stopped the subcutaneous bleeding. Pepper's sutures were beautiful, small and careful, a neat line of nylon stitching that crossed the irregular red mark of her wound, twisting down her forehead through her eyebrow. She swallowed three ibuprofen and left the mirror to itself.

Within a few hours, a parade of visitors began arriving. Dolores tapped on her door and brought her a small bottle of pain pills signed by Pepper, low-dose hydrocodone. Abby put them aside. Dolores checked the wound, checked the splint, and visited a while. When Abby asked her if she wasn't needed back at the clinic, Dolores said tartly that they could manage without her just fine for a little longer.

Shortly after she left, Ginger appeared with cookies, which she had stayed up baking all night since she couldn't sleep. She burst into tears when she saw Abby's face, but quickly recovered after a hug. Though Ginger still looked haunted, she found something to laugh about, mostly Priscilla, who was endlessly talking about how and when she pushed the emergency panic button that summoned the rangers so quickly.

Although Pepper told everyone they could take the day off if they wanted, that he would manage the urgent cases and emergencies by himself, no one decided to stay home. Pepper looked in on Abby briefly at lunch, checked her wound again, said a sympathetic "Yikes" at her bruises, and ran back to work. Then a sheriff showed up with reports to fill out; he grumbled that they should have been done the night before but Pepper put them off by saying Abby was not medically stable. Really, she thought.

By late afternoon, after Chef Nutter brought her a savory meal of pasta, Abby found herself exhausted and queasy. She put the pasta in the refrigerator for later and napped fitfully, jerking awake every few minutes with the pounding pain in her forehead. She was up when Pepper appeared again that evening.

"Have you slept?" he asked with concern, taking her pulse. "You don't look so good. Have you eaten anything?"

Abby started to shake her head no, then stopped because the motion hurt and made her dizzy. "Just a few cookies. This morning." She saw his scowl and continued in her defense. "But they were really good cookies. Homemade. Ginger stayed up all night making them."

"You've got to eat something and get your fluids up." He found the pasta and sat with her while she slowly ate some, made her tea and watched her drink it. He looked worried and drained, and Abby felt badly that she was adding to his burden.

"Better," she told him. Her stomach settled and the dizziness disappeared, although the pain hounded her face like a dog gnawing a bone.

He found the bottle of hydrocodone and tapped one out for her. Abby looked at him and shook her head.

Pepper sighed. The lines around his mouth were etched deeper than usual, his eyes darker. "Look. I respect why you're reluctant to take a narcotic. But you've got a good medical reason to use it and you're kind of a wreck right now, and I can see from your expression how much pain you're having. You look like you're being tortured. You can't go another night without much sleep."

"Why is it so much worse today than last night?" she asked, a little fretful despite herself.

"You had the lidocaine injection for getting stitched up, so that kept it numb for a while." Pepper paused. "What if you'd just had major surgery? Appendicitis, or a hip fracture. Would it be okay to take pain meds then?"

"Maybe . . ."

"This is no different, Abby. I think you're making yourself sick." He put the capsule in her hand. "Today is probably the worst day for the pain, and then it will slowly start to get better. But it's your decision. I'll be back in an hour to spend the night on your couch."

"I don't need monitoring. And you could use some sleep too."

"I just want to be here in case you need something. For a nightmare or panic or whatever. Is that okay?" For the first time he was asking her permission. He ignored the part about his own sleep.

Abby remembered the terror of last night and gave a little nod. After he left, she sat for thirty minutes trying to meditate the pain away, without success. She thought of calling Lucy but knew what she would say, so she finally picked up her cold cup of tea and shut her mind and took the medication.

She was already falling asleep when Pepper returned, and she slept through the night. He was gone when she arose in the morning, but he was right. The pain was a little better and she had some energy and appetite at last. Then she saw what he had left for her on the kitchen table. He had photocopied the pencil drawing of her face and he had carefully added the laceration on her forehead, complete with tiny marks for the stitches. Abby smiled. She wasn't sure everyone would find such a gesture humorous, but he had read her correctly and it was exactly what she needed.

She got out a sheet of paper and drew a stick-figure cartoon of him sprawled awkwardly on her couch with his legs and feet hanging off one end and his head hanging off the other. She gave him a grouchy expression and a word bubble saying "Go to sleep!" Then she walked down the street to his house and slid the page under his front door.

It felt good to be outside, the sun warm and soothing, dust dancing through the air and iridescent hummingbirds zipping past her head. It felt so good that she went for a real walk. The sky was piercing blue, crisscrossed with delicate veils of cirrus clouds. She texted Pepper that she was feeling much better and he didn't need to come over today. He'd looked exhausted last night, and she knew he needed time off from Abby surveillance.

Abby stayed home one more day, took a few more walks, and then went to the clinic the next day, the fourth day since Lubbock. She waited until midmorning, when she knew Pepper would be up to his ears in patient care, and quietly slipped into the little office after giving Dolores a hug and letting her check the wound. Abby settled into the corner with a laptop and worked on her messages and labs and notes.

It felt so good to be doing something, to be productive, out of the house. Her head truly only hurt medium, and a low medium at that, as long as she didn't touch the wounded area. The bruises were finally beginning to change, turning toward yellow and greenish, unsightly but improving. She heard Pepper and the new medical student discussing cases between appointments. Maybe she could start working with the student tomorrow.

The wrist splint slowed her down, making typing slow and clumsy. Just to see how it would go, she unfastened the splint and slipped it off. Much better — her typing speed and accuracy improved considerably, though her fracture soon began to ache. Absorbed in responding to a message, she looked up when a shadow fell across the desk, and there was Pepper glaring down his nose at her, his face a thundercloud.

Without saying a word, he pushed the laptop away from her and lifted her left arm, putting the splint back in place and strapping down the Velcro. Abby flushed, feeling like a child reprimanded by a parent. He turned silently, his back stiff, and stalked from the room. Abby knew that he would look in again soon, so she made sure he could see her sitting there, pecking awkwardly at the keyboard with the index finger of her right hand.

The next day Pepper unexpectedly summoned all the staff to a meeting at noon. He raked his long fingers through his hair and the chill in his eyes was glacial.

"I wanted to be the one to tell you," he said, looking at each one in turn. "I've talked with the ICU docs in Flag, and it looks like Lubbock is going to survive. It will take a while still for him to recover, and then he'll be going back to prison for a very long time."

Tears ran down Ginger's cheeks, and Dolores put an arm around her. Priscilla folded her arms and shook her head. Pepper's mouth was a thin line, and Abby felt such a mix of convoluted emotions that she closed her eyes.

Ginger gulped and started talking, sniffling after every few words. "I hate. Him so much. I can still. Feel his arm. On my neck. I can still. Smell him on me! What if he. Escapes again?"

"Not likely," Pepper said grimly. "He'll be in maximum security."

Abby opened her eyes and said what everyone had been thinking. "How horrible of a person does it make me if I wish you hadn't saved him?"

Dolores, Ginger, and Priscilla all nodded in dismay, looking at Pepper.

"I wish it too," he said quietly. "I wish it all the time, and it makes me crazy, because it's not something I should ever want. But I also think it's a normal thing. That's why we're here to talk about it."

No one wanted to talk much, but everyone felt better. As the meeting broke up, Pepper pulled Abby aside, told her she looked tired and to go home and rest, instructing her to come back at the end of the day so he could remove her stitches. She was about to launch into an argument that she felt fine and would simply stay until then, see a few patients, when a shriek from the front desk threw panic like a spear through everyone's heart.

They rushed to find Priscilla standing on the counter, her eyes wide with terror and pointing at the floor by her chair, where a small gray mouse cowered in the corner. She wobbled on her strappy high-heeled sandals, and Abby could see right up her short skirt to where she might or might not be wearing a scrap of thong underwear. Fortunately it was still lunch break and there was no one in the waiting area.

"Oh, for goodness sake," said Dolores with relief, reaching for a broom. Ginger grabbed an empty box, and the two of them managed to corral the frightened little creature, which darted back and forth and then scurried right into the box while Priscilla peeped and squeaked and nearly toppled off the counter. They took the box outside to release the mouse, and Pepper reached up to take Priscilla's hand.

"Come down before you fall and break something," he admonished, and with that Priscilla bent toward him and launched herself at his chest. Pepper was tall and strong, but he had to grab her and take a few quick steps back to balance himself as she wrapped her arms around his neck. For a long moment they were face to face, Priscilla's expression suddenly soft and swoony, until Pepper recovered his equilibrium and set her down. He hastily retreated to the back as Priscilla teetered over to her chair, watching him with flaming eyes.

Abby stayed the afternoon, trying her best to avoid Pepper, but even when he did see her, he shook his head and said nothing else about sending her home. She saw two patients, apologized to them for the appearance of her face, and felt so much better for the activity.

He was meticulous in removing the stitches, minimizing the tug on the healing edges of the wound. "The scar will be better," he reminded her, "if we get the sutures out early." Then he took off the splint and examined her wrist. She winced when he gently probed over the fracture site and the swelling there.

"Sorry," he murmured as he carefully flexed and extended her wrist. "It's getting stiff here. You need to take the splint off every few hours and put your wrist through some range of motion."

"Oh, so now I'm allowed to take it off? I won't be in trouble?"

A smile pulled at the edge of his mouth. "Notice that I didn't say you should take off the splint and start typing all day. I don't know what your middle name is, but you should change it to Defiance." His face sobered. "How are you doing, really?"

Abby waffled her free hand back and forth. "Pretty good, all things considered. I do better if I'm busy." She paused. "How about you?"

"Like you said. Better if I'm busy."

She studied him frankly for a long moment. "Do you really wish he was dead? Or did you say that just to make me feel okay?"

"Yes, I wish he was dead." It came out bitter and hard. "I've got a lot of hate inside me right now, and it's not good. It's not the person I need to be, or want to be. I'm kind of a judgy guy in my normal state, in case you haven't noticed, not to mention under stress. I hate him for a lot of reasons, and they're all good reasons, but I really hate him for what he did to you." He reached out and touched her wound so delicately she could barely feel it, then his fingertips traced the outline of her bruises. His face was an impossible mix of anger and tenderness.

"Did you . . ." She wasn't sure how to ask, but she had to. It had weighed on her since that night. "Did you mean for him to shoot you? Is that what you were thinking? When you stood there so defenseless . . . I don't know. Like you deserved it? Some kind of atonement?"

His eyes found hers. "I don't think so. No. I was just so desperate. Desperate to do something, to fix it. Because I felt like I'd caused it. Caused him to be there, I mean. That it was my own stubborn fault, the way I insisted on testifying in person last year. That because of me he was going to hurt others. And he did. I mean, look at you. That's my fault, and I'm so sorry. There's a lot of complicated stuff in my head these days."

Abby looked away, concerned about him and unsure how the pieces fit together. She wanted to help him but she felt too unsteady herself.

"It's not your fault," she said. "You can't predict or control someone like that." Her wrist ached from his exam and she suddenly felt exhausted and a muddy wave of confusion and compassion washed through her. She tapped her temple, not wanting him to feel alone in his distress. "And talk about stuff in your head? You don't want any part of what's going on in here either. Don't even ask."

He sent her a penetrating blue gaze and Abby realized that was a mistake, that he was clearly going to ask anyway, when there was a scuffle in the hallway. Dolores and Ginger were scrambling and shouting and suddenly another tiny gray mouse sprinted past the doorway, Ginger in pursuit wielding her box, Dolores following with the broom.

Abby and Pepper exchanged a laugh. It had been a while.

CHAPTER 21

A month went by. The season moved into June and the summer turned brutally, unusually hot. Although the South Rim always cooled off at night, thanks to the elevation, the days broiled up to nearly ninety degrees, and the deeper anyone ventured into the canyon, the hotter it became. At the river, temperatures mirrored the weather in Phoenix, sizzling at or above 115 degrees. Few visitors had ever experienced such desert extremes, and they had no idea how much water it took to keep blood flowing through a human body. The body must perspire to cool off, and it needed ample internal water to perspire.

Abby and Pepper worked long hours now because of high summer volumes. Today they had three tourists with dehydration and heat exhaustion, people who had taken a short stroll down the trails with thin shoes and little water, and had delayed turning around.

Abby understood. Standing on the rim was enticing, the pale threads of trails visible below. Tee shirts on every shelf proclaimed *I Hiked the Canyon*, and people wanted to be able to wear one. For the casual walker, it was hard to resist the allure of just one more bend in the trail, one more switchback, one more spectacularly revolving view of cliffs and color and time. It was so easy to put another foot forward and let gravity pull it down.

Then your water was gone and you were desperately thirsty and your feet were raw, and you turned around to face a steep rocky mile or more up in the blinding sun, without a shred of shade for relief. Soon you were faint and short of breath and your pulse pounded, your legs trembled, and each step took all the strength you had. You had ignored the ominous warning signs at the trailheads, clearly meant for someone else.

The overheated patients at the clinic that day slowly recovered with IV fluids, a little food, and a long rest under the air conditioning vents. One older woman had arrived at the rim that morning on the daily vintage train from Williams, then missed the return train because she was lying in the clinic with an IV in her arm.

"I have to go. The ship will leave without me," she kept insisting weakly, tugging at the intravenous line that anchored her to the bed. Her blistered feet had been cleaned and dabbed with antibiotic ointment. She'd been found near the top of the Bright Angel Trail, bright red, panting and clutching at people, asking them how to get to the cruise ship. Dolores stayed in the room with her to keep her hands off the line.

"She's still a little confused," Dolores told Abby.

"What's her body temp?"

"I just checked and she's below one hundred, so that's good."

They had located a niece in Denver who was on the way, but she would have to fly into Phoenix, rent a car, and drive up for hours in the stultifying heat. It was already late afternoon, so Ginger was calling to arrange transportation to Flagstaff Medical Center, since the clinic would be closed long before the niece arrived.

In the meantime, Abby managed a case of chest pain that fortunately turned out not to be cardiac, treated a gallstone attack and diagnosed a kidney stone, and stabilized a man with a blood sugar of six hundred who'd left his diabetes meds at the MGM Grand in Las Vegas. She sewed up a head laceration on a teenager riding a bicycle without a helmet, talked a long time with a depressed man who had fled from a toxic job and couldn't sleep, and treated a young woman who was anemic from heavy menstrual bleeding that had started five days ago. Pepper's schedule was similar.

They hadn't talked much lately. Both kept busy, both kept their heads down. Abby's bruises finally disappeared and her head only hurt when she touched the scar, and her wrist was nearly painless now. Pepper kept leaving her little gifts of healthy food, fruit or peanut butter crackers, sometimes accompanied by a small drawing of a healthy meal based on the national nutritional food plate. To reciprocate, Abby left him candy bars and more stick-figure drawings that showed him scowling and pointing and giving orders. But neither ever mentioned these.

The transport to Flagstaff was late. Wishing they would hurry, Abby went into the office and found Pepper sitting with his elbows on his knees, rubbing his face in his hands.

"What happened?" she asked, alarmed at his expression.

There had been a death at the river from heatstroke — a young man from Montana, just twenty-five years old, who hiked down the South Kaibab Trail with some friends and one bottle of water. He was a climber, fit and healthy, and he scoffed at the pansy warnings of the park service for a trip just under seven miles, and downhill on a wide trail at that. When he found himself slowing down, he just thought he was tired, too much beer the night before, so he told his friends to go ahead and he'd catch up soon. He made it across the suspension bridge before he collapsed, lying in the ruthless sun until his friends returned to find him unconscious and got rangers involved. His core body temperature was 108 degrees. Then seizures set in and his heart stopped. Prolonged resuscitation was futile.

"It's just such a waste. Twenty-five years old." Pepper shook his head, his eyes dark. "And I think it also bothers me even more because it's my brother's age and it sounds like something he would do, except he wouldn't have any friends looking out for him."

"Your brother would know better because he lives in Phoenix," Abby pointed out.

"Maybe you're right. It's just so depressing." He pondered for a moment, then his eyes jumped up at her. "I really need to do something different. I want to go look for condors tomorrow. It's Sunday, and we're both off. You should come with me."

"Condors?"

"I'm sure you've heard of them." He opened his long arms and flapped them, filling the office.

"Of course. I just didn't . . ." Her words faded. She knew next to nothing about the condors and felt stupid about it. But why was he asking her? She suspected he was worried about her again. Great, another Pepper pep talk.

"You really should see one. It's a great story, how they've survived. They were nearly extinct. Come with me, please. What else do you have to do?"

That was a rather disparaging thing to say, Abby explained sternly, and so he dutifully apologized and asked again, looking so determined that she finally agreed, even though the last thing on her mind was to spend an afternoon looking for large carrion-eating birds. A string of people were coming to visit her soon, Lucy and Rebecca and Bonnie, practically one after the other. No doubt because of the Lubbock publicity, and they probably just wanted to check on her, but she had hardly had visitors all year and was looking forward to it, which meant she needed to get her household organized and go to Flagstaff for food and supplies.

Still, Pepper had done so much for her lately, and now he wanted company. She knew he still felt responsible for what had happened to her. This was a small thing, truly, and he had said please twice, which for him was downright disarming. Or maybe downright alarming.

"All right. I'll come see your huge dead-flesh-devouring birds," she conceded.

A front was coming through, breaking up the heat. Big cottony cumulus marched across the sky with purpose, places to go, pushed by a steady breeze from the north. Cloud shadows climbed and fell up and down the canyons with roller-coaster giddiness, reds and golds and greens turning alternately bright and muted, over and over. Pepper led Abby to a secluded spot far along the west rim, with a small cluster of comfortable rocks at a cautious six-foot distance from the dreadful drop, one of the sheerest precipices in the park. The Abyss.

"I saw a condor here one time," Pepper said, sitting down and pulling binoculars from his pack. He looked younger and more at ease than she had ever seen him, and she saw how good it was for him to get out here.

"It flew right over me," he went on. "Looked at me, I swear. I could see into its eye in its ugly orange head."

Abby smiled, settling into a hollow of stone. "All right. Tell me all about the condors."

"First let's establish parameters. I don't suppose you know your wingspan?"

When she gave him a look and shook her head no, he pulled her up and took her hands, extending her arms straight out from her sides, parallel to the ground. He straightened her fingertips so they stretched as far as possible. Then he leaned back to appraise the distance, running his calculating blue eyes from one hand across her to the other. Abby felt oddly exposed and had to suppress an instinct to fold her arms across her chest.

"I'd guess about five feet or so," he said at last, nodding. "A respectful wingspan, if you're a big raven."

"Caw, caw," Abby said, trying to make that coarse raven sound, then dropping her arms. "Now you."

He obediently spread his arms, the wind tousling his hair. She felt suddenly reticent and wondered what the heck she was doing, but after all, he had once helped her change her slacks and spent the night in her bed. So it really was not a very big thing. She placed her left fingertips against his right fingertips and stretched as far as she could toward his other hand, barely reaching his inner elbow.

"I'm a little over six feet across," he said, looking down at her, his arms still out, hers still reaching. They were very close. "Almost a turkey vulture wingspan, but not a condor." He paused for dramatic effect. "They've got almost ten feet of wingspan."

Abby was impressed. Then she felt an impulse to touch the soft blue veins in the bend of his elbow and she stepped back. She couldn't read him and felt cautious. She sat back down on her stone and he sat next to her, slightly shoving her over. She tried to move and create a little space, but she had run out of rock.

"Bird-watching takes patience, and you can never count on success," he remarked, stretching out his long legs and looking over the canyon. He pointed to a faint filament of trail wandering across the dusty greenish plateau far below. "Tonto Trail. That green layer is Bright Angel Shale, over five hundred million years old. You can find brachiopods and trilobites in that. Trilobites . . . can you imagine? Pretty cool, huh."

Abby peered at the lengthy meandering trail. "How long is it? Where does it go?"

"Not sure exactly how long. I think this section is about fifteen miles, from Indian Gardens to the Hermit Trail. But it goes on farther than that. Not really much water along the way either. Not your friendliest trail."

Abby mentally flinched at the mention of Hermit Trail. The first time she and Jake slept together.

"What?" Pepper asked.

"What do you mean, what?"

"You twitched, or something."

Abby hated herself for that reaction. She thought she was past this, yet here she was acting like an emotional dingbat in front of Pepper. He probably remembered, though, since he remembered everything, so she just said it to get it over with.

"Hermit Trail. It's where I first . . . you know. With Jake." Her hand made a vague gesture toward the trail.

Pepper snorted softly, and she whirled on him, furious. "So help me, John Pepper, if you are laughing at me I will shove you right over the edge and never look back." She started to rise.

"No, no. Are you crazy?" He grabbed at her. "I'm not laughing at you. It was just the way you said all that. So . . . theatrical, and humble and funny, all at the same time."

Abby slumped and looked away. "I hate to let you down, but I haven't yet evolved to being funny about this. I'm better, a lot better, mostly normal. But sometimes I just still feel like I let myself down."

His put one hand on her shoulder and cupped her jaw with his other, turning her face to him. "Look at me."

Her eyes reluctantly moved to his.

"Stop it," he said harshly. "Just stop it."

"Oh, come on," she muttered. "You must think I was a fool. Everyone else does."

They sat uncomfortably for a few moments, and then he said, "No one cares, Abby. It's water under the bridge. And just so you know, I was sort of . . . a little bit . . . jealous of him. Or resentful. Annoyed. Something like that."

Abby twisted to stare at him. "What?"

He shrugged. "It's a guy thing. The way he came in and stood next to you, the way he leaned on you and touched you, like he possessed you, all that. I wanted to protect you, I guess. Shelter you. But I knew then, and I know now, that it was absolutely none of my damn business."

Abby recalled how she always thought Pepper never seemed to notice, never looked up when Jake came in and did his things. She felt unbalanced now, knowing that Pepper had been acutely aware, caring about her.

"So. You could see it coming." Everyone knew but her, she thought for the millionth time.

"No, of course not — don't give me so much credit. It was just my male reaction to him. Be glad you don't own any testosterone. And remember, I'm no poster boy for what makes a relationship work, pretty much the opposite. For all I knew, you two were the pinnacle of perfection for what it takes to live happily ever after."

Abby frowned at him. "And now who's being hard on himself?"

He shook his head, looking so distant and uninviting that Abby said nothing more. Small birds flitted through the trees, and now and then ravens called out in their graveled voices, diving past them, checking themselves so they hung in the wind before tilting and swooping off into the immense open space below them.

"Tell me about the dang condors," Abby finally said.

So he told her all about California condors, how their huge silhouettes almost disappeared forever from the skies. How they were the largest bird in North America but had dwindled to only twenty-two by the 1980s, clearly headed for extinction until some determined humans captured the last wild survivors and started raising them in captivity. How the reticent condors laid only one lonesome egg every two years but could be seduced into laying a second egg if the first one was secreted away, to be hatched and raised by people wearing condor puppets on their arms to keep the chicks wild, thus doubling the condor population. That there were now over two hundred condors flying wild across the southwest, soaring as high as fifteen thousand feet and ranging over a hundred miles a day searching for carrion. That a healthy condor could live as long as sixty years, and that now their greatest threat was lead poisoning from eating carcasses killed by hunters using lead bullets. How the lead bullets were killing bald eagles as well in the same way, and the hunting industry curiously had no will to make it stop. As he talked, Pepper waved his free arm in the air, tracing the breeze, gliding up and down as he mimed his tale, his other arm resting lightly on Abby's shoulder.

"Quite a story," she breathed, captivated. She felt an impulse to reach up and grasp his hand, but she resisted. He had just admitted his doubts about relationships. Probably he was simply lonely, maybe he mostly wanted a friend, maybe she was his pet project: Fix Abby. Build her confidence. Keep her from falling off the deep end.

Pepper was still talking. "People think condors are like hawks or eagles, but of course they're not. They don't capture live prey. Even their feet are different. Look."

He took her left hand and shaped the fingers into claws, bending the tips into talons. "This is a grasping, killing claw," he said, "but the condor doesn't kill, so it has a more level foot, for walking—" he flattened her palm and stretched out her middle finger—"and a long middle toe for balance."

Then she wasn't sure what he was doing because he quit talking but was still slowly manipulating her hand, stroking the length of each finger as he shaped them all back into claws, then flattened them out again. His thumb rubbed her palm to relax the tendons, an unhurried massage that managed to feel both soothing and stimulating. He took his time, as if exploring. She closed her eyes. When he eventually stopped, his fingers were wrapped around her wrist at the fracture site.

"So," he said, "that's the difference between hawks and condors. Their feet, anyway."

"Right," she said faintly, wishing he hadn't quit.

He flexed her wrist up and down, then frowned. "It's really stiff here. You haven't been doing your stretching, have you? Damn it, Abby."

"Really? You're going to go all doctory on me right now?" She thudded back to earth and pulled her hand away. He was driving her crazy. She felt aroused and unsure, half of her wanting to touch him all over and the other half wanting to smack him.

"Sorry," he said, "but really, Abby."

"Really what? What are you doing, John?"

"I don't know." He ran his fingers through his messy hair. "I suspect there's a fair amount of something wrong with me." He looked at her uncertainly, hesitant. "Listen, Abby, do you think—"

Abby abruptly stood up and pointed across at the sky. "Look at that plane. It's coming in awfully low, coming right at us."

Pepper turned and his eyes lit up. "That's no plane. These distances play tricks on your perspective. That just happens to be a really big condor."

The enormous bird sailed on and on toward them and passed right over them, filling the air with its colossal wingspan, its naked pink-orange head tilting to regard them with a dismissive red eye. They could see the long flight feathers at its wingtips stretch apart, working the wind, the tail feathers broad and stiff for stability. It was so close they could read the numbers on the tracking tags attached to its wings.

Abby and Pepper looked at each other and grinned. They wrestled on their backpacks, and Abby thanked him for making her come with him. As they walked along the path, he helped her over a rough spot and they found themselves holding hands, and Abby couldn't say for sure if she had reached for his hand or he had taken hers, but for some reason neither let go until they reached the road and saw the shuttle pulling up, Ada Cheshire behind the wheel, waving at them cheerfully through the windshield, ready to board a group of tourists.

Their hands fell apart, and they never did get back to what he had been about to say before that magnificent condor stole the moment and kept it.

CHAPTER 22

Abby spent her next day off shopping in Flagstaff. She and Pepper had been friendly but reserved, both too guarded to make another move, neither quite willing to step off the edge they balanced on. One always pulled back when the other leaned forward, leaving Abby feeling unsteady and doubtful. So today she put it all out of her head. With her car full of fresh linens and creative foods she couldn't buy at the canyon, she stopped by the observatory to see Bonnie since she'd missed the last two star sessions. Luther Lubbock had disrupted her life in more ways than one.

Bonnie scrutinized the scar on Abby's forehead and pointed to her own slightly crooked nose. "Now we match, sort of."

Abby smiled. "What happened?"

"Mountain biking. I ran around with a group of bikers who were a lot more skilled than I was, and I was too stupid to know when to back off. I launched off a ledge with a rocky landing, only I landed on my face. Poor form."

"Maybe we'll make it to old age if we learn anything along the way."

"Well, I learned not to get in over my head on technical trails. What did you learn?" Bonnie looked at Abby over her glasses.

"How to duck faster?" Abby had never joked about it, and she discovered that it felt good; it lightened her. "So, how's it going with the long-period comets?"

"They're still out there. *Way* out there." Bonnie had just returned from the Very Large Array of telescopes in New Mexico with new data that would keep her busy for months. "Maybe the VLA will teach us something."

Abby had supper with Bonnie, and they made plans for Bonnie's upcoming visit the next month. By the time she returned to the canyon and pulled up to her house, dusk was fading into night and stars were beginning to pierce the dark blue curtain of sky. An owl hooted over and over again, its brooding tones drifting through the trees, making the moonless night feel soft and melancholy.

Something fell on her foot as she opened the door with her arms full of shopping bags. It made her jump, like everything made her jump these days since Lubbock. Then one of the bags caught on the door handle and spilled, and Abby slipped on a jar of tomato sauce and she thumped onto the floor. Her left arm flew out to brace her fall, and pain spiked her wrist as she landed. Her first thought was that Pepper would have a fit if she cracked that fracture again. She sat there amidst her groceries, the door still open and moths flocking inside as she palpated her wrist and bent it back and forth. Fortunately it seemed intact, and the pain did not persist.

She saw the small box lying in the doorway. It must have been wedged inside the screen, and it must have been what fell on her foot when she opened the door. She picked it up, still sitting on the floor. A small package, *Fancy Dates, Grown in Arizona*, the kind they sold in the gift shops.

She pried open the lid and found a tightly creased piece of paper on top of the cellophane-wrapped dates. She unfolded it to reveal an ornately drawn scroll headed with "Important Question for Abigail Defiance Wilmore MD" followed by the calligraphic query "Will You Have a Date with Me?" and a checklist with boxes for responses. A border of tiny ink condor footprints with long middle toes ran up the left margin.

A moth fluttered in her face, and Abby distractedly gathered up her groceries and shut the door. Then she sat at the kitchen table to study the answer choices to the date question, a smile touching her face.

☐ (1) No, of course not, not in a billion light-years, are you insane?
☐ (2) No, life is too confusing right now, maybe later.
☐ (3) Maybe, what's for dinner?
☐ (4) Maybe, if you promise not to invite any huge dead-flesh-devouring birds.
☐ (5) Yes, if you do that claw thing with my hand again and promise not to act doctory.
☐ (6) Yes, but only because we're getting older every second and our choices are dwindling.

Pepper had done it. He'd stepped beyond the edge, and now it was up to her to follow or not.

Careful, she warned herself. Careful.

She looked at the paper again and saw a note below the list: "If you select any item(s) 3 through 6, please enter details below of your preferred day and time regarding the aforementioned having of a date."

Pick number two, Abby told herself firmly. What if things didn't go well? What a monumental disaster that could be. She might have to quit the job, leave the canyon. This daring step by Pepper, as charming and appealing as it seemed, was probably premature. She should give it more time, get more distance from Jake, from Lubbock, from all her baggage. Get her head straightened out. Just recently she couldn't say "Hermit Trail" without angst.

What moved her most was knowing how hard this must have been for him, how long he must have debated, considered. How vulnerable he'd made himself. He was a touchy, solitary man. If she turned this down, he would be unlikely to ask again.

If Pepper had been more certain on the condor day, she would have been ready. Now, with more time to think—and overthink—it, she hesitated. There had been so many flawed decisions. So Abby did the only thing she could think might help her, and called Lucy. She had to talk to someone more objective than herself.

"So," summarized Lucy. "He's basically a good man?"

"Yes." Abby was certain. "I'd guess, better than most."

"Go on."

"He's very thoughtful." She remembered how he insisted on that walk with her, made her sit down and assure him she was handling her breakup okay. The odd way he had put the dirt and pebbles in her hand. How he distracted her the night of her injury, telling stories and asking her about the moon. "And he cares about people."

"Mm."

"And he cares about other things. Like the condors." She thought about him standing with his arms out, the breeze playing with his hair. "And he's been through some tragedy."

"I'm sorry to hear that." Neutral.

"I think it's made him more careful, more cautious."

"Hm. Kind of like you."

Abby was silent, digesting that. "Well. I wasn't exactly cautious and careful about Jake."

"Weren't you? Didn't it take you months till you went out with him?"

"More like weeks," Abby said. But maybe it was months; that time had blurred in her head. Because after waiting, she just mindlessly dove in head first until she realized too late it was a shallow pond and she'd hit her head on the bottom. But she didn't say that. "I don't know what the hell I was thinking. I wasn't thinking."

"You're allowed to have a fling, you know. Maybe you were feeling more than thinking. Do you think that maybe that was okay, for you to let yourself go, have fun? Maybe it doesn't have to be so deeply meaningful every minute. Or does it, for you?"

"Gee, Lucy, I don't know. Maybe it really bothers me to be lied to. To be such a sucker."

"That's not what I meant. That's hindsight. I know this will come as a shock to you, but it's not the first time someone has done that in a relationship. Yeah, it bites. And as soon as you realized it, you took control and broke it off."

Lucy was right. She had taken care of it, immediately. Suddenly Abby felt better.

"I guess I worry because he's kind of touchy. Solitary." Now Abby wondered if she was trying to invent a way out of this.

"Hm. Maybe someone lied to him once."

Abby was no longer surprised at how Lucy figured things out. "That did happen. He told me."

"There you go. Maybe you two aren't so very different. Maybe there's a reason you're both so cautious. Maybe he thinks you're kind of touchy and solitary."

"Maybe," Abby said slowly. She was trying to adjust, for something new had taken hold of her. Something bold, that seemed like certainty. It felt downright strange and a little dazing. "And at least he has one other positive attribute."

"Which is?"

"I'm pretty certain he doesn't believe that UFOs are trying to contact us."

Lucy burst out laughing.

After they hung up, Abby imagined Pepper. Visualized him sitting at the table with his calligraphy pen, writing the invitation. She saw the line of concentration between his eyes as he shaped the elegant letters, a thoughtful smile pulling the corner of his lip as he created the checklist. She pictured him standing in the gift shop, taking out his wallet and buying that silly little box of dates.

She felt like she was there with him. She knew what he would say, how he would crimp his mouth at a funny thing, the way he would fix her with his cool eyes as he listened to her talk.

Abby took a black pen and carefully put an X in boxes 3, 4, and 5. At the bottom of the page she wrote in *Wednesday, 7 PM, your place.* She was taking Thursday off as a work-at-home day to clean her house and trim her yard to get ready for her guests, so Wednesday was perfect. She had quite a few vacation days that she had never used. Then she added a stick-figure Pepper with a crabby face, pointing at the sky and saying "Go Away" to a stick-figure condor hovering over him, the condor saying in a bubble "I want dead flesh for dinner! I'm hungry too!"

Abby waited until he left on his walk, made certain she saw him cross the road and head into the woods before she slipped out of her house and down the street. She slid the paper under his door and went in the other direction on her own walk, too restless to go back home.

The next day at work she barely saw him. One of the doctors collaborating with him on the sodium study came to visit, and they spent a great deal of time at the computer with spreadsheets. He met her eyes a few times, his expression pensive and neutral, and Abby truly couldn't tell if he was thinking about her or the sodium study. She hoped that what she saw was not regret.

On Tuesday, Abby overheard Dolores talking with him. "Dr. Pepper," Dolores said, a little surprised. "Did you forget to shave today?"

There was a pause. "Yes," he said slowly. "I guess I did."

Abby saw Joey Younger, whose mother brought him in for the third time in the last six weeks. Joey was a thin twelve-year-old with difficult asthma. His parents fought over his treatments and whether the dog was part of the problem and whether his mother cleaned the dusty house enough and whether the windows should be open or closed and whether he should play sports or drink milk or eat tomatoes. They fought over pretty much everything except how much his father smoked in the house, because that discussion was declared off the table.

"How's the breathing?" Abby asked, handing him the peak flow meter and watching him exhale into it as hard as he could. The little red marker moved weakly upward a short distance. Joey stared at it and shrugged his shoulders — he knew what it meant. His face looked pinched and tired, with blue smudges under his large brown eyes. Even without her stethoscope against his chest, Abby could hear the faint whistling wheeze in his lungs.

"Okay, I guess. Not great."

His mother worried at her lower lip with her teeth. "It got a lot worse last night."

"Are you using your inhalers like you're supposed to? Twice a day, no matter what?" Abby asked.

"Pretty much." He shrugged one shoulder this time, looking at his knees. Abby glanced at Mrs. Younger.

"He's really good about it. He almost never misses. Are you sure there isn't something better he can take?" She looked exhausted too, and Abby knew she'd been up with him most of the night.

"He's on the best meds there are. Joey, you're going to need another steroid burst right now to quiet things down, but I don't like it because you just had steroids two months ago." Abby hesitated. "I know this is a sore subject, but is there still smoking in the house?"

Joey and his mom traded glances. "Sometimes," she said.

Abby felt defeated and upset. Last winter, Joey's father promised to quit smoking inside and to always step out in the yard to smoke, but that didn't last long.

"Can Joey's dad come in?" Abby asked. "Can I talk to him about this again?"

"He won't. He's too busy at work. I've tried, Dr. Wilmore. He's really stubborn about this. He thinks . . . he thinks Joey needs to be tougher."

Anger flashed through Abby. "This isn't a mental condition. It has nothing to do with willpower or toughness. Joey's lungs react to irritants — that's all there is to it. And cigarette smoke is extremely irritating." She wanted to say that maybe his dad should be tougher and find some willpower to take ten steps out the door to smoke, away from his sick son.

"We have an appointment coming up, in a few weeks, with that allergist in Flagstaff," Mrs. Younger said hopefully.

"That's good, and maybe you can get some help there, but there's no allergy shot or medication for smoke inhalation. The treatment is avoidance. Will your husband at least go along on that appointment? So the allergist can talk with him?"

"Probably not." She looked weary.

"Joey." Abby turned to the boy, who sat dully, hunched. "What happens when you get out of the house? Spend the night with a friend? Do you do any better?"

He looked thoughtful. "I like it when my friend Bobby comes over and we spend the night in the back yard in my tent. It's just him and me and my dog. And then I don't cough and wheeze as much."

"Interesting. So it sounds like it's not the dog, huh?"

A smile lit Joey's pale face. "That's *right*," he said with some force.

"Would your dad mind if you slept out more often in your tent?"

Joey looked at his mother.

"No," she said, the light dawning, "he wouldn't mind at all. He thinks it's good for Joey. He always talks about how when he was Joey's age he would spend the whole summer out in a tent. Roughing it, you know, cowboys and superheroes. Boy stuff."

Abby raised her eyebrows. "It might help. Well, a little bit."

Mrs. Younger actually laughed. "I think we just might make this happen."

"I need to see Joey tomorrow to be sure he's turned the corner, and then again in a few weeks," Abby instructed. "Sooner, of course, if there's a problem."

Joey was quietly beaming as they left, but Abby remained profoundly upset. She waited till Pepper came out between patients and asked if she could talk to him.

"I know that guy, his dad," Pepper said, frowning. The trace of beard looked darker than she expected. "Kind of a hard-ass. Thinks he's tough. He almost never comes into the clinic unless he needs stitches or X-rays, which he seems to need more than normal."

"Can you think of anything else I should have done? I'm really worried about this. Joey's going to end up in the hospital."

"It's a tricky situation. You actually came up with a pretty creative way to dodge the secondhand smoke, at least. For now, until it gets too cold." Pepper sighed. "A study showed that parents who smoke and have kids with asthma usually don't quit, don't usually even smoke outside, even when doctors ask them to. Some people say it's child abuse."

Abby's eyebrows raised.

"Think about it. If you do something that makes your kid sick, so sick they can't breathe right or they have to take medication or end up in the hospital, is that abuse? If you do something that might give them cancer later in their lives, is that abuse? You can make the case." He shook his head. "It's messed up."

Abby didn't say anything, just sat there staring dismally at her half-written note. Pepper put his hand on the back of her neck and gave it a gentle squeeze. "Yeah, it sucks," he said, and went in to see his next patient. Abby felt like calling Mrs. Younger and offering to let Joey stay at her house.

On Wednesday morning Abby overheard Dolores again.

"Dr. Pepper, are you growing a beard?"

"I don't know, Dolores. Do you think I should?"

Dolores chuckled and said something Abby didn't catch. Abby found herself smiling though she didn't know why. Again she barely saw Pepper all day. The researcher had left. It was almost as if Pepper was avoiding her.

Joey Younger came in with his mom. His lungs were clear now, and he looked happy and normal. He was excited about the new tent his dad had just bought him and told her that he would live out in the back yard with his dog for the rest of the summer. He was busy making a list of the items he needed, which his dad had promised to get for him. Abby felt a little better, even though she knew it was a partial and temporary attempt. After all, it's not like Joey didn't still need to go inside the house.

At the end of the afternoon Pepper found her in the office at the computer, reviewing asthma treatments, making sure she hadn't overlooked anything for Joey. He stood in the doorway watching her before she realized he was there, and even when she turned to him, he studied her a moment before speaking.

"Last chance," he said, an impartial expression on his face. "If you want to back out, it's okay. I'll understand completely."

Abby stood and closed her computer, put her bag on her shoulder. So far all the risk had been his. She raised her hand and lightly touched the new beard.

"I like it," she said. "See you at seven."

CHAPTER 23

Abby wanted to be different tonight. If Pepper could change things up with the beard, she could change what she wore. She remembered telling him months ago that she missed the beard he'd grown, back when he was too ill and exhausted even to shave. She knew this was for her, and she wanted to do something — something physical, tangible — for him in return. The impulse felt so foreign, so unlike her, that she almost didn't follow through.

She rummaged through the back of her closet until she found her old favorite maxi sundress, unworn in over a year but perfect for a warm summer evening. Except for the time last winter at the office holiday party when she wore a wool skirt and boots, he had never seen her in a dress. The canyon was not a fancy place.

She slid it on, smoothed out a few wrinkles. Soft silky fabric, watery blue colors. The top half was a sleeveless halter, the long skirt split partway up the leg. Abby felt not quite herself wearing it — it had been so long since she'd purposely attempted to be attractive. With Jake she barely tried because it never mattered; he came after her like a wild beast regardless. If anything, she had played it down, tee shirts and sweatshirts and hiking shorts and jeans.

Now things were different. She wanted to surprise Pepper, catch him off guard, just as he had surprised her with the checklist. She wanted to take a chance at delighting him, if he was capable of delight. Maybe he was not able, not right now, but that wouldn't keep her from trying. She pulled her hair loose and brushed it out, let it float across her shoulders and down her back. Washing her face, she reached for some cosmetic concealer to dab on her scar, then stopped. The scar was fading, only light pink now, and there was that slight crooked step where it ran through her eyebrow. She hadn't really studied it in a long time, had dealt with it mostly by snubbing it. She supposed that maybe someday she might consult a plastic surgeon — the scar could likely be diminished, the eyebrow straightened out. But for now it was still improving, still waning, and it didn't feel important. She put down the concealer and decided to leave it alone. After all, he knew it was there.

On the short walk to his house, the evening sky looked unsettled. Dark gray clouds stacked up from one horizon to the other. No stars or moon tonight.

When Pepper opened his door for her, he stared. Abby smiled demurely, feeling unexpectedly shy. He took her hand and led her inside, then walked around her, as if inspecting a remarkable new invention. Then he walked around her the other way, as if to find any angles he might have missed. He raised her hand and lightly turned her so that the skirt flared and swung open, revealing her leg. She heard his breath catch.

"Excuse me," he said politely, finding his voice, "but who exactly are you? I was expecting someone else."

"She couldn't make it tonight. But we're close friends — I'll tell her you asked about her. She'll probably be sorry she missed you."

"I intend to make sure she will," he said, drawing her through the house to the back porch. He wore soft light blue jeans and an untucked white collared shirt that set off his tan. The dark brown beard looked fuller already and highlighted his smile. It made his face seem a little unruly, and she wanted to touch it again. He saw her looking at him.

"So do you still like it? Because I can go shave it off right now if you want."

"Don't you dare. It makes you look all dashing and piratey."

Abby stopped to admire his back porch, which had been enlarged into a spacious deck extending into the trees. A platform lounge scattered with cushions stood invitingly in the center, next to a low table spread with supper.

"This is wonderful," Abby said, looking up at tiny white lights twinkling along the porch rafters.

"I spend a lot of time out here. Reading, listening to music. Trying to think. Or sometimes trying not to think. I usually sleep out here, to tell you the truth. That's why I built the deck and the lounge." He paused, looked a little sheepish. "But the twinkly little lights are new."

"You did all this yourself?" Abby was impressed. She considered it an accomplishment to staple two pieces of paper together evenly.

"Remember what we said? I'm better when I'm busy. Anyway, are you hungry?"

"A little."

Food was the last thing on her mind, but he had gone to a great deal of trouble. They sat next to each other on the lounge and he pointed out the delicacies. He filled a small plate for her with stuffed dates, and a cracker spread generously with chicken salad and paper-thin cucumber slices.

"Would you care for some fruit and dead flesh? Dead chicken flesh, I believe."

A laugh burst from Abby, and she found herself hungry after all, and she ate his offering and more. There was salmon and avocado, goat cheese and dried apricots, small roasted potatoes with grilled bell peppers.

"It's all so good. Did you make this too?" Abby asked, incredulous.

"Heck no. It pays to know people in the gourmet restaurant business. Compliments of Chef Nutter." Pepper handed her a tall champagne flute and toasted to her year at the canyon.

"Um." Abby looked at the drink in her hand.

"It's sparkling apple juice. Drink up." His glass tapped hers.

She sipped, watching him. "Do you mind? You can have a drink if you want, you know. I don't care — it won't bother me."

"I don't drink much." He shook his head. She raised her eyebrows, sensing something more, so he went on. "I lost a friend in college to a drunk driving accident. After that it just wasn't very appealing."

She set down her glass and leaned against him. How many times could her heart go out to him?

"Well, that was grim enough, don't you think? What else should we talk about?" He slid his arm around her shoulders. "Cancer? HIV? Maybe Ebola virus?"

Abby laughed. "No! No medical talk. The next person who says anything medical or doctory has to . . . has to . . ." She couldn't think of a proper consequence.

He turned to face her, ran his hands slowly up and down her bare arms. His eyes were smoky. "They have to do whatever the other person says."

His hands entered her hair and he tipped her face, softly pressing his lips to the scar on her forehead. He lingered there, while a rush of warmth and complicated release flooded through her. He touched the scar lightly with two fingers and stroked the crooked part of her eyebrow, then kissed the spot again. The sensitive skin tingled under his touch.

"I've wanted to do that for so long," he confessed. "But I can leave it at that. If you think that's enough for right now."

Abby brushed her fingertips against his beard, barely feeling his lips.

"Influenza," she said quietly.

"Did you just say something doctory?" he accused, trying not to laugh.

She nodded cautiously, their foreheads nearly touching.

"Are you sure? This might make things pretty complicated." His fingers grazed her ear.

"Are *you* sure?" she replied. Her thumb moved back and forth on his jaw, his bristle. "This might make things really really complicated."

"Yes. No. Maybe." He grinned. "Unchartered waters. Sunken reefs. Sailor beware."

"Deep?"

"Very deep. Grand Canyon deep. No, Mariana Trench deep."

Abby nodded again, acknowledging, waiting. She gathered her brows. "Are you going to make me say something doctory again, just to be sure?"

"No way," he said. His fingers kept tracing her ear. She felt her breath quicken as he went on. "So here's what. You have to let me really kiss you, and you have to kiss me back."

"Wait, you only get one command. That's two things," she protested.

"I don't think so, not really. Let's see."

He started with her forehead again and worked his way across her nose and cheeks, his mouth moving unhurriedly while his hands explored her bare shoulders and drew her to him. The short beard tickled and made her smile. Then he was at her lips, barely touching them at first, then teasing them apart, tasting her, slowly investigating and finding her tongue, and she moaned softly and opened to him, and of course she couldn't help kissing him back, timidly at first, then more fervently as his urgency increased. They lay back on the cushions then and she lost track as his hands went on tirelessly traveling and discovering. Minutes passed, maybe hours, she had no sense of it. It seemed endless, infinite, wandering weightless in space. He lay partly on top of her now, and heat rose through her groin as his thigh shifted against her pubis, high inside her skirt. She felt his soft denim against her there and she writhed.

"I think you're almost there," he murmured. His long fingers slipped beneath her halter, and Abby was beside herself, fevered and crazed and about to overflow. It felt like he had been tantalizing her for days.

She sought his face, her eyes unfocused, and almost inaudibly she murmured, "Appendicitis."

"You first," he commanded quietly, and he drew his leg up and down against her. The friction ignited her, and she quaked against him, rocking in his grasp. He held her close until she subsided, then let her down. Wilted, she watched him bend over her and skim the dress and everything off her, then slide out of his clothes. He covered her with the bare length of him and kissed her deeply as his eager hands searched her again, and when she surfaced and began to quiver and catch, he nudged her open and eased himself in and she made an incoherent sound and rose to him. He groaned and moved himself with her until she erupted once more and he followed.

It was very late, close to dawn, when Abby awoke to a flicker of light against her eyelids. A cool wind had sprung up, tossing the pine branches, and a grumble of thunder crawled across the tattered sky. Pepper lay sleeping, his face in her hair and his lean body curled against her under a cotton blanket. Abby shifted to see the sky better and was rewarded with a web of lightning that scampered between clouds, followed by low trolling thunder that took a long time to fade away. She watched the lightning play in the scrum of dark clouds, and she thought about John Pepper and how he was good in all the ways that mattered, and she thought about herself and made no decisions except to keep trying her best. Not very profound, she thought. But sometimes profound was overrated, sometimes it only sounded good.

He brushed the hair off her face, and she realized he had been awake for a while, watching her. His face was solemn and kind and heartbreaking, and she turned and put her arm around his neck and kissed him on the cheek then buried her face in his chest. His arms folded her close and she felt his breath snag and felt him kiss the top of her head. The lightning capered and the thunder muttered until they both fell back asleep.

CHAPTER 24

In the morning, Pepper showered and dressed for work. It was raining steadily, a gentle gray.

"We can't have slept more than a few hours," Abby said, concerned for him. He looked peaceful, and his smile nearly devastated her, but he also looked very tired. "Your whole day is probably booked with patients."

"That's why coffee was invented," he said, pouring a cup from the pot. "It's not so different, anyway. I haven't been sleeping well since Lubbock."

"Has anyone?" She slept poorly too, but probably better than he did. She wasn't surprised at his insomnia. It explained his accumulated fatigue, night after night. Trying not to think, as he said.

"It will get better—it always does." He shrugged. Because of the rain, he drove to work instead of walking and dropped Abby at her house on the way.

"Take a nap," he suggested. "It's a great morning for it. I'm jealous."

"Is that an order?"

"It should be an order, but if I say it is, it'll probably show up in some damn cartoon."

Abby smiled and scurried through the rain into her house. She began her cleaning but made little progress. Soon she was on the couch instead, making lists of things to get, things to do. Then she abandoned that and drew him a new cartoon. When she leaned her head back to listen to the rain she was lulled asleep almost instantly. She awoke refreshed just before noon and thought about him and made a decision. First she stopped by his place to deliver the cartoon, then went to the clinic.

"What are you doing here today, Dr. Wilmore?" asked Dolores when Abby slipped through the back door at lunchtime.

"Just checking on a few things."

She found him in the office, slouched in his chair. His legs were stretched out on the other chair and his eyes were closed, his head nodding sideways. Abby touched his arm and quietly said his name.

His eyes opened slowly, and then he saw her and startled awake, yanking his feet from the chair. "Sorry," he said, pushing it toward her. "Nodded off, I guess."

"Um-hm." Abby pulled his computer over and looked at the schedule.

"Hey. Why are you here?"

"I really want you to let me do something for you," she said. "Will you?"

"What?" he asked warily.

"At least promise me you'll seriously think about it before you say no."

He tilted his head playfully, looked at his watch. "Not right now, Abby. There's just not enough time to do you justice. I mean, I know it would be exciting and all that, but the walls here are pretty thin and people would hear us and--" He stopped at her scandalized glare.

"Not funny. Go on, promise me."

"All right, all right. I promise to seriously consider." He tried to look contrite.

"So listen. I just checked, and the afternoon schedule looks really light, probably because of the rain. I've had a great nap, so I'll take over, and you can go home and get some sleep."

"That's nonsense." He was offended. "I'm totally fine."

"You were just now sound asleep in these horribly uncomfortable chairs. I really want to do this for you, John. Please let me."

In the end, Abby could only convince him to let her see one patient, little Trudy Blue, one of her favorites. She went up front to tell Ginger and Priscilla that she would be seeing Trudy, and Ginger nodded and tapped it into her computer while Priscilla regarded her with narrowed eyes. Today her lips were pearly lavender and her eyelids bright purple edged with green. Peacock, Abby thought.

Trudy was a small six-year-old with type 1 diabetes. Her mother took her to a pediatric endocrinologist at Phoenix Children's Hospital every three or four months, and brought her to see Abby or Pepper monthly to review her sugars and insulin doses. Trudy had wispy blond hair and a curious mind and an infectious giggle; it had been several months since Abby last saw her.

As they talked, Abby noticed that Trudy was staring at her face. "What is it?" she asked.

Trudy's mouth fell open in awe, and she pointed at Abby's scar. "Are you related to Harry Potter? Because that would be awesome!"

Trudy's mother, who clearly knew the real story, tried to hush her daughter, but Abby and Trudy shared a big laugh.

"No, I'm afraid not," Abby said, "but I sure wish I was."

By the time she was done, the rain had stopped and weak sunlight was breaking through the clouds. Abby could hear the staff talking up front.

"But why did she come in?" Priscilla asked in a wheedling tone.

"I don't exactly know," replied Dolores. "Dr. Wilmore said Dr. Pepper wasn't feeling well, or he was tired, or something like that. Something about he didn't sleep much last night. He does seem very tired today. Of course, he usually does—"

"How would *she* know?" Priscilla demanded.

"Why don't you go ask her yourself, Priscilla?" Ginger suggested, clearly done with the conversation.

Dolores came back past Abby and shook her head.

"You didn't hear that, did you?" she asked.

"Hear what?"

Dolores gave her a look that showed she knew better.

Pepper had only a few more patients to see, and he promised Abby he would go home to sleep the minute he was done. Abby felt restless, so she took a long walk out to the rim. After she drew a stick figure of him asleep in his chair and left it for him, propped up in the office where he couldn't miss it.

Pepper being not tired

Tourists were starting to venture outdoors again after the rain, but so far the path was mostly empty. Abby walked and walked, smiling when she passed Pepper's bench where they had their first talk and he made her sit down and put the dirt in her hand. Bands of sunshine lit the canyon's tinted layers, the dust washed away. Deep reds and bright creams and scorched golds glowed up and down the canyon, patches of mist still lingering in the gorges, the leftover scraps of cloud.

Abby felt like she could walk along here forever. She looked down through the striations, feeling the eons piled up under her feet, the evaporated seas and the crumbled mountains, the flattened dunes and ashy lavas, and the long-gone creatures that swam and wiggled and crawled along on their business hundreds of millions of years ago.

She couldn't see it from here, but she could sense the great dark river below, slowly slicing away into yet another layer, dropping into billions of years ago, working into the heart of the planet.

She looked up and saw Venus in the western sky, just beginning to glimmer between clusters of pale gilded clouds. Venus, their nearest planetary neighbor yet still an overwhelming one hundred sixty million miles away. It turned her mind inside out, to go from those primordial canyon depths to the accelerating, unfolding universe and its excruciating distances. She stood on the brink, embracing the extremes, which were really all part of the same display. Time moved and plunged and stopped and soared all at once.

All of it mattered, she thought, and none of it mattered at all.

Her phone chimed and she pulled it out, looked at the text.

Slept like the dead, he said.

She smiled, then another text came through.

By the way, penicillin.

Abby turned on her heel away from the edge and headed for home. That was undeniably a doctory thing to say.

Venus brightened and burned like a torch.

Special thanks
This would not have been the same book without the knowledge and support of Cheryl Pagel MD, Grand Canyon Clinic physician in the 1980s — long before cell phones and computers, when it was a grueling 24/7/365 endeavor. At the time, only 10% of the physician workforce was female.
Dr. Pagel is an American hero.

Many more thanks:
Thanks to Lindsay Alaishuski MD, physician at the Grand Canyon Clinic 2013-2016, for her support, information, and tours of the clinic.
Thanks to the painstaking research from Tom Myers MD and Michael Ghiglieri in *Over the Edge: Death in Grand Canyon* (especially sections on suicide and the Hermit Trail area).
Thanks to physicians who have shared their knowledge and experiences: Cheryl Pagel MD, Kelly Luba DO (the influenza rant), Lisa Villarroel MD, William Dabbs MD, Lindsay Alaishuski MD.
Thanks to the excellent family physicians Jacob Anderson DO and Luke Peterson DO, for creating enough name confusion during the three years of residency to inspire Ranger Jake Peterson's name.
Thanks to my wonderful first-draft readers, for keeping me on my toes: Ted Cavallo, Cheryl Pagel MD, Kelly Luba DO, and Cindy Alt.
Thanks to my gracious editor Joy Johannessen, for her support and endless supply of red ink.

Thanks to the many resources and web information that helped inform the medicine, geology, and astronomy included in this story: the CDC and USPSTF on suicide; the Arizona Department of Health Services on rabies in squirrels and on STDs; the CDC on bubonic plague; *Over the Edge: Death in Grand Canyon*: Myers and Ghiglieri; the National Park Service/Grand Canyon; Lowell Observatory; Homolovi State Park; NASA; www.space.com; www.moonconnection.com; www.defenders.org/california-condor/basic-facts; and the South Rim ranger talk on condors May 2016.
And yes, the Wallyball games over the Arizona-Mexico border fence have been a real thing.

Want more about Abby and Pepper?

Stay tuned for **CROOKED TRAILS**
Keep reading to see Chapter One ....

CROOKED TRAILS

Sandra Miller

May your trails be crooked, winding, lonesome, dangerous, leading to the most amazing view. May your mountains rise into and above the clouds. -- Edward Abbey

CHAPTER 1

Spring came to the canyon. The last snow slowly aged, turning gray and disappearing, little by little, and soon pale green shoots pushed up through the rocky soil. The black nights lost the sharp edge of frost and people began putting away winter coats and boots. Miles deeper, far below the tinted layers of rock, miles even below the great dark river that snaked along the red twisted chasms, little rifts and broken shelves of the planet's crust shifted and collided, sending out unsettled vibrations, little rocky ripples. Vibrations too faint for humans to feel, but the seismographs caught them and their needles waggled up and down, tracing a jagged image of shifting stone. Geologists sat up and took note.

The physicians at the Grand Canyon Clinic on the South Rim had no time to contemplate such subterranean developments. For the last few weeks they found themselves in the middle of a measles epidemic, responding to frantic parents and treating sick children and caught up in a media blitz of attention. The outbreak began seventy miles away in Flagstaff where a cult of families who did not believe in vaccinations suddenly started getting very sick. Shortly before the epidemic was realized, many of the children took a field trip to the canyon for their science lesson, visiting the gift shops and stores and restaurants. Fortunately for the survival of the measles virus, though unfortunately for humans, infected people could shed and spread the infection for days before becoming ill and developing the sandpapery rash.

"We've got another one," said Abby as she exited the isolation room in the back of the clinic, pulling off her face mask. "She's really sick."

Dr. Abigail Wilmore rubbed her nose with the back of her arm. Face masks always made her itch, and even though she had just washed her hands before leaving the room, then applied alcohol gel for good measure, the ingrained arm-rubbing habit had kicked in anyway, keeping her potentially-contaminated fingers away from her face. While she should be immune to measles because of her childhood vaccines, there was still a small chance of infection and everyone was encouraged to protect themselves.

"So. Not quite out of the woods yet," said Dolores with a sigh, printing another measles handout from her computer. One of the best nurses Abby had ever worked with, efficient and competent, Dolores Diaz frowned with frustration and pushed her dark hair back from her face. Abby noticed there were more silver strands this year. "I remember you talking with Angela's mom just last fall about getting caught up on her shots."

"Yeah. I guess I didn't talk quite enough about it." Abby always wondered if there was something else she could have done, another way she could have said it, that would have been more convincing. She wondered if all physicians harbored as many self-doubts as she did. *They get so many shots,* Angela's mother had wailed, *it just doesn't seem right. Let's wait till she's a little bit older.* Abby assured her that vaccines are often better tolerated when kids are younger, but the mom's mind had already been made up. Now little Angela was two years old with a fever of 104, red runny eyes and a drippy nose, coughing and crying nonstop, the inconsolable picture of utter misery. The rash was just beginning to scatter across her face, and Abby warned that it was about to get much worse.

Abby pulled the mask back up over her nose and mouth and took the handout into the room, going over the precautions personally in case the mom was too distracted to read them. Acetaminophen for fever, and watch out for dehydration or worsening symptoms. The chance of developing complications with pneumonia or encephalitis — brain inflammation — and when to be concerned. Encephalitis occurred in only one case in a thousand but was still a distinct possibility. Her face stiff with worry, Angela's mother clasped her child closely and Dolores ushered her out the back door, avoiding the patients who were waiting in the lobby. They closed up the exam room and taped a sign with the time on the door. The measles virus could hover in the air and remain contagious for several hours; nearly every susceptible person exposed to the virus would catch it. The virus was a very determined organism.

Here came Priscilla from the front desk, stepping down the hall in her tiny skirt and black tights, her spike-heeled boots clicking quickly on the floor, her snug scoop-necked top reaching a novel low position on her ample bosom. Abby's eyes widened and she made a conscious effort to look away from the deep cleavage approaching her. This was a brave new stance even for Priscilla, long known for her provocative attire and attraction to Dr. John Pepper. Another few millimeters, and there would be nothing more left to the imagination. A medical mask dangled around her neck, and she held a handful of papers and envelopes. Her eye shadow was bright blue today and her glance flicked past Abby as if she wasn't there.

"I need to talk with Dr. Pepper," Priscilla said to Dolores, craning her neck to look in the doctors' office where he could be heard talking on the phone, his voice low and serious. "He needs to sign these disability papers."

"You can give them to me," Dolores offered, reaching for the documents. "I'll be sure that he sees them."

Priscilla snatched the papers away, then seemed to realize how that looked. Her voice sweetened. "Thanks so much, Dolores. But I told the patient I would take care of it myself. She had a message for the doctor, and she asked me to tell him."

"He's talking with the medical company manager," Abby put in, keeping her head down and tapping on her laptop. "The FirstMed guy. And he doesn't sound very happy. It could take a while."

"Well," Priscilla huffed.

Abby could feel Priscilla looking her way, sensed herself being measured and dismally failing the evaluation like she felt at least a dozen times every day. This had gone on now for months, ever since Abby and Pepper started dating last summer and were now more or less living together. As if Priscilla could not fathom why Pepper had chosen Abby over herself. As if it was only a matter of time until he came to his senses and dropped Abby and started looking around with his eyes wide open.

"Well," Priscilla said again. "I'll come back in a few minutes." And she stalked up front to her desk, loudly asking her counterpart Ginger if Dr. Wilmore didn't have another patient to see.

Dolores sighed. "She is very good at her job."

Abby nodded, leaving it at that. She was tired and wanted to go sit in the office to work on her notes, but from Pepper's tone in his phone conversation, this was not the time to distract him. She worried about how many more measles cases they might see and whether they should put up more signs around the village, urging vaccinations.

Everyone in their patient database had already been contacted by mail or email, or both, but that was only a portion of their clients since they had so many one-time and temporary patients who visited the park from all over the country. From all over the world. More than four million visitors a year to the canyon, and some days it felt like every single one of them managed to get sick or injured while they were there.

Abby heard Pepper hang up, dropping the phone into the cradle a little harder than necessary. She grimaced, wondering, and gathered up her computer and mouse to move to the office but Priscilla's radar was operating at an impressive stealth level and she suddenly appeared and whisked into the little room with her papers. Abby could see her bend over him, her little stretchy skirt hitching up her behind, her hand on his shoulder and her pale blond hair falling against him as she pointed to the papers and tilted her chest toward his face. She was an attractive woman, Abby had to admit. Pepper straightened his back, pulling away a little, but Priscilla moved right with him, talking earnestly in a quiet, private voice.

Eventually Priscilla exhausted herself and returned to the front desk. Abby moved to the office and sat down beside Pepper, who was quietly fuming.

"What's going on?" she asked.

"Nothing," he said shortly, vigorously rearranging a messy stack of papers, tearing a page in the process. "Everything is just peachy."

"Come on, John. Talk to me."

He exhaled heavily and finally looked at her, his blue eyes frosty. "You want to take a walk? Not much privacy here."

Abby glanced at all her unfinished work. "Of course."

"Don't worry. I'll come back with you and we can both wrap up then." Pepper stood and put his hand on the back of her neck, just under her hair where she gathered it into a low twist, and squeezed gently. He was a reserved man and rarely displayed affection for her at work, but he allowed himself that one gesture, that soft grip on her neck, and she loved it.

They pulled on their jackets, asking the staff to lock up when they finished, and cut through the woods to the rim trail. Abby slipped her hand in his and he gripped it hard, a sure sign of his stress.

"Ow," said Abby mildly, wiggling her fingers.

He looked down at her and smiled, relaxing his hand. "Sorry."

When they reached the rim they stood silently, taking it in. The sunburnt canyons fell away at their feet and the stone mesas paraded off in all directions, striped with bands of rust and cream and dusky green. Hundreds of millions of years, the planet's history laid open below them, the raw exposed specter of past ages.

Abby closed her eyes and inhaled deeply through her nose, savoring the scents of limestone dust and pine. She knew there had been a recent uptick in seismic readings and she tried to sense the shifting inner crust so far beneath her feet. She opened one eye, sniffed again, and glanced sideways at Pepper.

"So what do you think?" she asked. "Does it smell like earthquakes to you? One big tremor and this very ledge we're standing on could crumble and drop into the canyon. When was that last rockslide that was triggered by a quake — at Mather Point? 1959? Just a few seconds ago, geologically speaking."

John smiled, his brown hair tossing back and forth in the breeze, and one hand distractedly rubbed his short beard. "I wish it would. Then I'd have better things to worry about."

"Better than what? Let me guess . . . Priscilla?"

"Ha," he snorted. "Thanks for reminding me." His gaze appealed briefly to the dark blue sky as the color deepened, edging toward evening. "I suppose I need to say something to her about her tops. Or blouses, or shirts, or whatever you call them. Unless you want to? You know, woman to woman?" His eyebrows rose hopefully.

"Nice try. But since you're technically in charge of the clinic, I'm afraid that's up to you. Besides, it's mostly for your benefit, you know. If I said something to her about it, she'd probably take heart."

Abby sat on a bench and pulled him down next to her, snuggling against him, waiting for him to get to the real reason why they were there.

"How awkward can this get?" he asked. "Me having to tell a woman who's trying to seduce me that she has to dress less sexy. We need an office manager for these things. As busy as we are, it's ridiculous how they don't give us one. What has happened to FirstMed, anyway? Instead of helping, all they can do is come up with stupid new schemes to send us all over the country." He picked up a small rock and hurled it over the edge.

Abby gathered her eyebrows—there was no trail beneath them at this spot, but it was still a forbidden thing to do, throwing rocks. You could seriously injure someone below. Then what he said sank in.

"Wait. What?" She turned to stare in his face.

Pepper looked troubled. He palmed her cheek and pulled her to him. "They want to try out a new national park clinic this summer, just for three months. Where there's lots of visitors, where they can maybe make lots of money. There's been a small clinic there, staffed with mid-level providers. A physician assistant, I think. But they've gotten busier and want to see how it goes with a physician."

Abby let that digest. "Just you, is that what you're saying? Not me."

"Yeah." He pulled her closer. "You would stay here."

Abby bristled up, indignant. "There's too much work here for just one person, and that goes triple in the summer."

"And that's what I told them," Pepper agreed. "And they said they would approve the rotation for a third-year family medicine resident to help out here. You know, what I've been asking for the last few years? Someone who could function almost independently."

"Sure, if they're a good resident," Abby argued heatedly. "But if they're not, if they're struggling or not very polished, it takes a whole lot more time to do the supervision."

"Yeah, well, you're preaching to the choir." He picked up another rock to throw and Abby put her hand on his, prying it from his fingers and dropping it to the ground. He dipped his head at her and went on. "Besides that, there's my sodium study. We're just getting ready to start the next phase and I've got a professor and a medical student coming up here in June for six weeks to launch it. I have to be here."

"Surely they understand that?"

"That would be no. He said he couldn't authorize me working on a study during company time. The little bastard. I assured him that I only work on it during my own hours and I have never jeopardized the company's precious damn time."

Abby winced. How many days did they come in early and stay late, taking care of patients, wrapping up paperwork, following up phone calls and labs? Nearly every day; it was simply part of the job. While they theoretically worked an eight-hour day, most days it was more like ten, sometimes eleven. She took a deep breath.

"So. What are you — we — going to do?"

"I don't know." He shook his head, irritated. "If I insist I won't go, it actually might put my job at risk. Or so that little weasel implied."

Abby sat back in alarm. No wonder he was upset. "Surely not."

"I doubt it. He's just full of hot air, flexing a few muscles he doesn't have." He scowled, then peered at her closely. "I don't suppose you could work on the study?"

"Are you kidding? You want me to work with statistics?" Abby nearly laughed. "How much do you care about your study? If you recall, I originally wanted to make my career in astronomy but it was too mathy."

Then it occurred to her. She slid the idea back and forth in her brain a few times.

"What if I went instead of you?" she suggested cautiously, feeling her way. "That way you could stay here and work on the study and work with the resident. And I can run off and have fun in a new place that probably doesn't even need a doctor and I'll just sit on my hands all day watching the clouds go by."

He looked at her hard, his eyes brittle, and drew her tight, kissed the top of her head. "I don't like it. I would worry about you too much."

"But maybe it wouldn't be so bad, you know. It's only three months. Maybe we could visit each other. What's there to worry about? Where is it anyway?"

His expression was dark as he studied her, the sky nearly black now, with a few stars sparking above his head.

"Nowhere dangerous." He took her hands in his. "It's at Old Faithful, in Yellowstone. On top of the biggest active volcano in the world."

Made in the USA
San Bernardino, CA
28 May 2018